Middle
of
Nowhere

by Phania Lee

Middle
of Nowhere

by Phania Lee

ISBN 13: 978-1-955338-38-7

Cover elements, Canva Pro.
Design by Lori Graham (Pocahontas Press).

Printed in the United States of America.

POCAHONTAS PRESS

Floyd, VA
pocahontaspress.com

Dedication

To my girls, Maia, Sidney, and Alyssa.

PART I

Adrian

"But when the planets
In evil mixture to disorder wander,
What plagues and what portents, what mutiny,
What raging of the sea, shaking of the earth,
Commotion in the winds, frights, changes, horrors..."

Troilus and Cressida, I:iii,
Shakespeare

Chapter One

$\mathbf{S}$ix years ago, Raymond Hawke had been elected sheriff of Ridley, West Virginia, and he was proud to say that things had remained much the same as when he'd taken the oath. As Hawke made his rounds of Ridley's main street, he sighted one of the town fixtures on a bench between the Ben Franklin Variety and Fletcher's Hardware.

A wizened black man, still and silent as if carved from flint rock or obsidian: Hawke couldn't remember a day when he hadn't been sitting there, since Ray himself was a boy. Not a thing went on in Ridley and the surrounding county that Old Claude didn't know about.

Hawke speculated that Claude was Melungeon, what with all the different appearances of his tribe. Melungeons were said to be colored, white, Portuguese, Turkish, Gypsy, and Cherokee. Sam Fletcher, with his college education, knew all about them, and said they'd drifted here from Lee and Wise counties in southwest Virginia. Claude and his kind pretty much kept a low profile, probably to avoid a hateful world.

This morning, Hawke was thinking back to when the Negroes marched in Selma, stirring up violence and bloodshed with the Klan. Innocent people had died, white and colored, homes and businesses destroyed. Must have been a nightmare for local law enforcement.

At breakfast, tuned to the national news from the small television on the kitchen counter, Edith said, "Well, now they've started burning down Watts, wrecking Los Angeles. Won't be anything much left of America if they don't get their freedoms."

"LBJ passed the Civil Rights Act last year," Hawke said to his wife. "I don't know what else they want. Just goes to show if you give 'em an inch, they take a mile."

"Don't talk with your mouth full, dear."

Hawke might have his law enforcement problems, sure enough, but with gentle souls like Old Claude residing in his county, race riots weren't likely to be on the list. For the life of him, he couldn't understand why the races in the big cities couldn't tolerate one another.

"Hey, there, Claude."

"How you gettin' on, Sheriff? Fine day, ain't it?"

Hawke looked up at the sky for the first time that morning. Clouds fluffy as white lambs drifted high across the blue. "Yeah, but you know what they say. A mild summer makes a hard winter." Already he was thinking of more pressing matters, whether he could trust his chief deputy to transport a prisoner from Ridley to Harrisonburg, or whether he should do it himself.

"Yes, Suh. That be what they do say."

Suddenly a young woman fair as a single blossom on a dead twig popped out of the hardware store and smiled in their direction. Hawke touched the brim of his hat to her before she whirled away with a tinkling sound and sashayed up the street.

"Why, she got bells on, Sheriff, I do believe."

"Seems so."

"Sound like Christmas look, don't it?"

A tree bedecked with twinkling lights came to Hawke's mind, and he knew what Old Claude meant. He cleared his throat and hitched up his gun belt. "Well, I guess I better check up on things at the office."

"You have a good day, Sheriff."

"You do the same."

For nearly a year now, Hawke had kept half an eye on the comings and goings of the woman known as Lila. She was a pretty thing in her loose, flouncy way. Never seemed afraid of living alone the way she did, tucked in the woods by the Capon River far off the back roads, so no man but a poacher stalking deer out of season would stumble upon her by accident. One of those women left over from the crazy hippies out in California he'd read about in TIME magazine, was Hawke's private theory.

She hitchhiked into town for millet and wheat, garden seed last spring, Sam Fletcher from the hardware store said. You'd see her around town like a bright surprise, dressed in thin flowing dresses of shocking colors, a cape of long black hair, and sandals on her feet. Not a thing like regular women born and raised in West Virginia or the rest of Appalachia.

One thing you noticed right off was her flashy white smile. She had all her own teeth. She came from money, probably, good dental care and a healthy diet.

Running from something, or somebody? Hawke wondered if she'd been charged with a crime, maybe hiding out in the sticks, laying low until the smoke cleared wherever she was from, waiting to return. Why else would a stranger elect to come here?

Still, whenever he spotted her on the streets of town, she didn't appear to have a care in the world, just plain happy from the way she struck

Hawke. That set her apart as much as her gypsy clothes and the way she had of drifting down the sidewalk like there wouldn't be footprints, as if she could float in the very air, the same as those puffy white clouds in the sky.

When Hawke entered the Sheriff's Department, the first person he saw was the new dispatcher he hired last month, Ruby Whitlow, too fat for her uniform but stuffing pecan twirls down her gullet, anyhow.

"Hey, Ruby," he said, trying to sidle past the dispatcher's desk to get to his office.

"Mornin', Sheriff Hawke."

"Any messages for me?"

"No, Sir. Been real quiet."

One thing about Ruby, she was respectful, same as Hawke's chief deputy, Edgar Wills.

He eased down in his swivel chair at the desk, thinking of the one prisoner in the county jail who'd been extradited to Virginia. Safe passage for Lonnie Robinson, the alleged murderer, was the big item for the day.

But the image of Lila kept coming to mind, like a secret he coveted and nobody else knew about. So far as anyone could tell, there wasn't a man in her life, which put to rest Hawke's original theory that she'd come to town to set up a prostitution business for Ridley's love-starved married men. Though over the months it was plain she had no interest in finding herself a man, she'd shine that smile when she passed you on the street and you happened to catch her eye. Lila's appearance in Ridley was as interesting as it was peculiar, something Hawke had begun to look forward to.

Friendly but remote, as if she didn't want for a thing other than the supplies she paid for with honest money. Money she'd brought with her from somewhere up north or maybe out west, because Sam Fletcher told Hawke that Lila didn't talk like she was from anywhere close by, not any place they'd personally know of.

Which was true enough. Hawke had been over to Charleston a few times for the State Sheriffs Convention, and up to Cincinnati to see his wife's sister's family, the extent of his travels. Maybe he'd call Edith and tell her he needed to take the prisoner to Harrisonburg, after all.

Back in August last year, when his curiosity had been percolating for several months, Hawke followed Lila to the woods, keeping his distance so she wouldn't see his shadow. That's when he learned how she lived in a rusted-out school bus close to an active stream fed by the Capon River. The exterior of the bus was decorated with colorful pictures, faces, rainbows and such she must have painted herself, for company. At the far side of the bus, near the stream where the earth was most fertile, she'd planted an autumn garden, with turnips and kale, and a row of darker leafy greens that were probably growing into potatoes.

From his hiding place in a stand of pines, he noticed a curl of wood smoke against the gray sky. Her nearest neighbors would be the Funge family, but they lived over the next ridge a piece, not that her path was likely to cross with theirs. Backwoods neighbors kept to themselves.

Skulking down the rutted logging trail to his official vehicle, he estimated that Lila lived a good four miles off the beaten track, homesteading a scruffy patch of land. She had to walk out to thumb a ride to town on Route 50. Then she dragged her provisions to the abandoned bus in a wooden cart left in the blackberry bushes by the side of the road.

She'd been seen right often in the local library, too. Evidently, she did a lot of reading, which also set her apart. But Hawke couldn't help but wonder what else the young woman found to do with her time, and whether there were moments when she felt lonely out in the woods all by herself.

He hadn't seen any evidence to say she didn't live alone. A garden, about a half-cord of crudely sawn wood stacked by the bus, a rake and a hoe, some watering pails. Flowers planted in an apple crate and bushel baskets, pansies and red geraniums.

She had no telephone or electricity. Power lines didn't run this far, at least not down in her gulley.

When Raymond Hawke returned to town on an overcast August day, telling himself that as an elected official it was his business to be familiar with his county and who lived there, he went directly to the office. He knew he owned some information about the mysterious Lila to whet the appetite of men like Sam Fletcher, but Hawke had no intention of sharing it.

Lila. Short for Delilah, maybe, the woman from the Bible who stole Samson's hair and left him for a weakling.

It felt queer, knowing she could survive out there without the benefit of a man's company or a man's strength. What would she do for protection if an intruder happened by some dark night? Part of him began to worry for her, she seemed so fragile in her long lacy dresses. Innocent, almost, as if the risk she took was something she couldn't begin to fathom.

She was like a monarch butterfly gliding from flower to flower, blind to the jaybird circling in for the kill...

"Sheriff Hawke," Ruby called out. "Line two. It's your missus."

With a sigh, Hawke punched into the line and to his wife's worried voice.

"Spanky threw up," Edith said. "What should I do?"

As a childless couple, Hawke knew he and Edith babied the terrier too damned much, fretting over the dog's every burp and sneeze. But this morning he was in no mood to encourage it.

"Well, Edith, I don't know. I'm fixin' to transfer a prisoner to Harrisonburg, Virginia. Got other things on my mind."

So he drove to Virginia and back without incident, Lonnie Robinson in cuffs and leg irons, chained by his waist to the wire-mesh barrier behind the front seat. Edith said later that she gave Pepto-Bismol to the terrier, and by the dinner hour Spanky was right as rain.

Then the dog days of summer blended into a damp autumn, and the Mexican migrant workers trucked in to work the peach harvest in Hampshire County went elsewhere for the winter.

When he received the news on a snowy Saturday in February, a frantic call from Rebecca Funge about a fire in the woods just over the ridge from their cabin, Hawke radioed his chief deputy to ride with him and knew exactly where to go.

As they approached the site, black plumes of smoke clawed the sky above the line of bare trees. But by the time Hawke and Wills arrived, the fire had nearly burned itself out, leaving the school bus in ruins. There was no need to radio the fire trucks.

In the night the oil drum she used for a woodstove must have burned through. Hawke found her burned body half-melted into the glass doors of the bus, as if she'd been trying to get out at the last minute.

The flesh was gone from her face, the eyeballs missing. Two charred sockets stared through the jagged shards, the pretty black hair frizzed off the skull.

"Jesus God!" Hawke's deputy turned away to pitch a steaming heap of breakfast on the snow. Wiping his mouth with a blue bandana, Edgar said, "Guess we won't be seeing her around town no more. What should we do with the body?"

"Forget it," Hawke said. "Far as we know, she had no kin."

"But we can't just leave her here, Sheriff."

"Don't know what more we can do. Besides, it was here she chose to call home."

At the same moment the two men heard the reed-thin wail. As Edgar gawked at the Sheriff with startled round eyes, Hawke moved off in the direction of the tiny sound.

In the snow he found an infant lying on a blanket, cold and naked but unharmed. A baby boy, it was. Hawke bent down to scoop the child into his arms.

Black hair, dark eyes. Maybe six months old, not much older, he was sure. Dirt and a few seeds were stuck to the baby's lips. Thinking that was a little odd, Hawke brushed it off with his handkerchief.

'Well, if that don't beat all." Edgar touched the baby's thatch of dark hair. "I never knew she was expectin' when I saw her around town."

"I never did, either."

"Well, maybe he wasn't hers. Maybe she stole him from someplace. But what are we going to do with it?"

"Guess we'll have to scout for a decent home."

Raymond Hawke wrapped the damp blanket around the child and trudged through the snow, past the burned-out bus toward the logging trail leading to the car.

"But who'll want to take in an orphan baby in times like these, Sheriff? I mean, with jobs being so scarce and all. Hard times for folks to feed their own."

"I know some people just lost a grandbaby to influenza," Hawke said. "We can start with them."

"But if it don't work out, we'll have to call the welfare woman from over to Petersburg..."

Hawke waited while Edgar got in the car before gently handing over the baby now wrapped in the Sheriff's winter jacket. He went around to the driver's side, started the engine and began the slow, steady process of backing out to the main road. Edgar had neglected to fasten his shoulder harness again, but under the circumstances Hawke wasn't going to remind him.

"I swear, Sheriff, but if this baby ain't asleep already."

"Must have taken a natural shine to you, Edgar. Too bad you're still a single man." Hawke steered the car around a snowbank. "But a good baby like this, we won't have any trouble putting a roof over his head."

"Handsome little fellow, too. Almost looks like an Injun baby, don't he?"

Or Melungeon...

But Hawke was mourning the sudden loss of the woman who called herself Lila, missing the sharp sense of pleasure when she appeared on the shabby streets of Ridley. Now that she was gone, he wished he'd tried to discover more about her, who she was and where she'd come from.

Now he would never learn those things.

Nor could he know that the infant found in the snowbank was to haunt his life more obsessively than the strange young woman in flowing gypsy clothes forever hovering, just out of reach, at the edge of his dreams...

7

Chapter Two

Never mind she'd been sickly. He traipsed off and left her alone, thinking only of his own entertainments and pleasures, like every man alive. Wouldn't it just serve him right, though, coming home to her dead body sprawled across the bathroom floor?

Alma Lightfoot was miffed with her husband Ben, who'd gone fishing with Airlie Funge down by the Capon River. They were camping out in a little lean-to Airlie had built on the riverbank for his boys. Some mean, dark part of her half-wishing he'd step in a sinkhole told her she needed to run to church and beg for mercy.

Last week the Foursquare Church marquee said the sermon was called "Satan, The Chief Terrorist." She wondered why anybody bothered to show up, to be scared half to death by sin and damnation. She wanted a tamer, gentler church that talked about Jesus and the angels and preached the Commandments, which was why she didn't go to church anymore.

What would happen, one Sunday, if the pews at the Foursquare Church were empty, and that new Reverend Litchfield had to holler his sermon to a bunch of ghosts?

The heat of the day gave her a second excuse for taking it easy. The family knew she'd been feeling poorly for next to a week. Betty Ann, her youngest daughter, was supposed to care for Baby Winston until Alma got better, but she'd telephoned first thing this morning to say something had come up, and she had to bring Winston home today.

Alma sat on her screened-in front porch, listening to the drone of the seven-year locusts, and drank her glass of iced tea. She heard a suspicious chuckling, then a rattle and a whirring like a Mix-Master, growing louder. Betty Ann appeared behind the wheel of a decrepit pick-up truck, probably a loan from a worthless man who thought if she owed him a debt, he'd get to sleep with her. The Chevy skidded to a stop in the Lightfoot driveway.

Betty Ann was widowed at twenty-six, with five children already to her credit. Then she went right out and picked up some no-account who promised to take care of her and the kids forever, only to disappear after giving her another infant who died when it was three weeks old, God rest its tiny soul.

About then, Ray Hawke came by with a scrawny, naked baby, asking Alma if she would give it foster care until the welfare woman could find a proper home. Alma had named him Winston after her own deceased Daddy, and Ben was madder than she could ever remember in thirty-seven years of marriage.

Poor little Winston. He was born with something missing from his brain. If he even *had* a brain, Alma thought to herself, plumping out of her porch swing to unhitch the latch on the screen door, watching as Betty Ann hauled three-year-old Winston from the front seat.

"Hey, Mama!" Betty Ann dragged Winston up the walk like a pup on a tether. "I gotta do some things this afternoon, so I had to bring Baby Winston home early. Hope you don't mind. Are you over the sickness yet?"

"Little bit, thanks for asking. I thought Darla might watch him this afternoon."

"Darla don't want to, Mama. Winston makes her edgy, her being pregnant and all. I kind of think she's afraid her own unborn baby might catch it from him."

Darla was fifteen, some kid Betty Ann picked up on her travels who presently shared Betty Ann's trailer. The advantage to having a roommate, Alma could see, was that Darla was there to watch Elvis, Pammy, Tommy and Timmy, and Emma Jolene, so Betty Ann could carouse all hours with shiftless characters. Betty Ann was Alma's middle living child, and she always had been a handful.

With that one nervous foot of hers tapping a mile a minute, Betty Ann helped herself to a swig of Alma's tea, tossing out the wilted sprig of spearmint without asking. She started jiggling her car keys.

"Come to Grandma, Baby," Alma said, stretching out her arms to the child.

"Where's Daddy?"

"Gone fishing since yesterday morning. Supposed to be home tonight."

"Well, I gotta run, Mama."

"Where to, in such a hurry? You going to a fire? Best remember, Betty Ann. Just because you can't have no more kids don't mean you can't get into trouble."

"Oh, Mama." Betty Ann grinned with what might have passed for embarrassment, but Alma knew she enjoyed the attention. The girl put a hand on Winston's dark glossy head and said, "Bye, Sugar. You be good for your Grandma, now. Aunt Betty will come get you real soon, so you can play with your cousins."

"Be good for your Grandma?" Alma said to the child as she watched the pick-up snort up the hill in a spray of gravel and red dust. The lap of her housedress was getting wet from Winston's bottom. She suspected that when she went to change him, there'd be angry raw flesh where the boy was eaten alive by the diaper rash.

He couldn't complain, didn't know how to cry, and you had to spoon food down his gullet like you were nursing a sick baby bird. It was amazing he knew how to move his jaws to chew. Why, being good was all Winston knew, if being good meant pretending you weren't even here.

Not like Betty Ann, whose twitchy eyes darted around in search of something she should have learned by now would turn out to be nothing but dashed hopes and expectations. Alma worried that Betty Ann was the type of woman who'd be forever sniffing for excitement and new adventure, never mind the price she'd have to pay for getting it.

Alma gazed into the child's watery, empty brown eyes. He had a perfect round head, dark brown hair, and a strong little body. What a sorry shame there wasn't a working brain in his head. He was vacant as a doll.

"You're Grandma's little Winston Doll," she said, planting kisses all over his face. He didn't squirm or pull away, like the rest of her grand-children. He just sat there staring at who could know what.

Sometimes Alma caught herself wondering if Winston saw things none of the rest of them knew were there.

She took him into the house, removed his soggy diaper, washed him off in the bathroom sink and put cornstarch on his rash. The fact he never cried didn't mean he couldn't feel pain.

She set him down on his chubby bare feet, wondering whether Winston could really feel a thing. Did he like grits better than oatmeal, or orange juice over milk, or applesauce more than chocolate pudding? Did he know whether you were loving on him or pushing him down a flight of stairs?

Could he tell the difference between happy or sad? In a way, Alma considered the way Winston was as a blessing from the Lord. Didn't some people spend their whole lives trying not to feel a thing?

Betrayed by love, buried alive, forgetting how to hope for something better after years of disappointment, refusing any longer to dream, knowing not to expect even a little from a soul: Alma knew all about it. She guessed Betty Ann would finally learn the lesson, too. Most women did, as Alma could see by their wrinkled, pinched-together lips.

But she had enough problems of her own without worrying too much about Betty Ann. People made their own beds and then had to die in them.

She turned around to see Winston, naked and pink and powdered, gazing at the door of the refrigerator. As usual, Alma pretended he was telling her things. If somebody didn't act like he had some sense, how was he ever going to get any, to make his way in the world?

"You hungry, Winston?" She opened the refrigerator door. While the cool air soothed her nerves, she pointed out things on the shelves. "There's milk. Say milk, Winston. Here's a big bowl of raspberry Jell-O with fruit cocktail in it. And a macaroni salad for Pappy's supper. Grandma's got hoop-cheese, you want a hunk of cheese? Here's sweet apples, or maybe canned pears. Bet you'd like some of them, huh?"

She placed Winston on the kitchen counter, took out the can, and sliced a pear into slivers, threading them piece by piece into his mouth. She couldn't help noticing what a pretty, manly little body the boy had.

It was a crime Betty Ann had let him get eaten away from the rash. Ask the girl for a simple favor once in a blue moon, and this was the way it turned out.

Where did he come from, whose baby had he been? Sheriff Hawke said he really didn't know. So Alma took him in while they searched for a permanent home, trying without success not to get attached to the infant who soon grew into a toddler and then a small boy.

"What'd you like to do, Sugarplum? It's too hot to make mudpies, now ain't it? You want to play with some toys Grandma has? You would? Well, all right. Let's do that."

The heat was getting to her, making her feel queasy. Alma got a clean sheet from the closet, spread it across the kitchen floor, and set Winston in the middle. Then she surrounded him with plastic margarine tubs, measuring spoons, a saucepan and a wooden cook spoon.

She sat down at the kitchen table with a sigh and looked at the boy still as a statue. Well, he'd sit there all day, even if he messed himself. Dear Lord, but it was pitiful.

Alma felt nearly overwhelmed with sadness, picturing what would happen when Winston was older and not so pretty, and the rest of the world found out he was a big empty-headed baby.

People couldn't stand each other, anyhow, and if there was anything wrong with a person, they couldn't wait to be cruel, like they'd been saving it up, a pack of hungry wolves going for the weakest lamb. Somebody might even kill Winston out of meanness, and poor Winston wouldn't be able to protect himself much less know what had hit him and just forget about figuring out why.

Lord have mercy, but it was a scorcher! Alma's forehead was soaked. The kitchen was so stuffy she was afraid Winston might take sick from it. She rolled the floor fan from the bedroom to the kitchen door and turned on the fan to high.

Then she poured some apple juice into a plastic baby bottle and handed it to Winston. The bottle thudded to the floor. She picked it up, put the nipple in Winston's mouth and moved it around until the slack jaws began to suck.

No matter how sick or weak or empty a living creature might be, some part of it wanted to survive. Even Winston. At least he knew how to suck and chew. That was all he did, eat and sleep and soil his diapers, like a little machine.

Alma loved her grandchildren, but it was only Winston she truly enjoyed being with. He made her heart stir with a long-forgotten feeling. She wanted to hold him and protect him from the world.

Sometimes when the two of them were together like this, Alma felt completely at peace. Maybe that was Winston's strange gift, being a comfort to a dried-up old woman in her last years.

The thought made her feel selfish and greedy, knowing how Winston was by far the sorest point there'd ever been between Alma and Ben Lightfoot. When her husband's eyes fell on the child, he looked like nothing so much as a frightened rabbit snared in a trap. And that was the crux of it. Winston forced anyone who set eyes on him to consider things about the Lord and life and nature they'd rather not think about.

But Alma knew she was different. Once somebody told her Alma was Mexican for soul. She could bear the mystery of Winston's condition with simple faith the Lord had His reasons. If Ben couldn't, that was his problem.

Her garden needed watering, but she'd have to wait for the cool of an evening. She lifted Winston to set him on a bath-towel and gently pushed him over on his side. She got down and stretched out beside him.

"Grandma's real tired, honey," she said softly. "Let's take a nice nap." She closed her eyes, feeling the occasional gusts of cool air from the fan, thanking the Lord for the gift of sleep, when even your worst troubles could disappear for a little.

###

"Well, my Lord, woman! Would you go and look at this?"

Alma was pulled back by the sound of her husband's voice. Her eyes fluttered awake. She struggled to sit up. The air was moist and suffocating, the front of her dress wet. "What time is it? Ben, are you home for good?"

Noticing how the light had shifted, she realized she'd slept away the afternoon. Must be close to six o'clock, she decided, already dreading a sleepless night.

"Look at what he done!" For once, Ben's voice didn't sound the least bit harsh or angry, which was usually the case when confronted by Baby Winston.

She looked at where Ben was staring. Winston had made a cave of her body as she slept, fitted himself against her like a teaspoon inside a tablespoon. Even now he remained curved in her shadow, though his dark eyes seemed focused on his Granddad.

"Hello, little fella!" Ben extended his rough paw toward the child. "Do you know who I am? I'm your Pappy! Say hey to Pappy!" To Alma, Ben said, "Why, I declare, but I do believe the boy's eyes are right on me."

"What you think we ought to do?"

"Nothing yet. Let's see how long I can hold his attention. Winston, how are you, boy? Did you have a nap with Grandma? Hungry? Been waiting supper for Pappy to come home?"

Alma squelched a crazy desire to shove her own face between Ben's and the child's, to have Winston looking at her just one time.

She remembered the garden that hadn't been watered, the load of dingy diapers she'd meant to bleach. She was glad she'd made the macaroni salad before the heat of the day hit hardest, remembering to boil the noodles at seven in the morning. Then she wondered what else she could think about, to make time stop in its tracks.

But the spell was broken when Winston turned his face away and studied the wall.

"Shoot," Ben said dully, all the life drained out of his voice. "I coulda swore the boy was looking right at me. Musta been a trick of the light. What's for supper?"

"I'll set it out in a minute," she said, while sponging off Winston's bottom. Sure enough, he had peed all over the sheet and the front of Alma's dress. "Look at how Betty Ann let him get, Ben. I need to talk to that girl. She's had babies to tend to before. Ain't no excuse for a dirty diaper staying on for hours."

13

She plunked him down on a folded towel in the old highchair that had been in the same place for thirty-three years, one of Alma's babies or grandbabies putting it to use. Then she set a plate of yesterday's biscuits to warm in the oven. Soon a load of diapers churned in the washing mahine, and the fan turned to low to circulate the air while they ate.

Alma and Ben sat at the table with macaroni salad and Jell-O salad, buttered biscuits with homemade may-apple preserves, pickled eggs and a jar of Penrose sausages. She poured more iced tea with a sly glance at Ben whose hopeful eyes were trained on Winston. She fed a few noodles at a time on a spoon to the boy, waiting until the noodles slid down his throat and his mouth opened for more.

Alma remembered what her own mother had said about Ben Light-foot blundering into her daughter's life. "Sleep with him if you have to," her mother said. "Have yourself one of them affairs. But don't marry him or he'll ruin your life."

Well, not exactly the truth, as it turned out, to Alma's mind. There'd been some right happy years. But Donny grew up and went to Vietnam, he'd been the last, and things turned sour between Alma and Ben. They'd been thrown back on themselves, like two old dogs penned up in a cage.

Ben Lightfoot may not have amounted to much, as Alma's mother feared would happen. But neither had Alma. She was good with children, but she couldn't keep a clean house. She had to laugh.

Tearing into a buttered biscuit, Ben said, "What's so funny?"

"Oh, I don't know. I was just remembering how it used to be when we had a houseful of kids. Things were good then, weren't they, Ben?"

"And that made you laugh?"

"Well, life ain't no laughing matter, I guess. Still, though. If you can't laugh, most of the time you'd be bawling."

"That's the truth there. Alma, I coulda swore he looked right at me."

"Might have. Maybe we'll never know if he did or didn't." She picked up her fork to feed herself. As she finished her Jell-O salad, she heard a sound as ancient as life itself.

"Wah!" The sound had come from Winston's mouth. And he was staring at her, hard.

"Good gracious, he wants more food!" Ben said, his eyes popping. "I don't believe it!"

"Well, Mr. Winston, what you want? Jell-O? Well, here you are!" The little boy was chewing and gazing around the kitchen, and at Ben and Alma, as if noticing things for the first time.

In amazement, Ben said, "It's like he woke up from a deep sleep, like that Rip Van Winkle."

Alma was nearly beside herself. It was as if Jesus Himself had crept into the Lightfoot kitchen to breathe life into Winston, just like He'd raised the dead. She felt light as a feather caught in the currents of a stream, rushing toward a happy place.

Ben got up from the table and bent down for a minute to chuck Winston under the chin. "You want to go outside in the yard with Pappy and look around, son?"

"Wah!"

He lifted the boy into his arms. "Let's us go whiff ourselves a flower and chase after a honeybee."

Clearing the table, Alma marveled how any mortal soul could so easily forget the constant presence of The Almighty. Suddenly she felt so full of energy and life that she had to blink back tears. If ever two people had needed Winston, it was Alma and Ben.

Tomorrow she'd pull out the old blocks and toys from the chest in the attic. Winston could play while she cleaned the house. With every stroke of her broom and swipe of the dust-rag, she'd say "Forgive me, Jesus." Then she'd spend time with Winston. First, she was going to teach him how to talk. After he'd learned a word or two, she and Ben and Winston could have their cool summer supper.

When Ben brought Winston in from the yard, Alma propped the boy in her big double bed with pillows bolstering his side so he wouldn't roll off and hit his head. Stretching out beside him, she told herself she wasn't about to lose him for a moron, not again. Why, he might grow up to be a famous man, a doctor or merchant, a sheriff, or...

When Alma woke at sunrise, Winston's big brown eyes were peering straight into her soul, his little hand wrapped around her finger. Choking down a sob of pure happiness, she kissed his soft cheek.

And in the friendly, efficient tone always reserved for him, she said, "Welcome to the morning, Winston. Did you have yourself a nice dream?"

#

In the fall and winter months, the Sheriff's Department could count on dispatching the fire trucks to half a dozen houses tucked back in the hollows. People heated with wood. Chimneys harbored invisible wonderlands of creosote, stovepipes exploded.

When the call came in June, Edgar Wills was surprised. It was

Hawke's day off, and Wills hated to disturb him, seeing as how he was recovering from gall bladder surgery. To make matters worse, Edgar had to rouse the Sheriff from an afternoon nap.

"You handle it," Hawke said thickly. "Let me know about any survivors."

"I hate these damned fires, Ray. By the time we get there, it's always too late."

"Then why don't you hang up the damned phone and tell Ruby to dispatch the fire trucks?"

As the deputy could have expected, the house was an inferno. Some of the volunteer firemen aimed a few hoses at the blaze, but the weak streams of water pumped from the Capon River, low from the drought, were a joke and only seemed to make the flames shoot higher. The best they could do was wait until the fire burned itself out and soak the smoldering pile of ashes, the remains of the Lightfoots' life.

A dark-haired boy sat in a tire-swing under a sweetgum tree. Edgar guessed he was one of the Lightfoot grandsons.

"Boy, how'd the fire start, do you know?"

The small boy shrugged and said nothing. Deputy Wills figured the child must have been in shock. Quietly, he led him toward the patrol car, to drive him into town to the office until Ruby Whitlow could locate his next of kin.

"What's your name, son?"

"Grandmama called me Winston, she said after her own Paw. Never knew what my real name was."

"Oh? How so?" Edgar thought it would be a healthy thing to keep the boy talking, take his mind off the tragedy.

"Grandmama said she adopted me when I was a baby."

Then it all came back to Edgar Wills. An infant found in a snowbank after a fire at the old school bus, Sheriff Hawke taking the child to Alma Lightfoot after she'd lost a new grandbaby.

"How old are you, son?"

"Five."

"Five! For a fact? You seem older than five. Why, you're a big fellow now, ain't you?"

"Guess so."

"You got some relatives I can call you could stay with?"

"My Aunt Betty Ann. But she took her kids and moved away when she got married. Don't know where they went."

"Well, who'd she marry? What's his last name?"

"Don't know that, either."

"Well, you can come to my house for a while and stay with me and my new bride. We got a horse. Sound okay with you, son?"

No answer. Maybe the boy was afraid of horses.

Deputy Wills wondered what Angie would say when he brought home a five-year-old boy. Just temporarily until we can locate his relatives, he'd tell her. They'd only been married a month, but Angie was expecting their first child four months away. She stayed mad at him.

He couldn't see why. He'd done the right thing. When a decent man swells a woman's belly, he has an obligation to marry her. Besides, it was Edgar's own fault because he didn't cotton to those damned condom things. Like wearing a raincoat in the shower, he used to joke with her, but it didn't seem nearly so funny now.

Well, maybe she wouldn't mind if the boy stayed with them in the spare bedroom for a few days. But not any longer. They already had more than they could handle, trying to get along with one another. Married life was really different, took some getting used to. No doubt about it.

Anyhow, Edgar didn't want to make Angie madder with him than she had been since before their official wedding day. He kept telling her how much he loved her, but he suspected she either didn't believe it or didn't care. He hoped things would improve once the baby was born, but there was no guarantee of that, either.

When they were on the outskirts of the town limits, the patrol car hit a skunk straddling the middle line of the road. He looked over to see if the boy had noticed, but his eyes were pinned to the dials on the dashboard.

Later he'd talk to Sheriff Hawke and they'd figure out what to do. No telling where Aunt Betty had gone. Once somebody worked up the gumption to get out of Ridley, they seldom came back.

If this was the same baby they'd rescued from the school bus five years ago, the boy had lost people he loved not once, but twice. Not that he'd rightly remember his mother, though. What was her name? Edgar couldn't recall.

Edgar thought how, this time, it wouldn't be so easy to find another home for him. People around here were mighty superstitious, Appalachia steeped in folklore. After such tragedy in his tender years, he had to be marked.

Not so you'd notice to look at him, though.

When Edgar Wills glanced over at the boy again, he'd fallen asleep. The dreamless sleep of the innocent, Edgar thought to himself.

Poor little thing

Chapter Three

With a lurching gait thanks to his arthritic leg, Jenkins Mallory walked three blocks from his house to town. Funny how things had changed around Ridley in the past few years, yet the elderly colored man gnarled as a sycamore stump had never abandoned his bench. He waved at Old Claude before going inside Fletcher's Pharmacy that used to be the Ben Franklin Variety.

"Howdy, Sam." Mallory handed a prescription to the druggist.

"Fill 'er up again?"

"Might as well. Don't sleep without it."

"You mentioned that to Doc Watkins?"

"Sure. He says keep taking it. At my age, why not." The doc had also recommended knee replacement surgery, but Mallory had declined.

"Have a seat. It'll be a few minutes."

Favoring his bum leg, Mallory eased onto a stool at the soda fountain, dropped his elbows on the counter and thought about how once he'd expected to see the year 2000. Well, 2000 was twenty years away, and Mallory knew Hell would freeze over sooner than he'd witness a new century.

When he noticed the dampness of his shirtsleeves, he folded his arms across his chest. He read the hand-lettered sign that said *My boss told me to change this sign, so I did.* Fletcher's teenage grandson Marshal worked in the drugstore after school let out and in the hardware store on weekends. Someday this store, and the hardware next to it, would belong to Marshal. They called him Marsh.

Not a bad thing to leave to a boy, Mallory decided. Better than what he had, and then with nobody to leave it to. Chicken-shit piece of land, nothing'll grow on it. Couldn't live on it, if a man was in his right mind. Sixteen acres just past Overton, sixteen acres of nothing...

But when he thought about his land, the idea of leaving the white frame house where he lived three blocks from the Ridley post office was a temptation. He could drive out and walk the property for a change of pace, like Doc Watkins talked about as being good for a man's spirits.

"You may be seventy-two, Jenk," the Doc said. "But it's a sorry excuse for living in a rut, which is one step from being in your grave. Pry yourself loose from those damned television shows and get some exercise. Do something different, take some risks!"

Sam Fletcher set a white paper sack on the counter in front of him. "Put this on your bill?" When Mallory nodded, Sam said, "Hey, Jenk. What about the big shindig they're having up at Aaron's place tonight?"

He noticed the sparkle in Fletcher's eyes, plain devilment, it was – even as a boy, Fletcher had a mean streak – and Mallory didn't like to be toyed with.

"How should I know? He ain't no kin of mine." He slid off the stool, thanked Fletcher for the pills, and hobbled away.

Just past the town limits, Mallory took a deep breath and felt himself loosen up like a sapling released from the grip of a strong wind. Lately he'd been feeling out of sorts , and he knew it was partly due to his poor health. The rest was because of Aaron, the dirty son of a bitch. Why Elsie, God rest her soul, had ever taken him into their home…

But she couldn't bring herself to say no to Ray Hawke, that was the short of it, when the sheriff appeared on their doorstep one rainy night with a five-year-old boy, the only survivor of the fire at the Lightfoot place.

A temporary foster child, Elsie had said, her face all aglow with stored-up love for a boy who would fill the space of the child of their own they'd only been able to imagine. She named him Aaron, Elvis Presley's middle name. They'd been calling him Winston, but the boy said he didn't care if he was Aaron or Winston, because he didn't know what his real name was, anyhow.

They'd only had him four years, and those four years were a damned sight too many.

But he wouldn't let himself think about Aaron, which was the reason for getting away from Ridley in the first place.

Driving along at a cautious speed, he was glad the first killing frost hadn't come yet as he savored the changing leaves, seeking out the blush of dogwood from golden tulip poplars painting the hillsides. Once he'd planned to plant two dogwoods in front of the house they were going to build. But that dream died with Elsie. Cancer of the spine.

"Sweet Jesus," Mallory said, drawing the beauty of the mountains into himself. He relaxed behind the wheel of his Monte Carlo. The doctor had told him not to drive for a while, but Mallory trusted the old car. He had a healthy respect for machines.

If his blood pressure had been under control, he could have camped out under the stars. *The awful majesty of the night* popped into his head, a piece of Reverend Litchfield's sermon many Easters ago.

He wondered what Sam Fletcher had gotten wind of this time. How did news blow around to the whole of Ridley before it reached Jenk Mallory? Sometimes he felt as if his head was stuck down in slime. But he was used to keeping to himself, a habit from driving a rig along the Blue Ridge Parkway all the way up north to Cleveland, Toledo, and Detroit.

Then there was always Elsie to come home to. Just the two of them, until Aaron wedged himself in the middle.

She'd been gone three years, and still he listened for her sweet voice. The Good Lord never made a woman finer than his Elsie.

The woods began to thicken, a dense green-black texture giving off a scent through the open window that reminded Mallory of cedar shakes fresh-hammered to a roof. Virgin woods, but not for long, not if the land developers had their way about it. Mallory had gotten offers on his sixteen acres from two of them.

But he refused to sell. Sixteen acres wasn't much to show for a lifetime of farming and driving a rig, but it was better than nothing.

He caught himself thinking that way again. Lately he'd been weighing whatever he looked at or thought about as not-much-but-better-than-nothing, himself included. He considered asking Doc Watkins if it was a sign of the end drawing near.

What was a man supposed to do, anyhow, when he knew he was going to die? Mallory thought he'd keep planting his garden, feed the chickens and choose the plumpest for Sunday dinner, like nothing unusual was coming about at all.

What else could he do? Cry over spilt milk, over plans never hatched or dreams that would never be true? Over losing his wife or not having any natural-born sons? Hell, he could handle most of what was in his mind, even Elsie's death, if it just hadn't been for that dark, shifty-eyed little bastard who had tainted his married life.

God-given: that's what Reverend Litchfield had said about the way Elsie died. Which was what they'd told him about Aaron when the boy was nine years old. Some psychic fellow from the state university had been real interested in the strange things happening on Easter Sunday six years past *in the heart of Appalachia, at the home of Mr. and Mrs. Jenkins Mallory in an obscure, backwoods place called Ridley in the mountains of West Virginia,* as the big papers put it. Mallory was the only one who hadn't been particularly surprised. Shoot, but the boy had been downright peculiar from the first.

He turned the car into an overgrown path and drove through the wall of loblolly pines. Parking the car at the far side of a clearing, he dragged the canvas tarp from the trunk and spread it over the cold ground.

He sat down on the canvas, fumbled in his shirt pocket for matches and a forbidden smoke. Puffing, Mallory looked at the spot in the middle of the clearing where the cabin would have been. The ring of boulders Elsie helped him roll to the place would always be here.

"My kitchen," she had said to him with a shy smile.

Her kitchen.

He could hear Roy Litchfield preaching about what happens to sinners who question God's will. "She's gone to her Maker," the Reverend said to Mallory after Elsie's funeral. "Elsie's at peace. You should get down on your knees and praise the Lord for ending her suffering and taking her away from this woeful world of cares."

Then Roy Litchfield reminded Mallory of how God always works in mysterious ways, how only fools would waste their time trying to figure out the designs of The Almighty. It wasn't long after when, one by one, the members of Litchfield's church began drifting over to the Church of Mystery and Miracles, Aaron's church, so that Roy Litchfield had to pack his family's things in a U-Haul truck and move on to start another church somewhere else.

Mallory shook his head, took a last puff of his cigarette and stubbed it out on the heel of his boot. He tried to settle on a different topic to think about, something interesting and new, so his mind wouldn't dwell on Aaron.

He went back to the car, got the can of chicken and dumplings that he opened with his jack-knife and ate with his traveling spoon kept on the dashboard of the Monte Carlo as a reminder of the old trucking days.

Leaning against the left front fender of the Monte Carlo, he felt for his watch in the bib pocket of his overalls before remembering he'd left it on the bedroom bureau. But he could tell by the sun it couldn't be much more than two o'clock.

Mallory's stomach felt like a twisted rag, and his bowels were churning. Weakly, he crept over to the tarp to lie down and let his food digest...

...Elsie in her Easter outfit, a navy-blue dress and a white straw hat crowned with red flowers. She stands in front of the big bureau mirror, fixing her hair and trying on the new hat, then taking off the hat and arranging her hair again. Yesterday she went to the beauty parlor.

"You better hurry, honey," Mallory says with a grin.

"Don't you get to rushin' me, now," she says brightly.

"Then I'll hunt the boy and warm up the car." Mallory goes downstairs and out the kitchen door to the Monte Carlo. The car was only a few years old when he bought it used, and he's proud of how yesterday's wax job glistened in the April sun.

The day is warm and birds are chirping. Buds on the big oak in the backyard are anxious to be leaves. Red and yellow tulips blaze in Elsie's flower garden near the tool shed. Pleased by the morning, by the warm sunshine on his face, Mallory climbs behind the wheel of his car.

Aaron slumps in the back seat, wrinkling his new suit from the Sears catalogue.

"Hey, boy! Cheer up. Church won't last all day. I declare, but if you don't look like the devil's got your tail." He starts the car. "You best not let your mother see you sour as a lemon on Easter morning, boy." Mallory pushes the accelerator with his foot so the engine makes quick, startled noises ending in a high whine. He needs to adjust the idle.

"She ain't my mother."

Mallory turns around and stares at Aaron. "Well, where'd you ever get a fool notion like that?"

"The kids livin' down by the cider mill. How come it's them knows she ain't?" The boy kicks the back of Mallory's seat for good measure.

The expression in Aaron's dark, flashing eyes gives Mallory a strange chill. He releases his breath slowly, turns toward the steering wheel, and raps the horn twice. Not loud enough; maybe the horn needs adjusting, too.

"Well, boy. That's something we can talk about later. Right now we're going to hear Reverend Litchfield preach about Jesus rising from the grave. Now I'd say that's a mite more important than this problem you seem to be nursing pretty careful so it don't up and disappear on you. Wouldn't you say the fact that Jesus rolled away the rock from the tomb after dying in agony on the cross for the wickedness of mankind so all us legions can get to Heaven, whosoever believeth in Him, never mind what a sorry bunch we are, shouldn't Jesus rising from the grave be the main concern of every God-fearing man, woman, and child on Easter morning?"

Waiting for an answer, Mallory's face is hot. His voice sounded shrill to his own ears, and he has an awful urge to slap the boy until his ears rattle. "Well?" To the boy's mumbled yessir, Mallory says, "That's more like it."

He sees Elsie tiptoeing down the steps in her shiny new high-heeled shoes.

"Here comes Mother. You button your lip till we get home, and you smile and say how-de-doo to everybody we meet, or I'll give you the licking of your life. You can set your clock by it."

He reaches across the front seat and opens the door for Elsie. She gets into the car, patting at the springy curls that are visible beneath the wide-brimmed hat. He loves it when she feels pretty.

To Aaron, he says, "Well, boy? Don't you think we ought to tell Mother how mighty fine she looks?"

Then they are at the church, singing hymns and giving coins to the collection plate. Now they are shaking hands and sincerely complimenting Reverend Litchfield on his sermon.

"Uplifting, Reverend," Elsie insists, holding onto Aaron's hand at the doors of the little white church while Mallory walks ahead with some of the other men to fetch the vehicles...

###

The call of a beast, sharp and agonized, caused Mallory to sit up all at once. His ears burned with keen listening, his body taut as a snug rubber band. He wondered whether he'd heard a coyote, or maybe a bobcat. But his stomach didn't feel a danged bit better, not yet...

###

They have finished feasting on Elsie's ham dinner with mashed potatoes and red-eye gravy, sweet garden peas, fried apple fritters, butter beans and corn, coleslaw, cherry pie with vanilla ice cream, and Mallory is helping Elsie clear the table like he always does on holidays when things start sliding across the floor.

They hear it upstairs in their bedroom, the big brass bed upended and smashing through one of the bedroom windows. Then the refrigerator moves a good four feet chasing Mallory from the back door to the kitchen sink. Dishes hurl themselves from the kitchen counter and off the shelves of the china cabinet. Elsie screams and wants to run and find Aaron, but Mallory pushes her out of the house saying he'll find the boy.

Neighbors from both sides and from across the street stand around asking what's going on at the Mallory place. Mallory hears somebody shouting to call the sheriff, and on his way upstairs he thinks that's a durned idiot idea. He wonders what good the sheriff can do when he sees Aaron huddled against the side of an armoire on the landing at the top of the stairs. He grabs Aaron's arm and pulls him downstairs and out to the backyard.

The crashing inside the house comes to a stop. In silence, the people gape at one another. Mallory looks around at the crowd gathered on his lawn. To Elsie he says, "Well, guess it must be over."

"What was it, Jenk?" one of the neighbor men asks.

"Danged if I know," he says. "Never seen nothing like it in my entire life."

"Devils," Aaron says softly. "We got us a heap of devils."

"Hush, boy!" Elsie whispers. "You want our neighbors thinkin' something's wrong with us?"

The sheriff's car pulls up in front of the house. They watch as Sheriff Hawke strolls toward them with his holstered gun flapping on his hip. Mallory tells the story to Hawke. When Hawke asks for volunteers, Mallory and five other men follow the sheriff into the house.

Not much of the furniture is broken. Mainly it's the big pane in the bedroom window; that's gone. It doesn't take long to straighten the house.

But things start toppling over in the middle of the night, when Mallory and Elsie are asleep. It happens three times the next day, twice the third day, and seven times the day after. Most of their dishes are gone and Elsie's little knickknacks smashed to smithereens. By then the reporters and television people had set up shop on every square inch of Mallory's yard, taking measurements and whatnot.

Professor Barlach arrives and asks different questions from those Mallory has heard at least twenty times before. Then the professor asks Aaron a lot of questions about his feelings and his childhood, but to Mallory's relief Aaron says nothing about Elsie not being his real mother.

Slowly, Mallory and Elsie come to understand that the *phenomenon* only happens when Aaron is in the house. Barlach claims Aaron has *powers of the sort science has not begun to comprehend.* Mallory wants to know what else Aaron can do with those powers, and where it comes from, but he won't ask for fear of being taken for ignorant.

There isn't anything to do but keep Aaron out of the house, but the boy doesn't seem to care. He just stands there, glaring at Mallory. The same welfare lady who let the Mallorys keep Aaron takes him to Reverend Litchfield's house, because nobody else in town will have him, not even for a temporary foster child.

But over the next three years Elsie goes to see the boy every day. She gives him presents at Christmas and on his birthday, takes him sweet things she baked in the oven, just as if he never stopped being her son.

Then Elsie dies. Mallory sees himself going to her grave three Easters. Twice there's sunshine, once a warm rain, and Mallory leaves red carnations.

When he sees Aaron on the street, they stare at one another. Mallory turns his head and refuses to speak, pretending never to have laid eyes on the boy before. He feels like an old coward, a yellow belly, and has a suspicion people make jokes behind his back, people like Sam Fletcher.

The truth is, he's plum afraid of Aaron. The other people in Ridley don't know, Mallory never told them what he heard from Professor Barlach, about Elsie not being the *catalyst* to fire up Aaron's powers.

"In rare cases that have been well-documented, children under stress have been known to unleash excessive mental energy sufficient to move inanimate objects," Barlach said to him. "What kind of relationship do you have with your son?"

Mallory could only gape at the short, chunky man. "Why, I feed him and buy clothes for his back. What else is a man meant to do? Raising kids, that's woman's work, you ask me."

"Do you use corporal punishment with the boy?"

"Pardon me?"

"Do you spank the boy with your hand, or strap?"

After Barlach and the rest are gone from Ridley, Mallory is left with a gnawing feeling there's something he was supposed to do, but he can't figure out what in the world it could be...

A whistling wind came up and smacked a corner of the tarp against Mallory's face. He sat up with a groan, rubbing his eyes. The sky was a dark, peacock blue, with a bank of blackish clouds boiling over the treetops.

From a sense that something had slipped through his fingers like water through a sieve, he knew he'd had the old dream again, where everything was alive and in color and he could touch Elsie's face. Well, it was his own fault for letting himself doze off. After one of those dreams, he woke up feeling empty inside.

So he was going to die. Well, who didn't? Nothing to fear. The truth was, it might be better to go ahead and be dead than only half-alive and worried something terrible was fixin' to befall him, to boot.

He sat in the growing darkness of the late afternoon listening to the wind build up in the pines. Behind the pack of Viceroys in his shirt pocket was a folded square of paper. Mallory took it out, smoothed it flat, and read it again:

THE MESSIAH HAS COME! *And you can meet him! Bring the troubled, the sick, the lonely-of-heart. Tonight, at the Church of Mystery and Miracles, your questions will be answered, your bodies will be healed, your souls will be saved! No request too large or too small. Tonight at 8 o'clock. (Donations gratefully accepted.)*

He'd found the flyer jammed in the side of his screen door at sunrise, when he went out to scatter cracked corn for the chickens. At first it made him angry to find it, but as the day progressed, he caught himself wondering if it was a true sign of God's mysterious ways.

Even the name of the church set him to thinking. Mystery and Miracles. If Jenkins Mallory wasn't in need of a good, honest miracle, he didn't know who was. *Seek and ye shall find*; didn't the Bible say that, right out?

The Bible also said *Pride goeth before a fall.*

He wondered if he was the only man in Ridley who hadn't gone to the Church of Mystery and Miracles for a miracle of his own. Aaron was just sixteen, and already he had a following. For the revivals, people even drove in from out of state, foreign license plates sprinkled all over town.

A miracle: Mallory turned it over in his mind, trying to figure out what could be called a real miracle, and what was only wishful thinking.

Now, Jesus had given miracles to the nonbelievers to prove he was the Son. Water into wine, little fishes and a few loaves of bread feeding the multitudes. But that was Jesus, and to Mallory's way of thinking, God only had one Son.

Aaron couldn't be any real Jesus, but maybe he was like one of those impersonators, the fat guys in white suits who tried to pass for Elvis. People knew Elvis was dead, but when they were watching one of those impersonators singing *You Ain't Nothing But a Hound Dog* and swinging his fat hips around, they probably liked believing Elvis was alive again, and for a little while it seemed real.

Maybe that was the way it was with Aaron up at the church. People knew he wasn't Jesus. But to get their miracles, for a minute they were glad to pretend he was.

Well, Mallory had witnessed a lot of peculiar things in his time.

He'd seen a rabbit chewing off its own paw to get out of a trap. He'd seen it rain on sunny days, when people said the devil was beating his wife. He'd seen strong men turn tail and behave like crybabies over any number of things Jenkins Mallory would have hooted at, had he been in their place. And he'd watched the furniture in his own house hopping around like Mexican jumping beans.

But the strangest thing he'd ever watched in his life was the way Elsie died. She was a woman with spare meat on her bones, a woman you could hold onto, but the cancer, all it left was a skeleton with a bit of skin to cover for decency's sake.

He sniffed the crisp November air. Now the dark sky promised snow. Coming out to his land was an excuse, an escape. But suddenly he knew there wasn't going to be any escape, not for him. He'd been running away from it for too durned long.

Doc Watkins was right. Mallory had been keeping to himself too much, there was the problem. He managed to live like a hermit in the heart of a small but friendly town filled with people he'd known all his life. Sure, he missed poker with Fletcher and Timpkins and the boys. But what he had missed most was regular Christian fellowship.

Before Litchfield left town, Mallory had pledged he'd never darken the door of Aaron's church come Hell or high water.

"Don't deny Jesus on my account," Roy said. "It would make me really sad, Jenk."

"Yeah, Roy, but how am I going to know if that church of Aaron's preaches the Blood? What's to say there's any Jesus in Aaron's message a'tall?"

Litchfield thought for a moment, rubbing the top of his bald head. "The only way you'll ever know is to go and see for yourself. Listen to his message with an open heart. You can't expect other people to do your living for you."

"Well, if Jesus is in Aaron's heart, how come they both run you out of business?"

"Aaron must have a more powerful feeling for the Holy Ghost than I do," Roy had said. "Maybe it's because my message comes across too tame. You know that charisma they're talking about in theological circles these days? Aaron's got himself charisma. Maybe I'm supposed to move on and plant God's word in fertile ground. I'm going in faith, Jenk. Ridley belongs to Aaron now."

Before he could change his mind, Mallory gathered the tarp and threw it in the back seat of his car. When the Monte Carlo's engine started with one try, he gave a sigh of relief. The car was so old and moody, he never knew what it might do. Carefully, he turned around in the clearing and drove the two miles through his property to the road.

It wasn't as if he was greedy about hanging onto life. Even if he could be forty again, Elsie was gone, and what good would it be to him to keep on living? He'd done just about everything there was to do. And he didn't have the desire to travel, because he'd seen the sights for thirty-seven years from the cab of an eighteen-wheeler. So, what was left?

But what could he give in exchange? The flyer said donations were accepted, which meant expected.

When he'd seriously considered following Doc Watkins' advice about having the heart operation, Mallory went to the bank to see David Crenshaw who told him, "Jenk, you don't have any liquid assets to speak of. Medicare won't pay all the tab, so you'll have to sell something off to pay the difference or die a debtor. But since you have no legal heirs, at least you won't leave unpaid bills for somebody else to have to fret about."

He knew David had meant it for a joke, but Mallory didn't think it was funny. He'd always made a practice of paying his bills on time. He'd refused the operation.

As he drove along the highway, Mallory wondered how Aaron remembered him, whether the boy would even recognize Jenkins Mallory. Tears stung his eyes, thinking about the years Aaron had spent in the Mallory home. He and Elsie had tried to love the boy, hadn't they? It wasn't their fault Aaron started showing off his psychic powers.

Was it their fault? Or was Jenkins Mallory to blame? The things Professor Barlach said had come back to haunt him more than once, though he couldn't understand what hidden truth there was behind those educated words.

When he really stopped to think about it, he realized that Aaron was the closest thing to a son Jenkins and Elsie Mallory had ever had.

Since he didn't have much in the way of liquid assets, the only donation he could offer was this car. It was old, but it ran. Better than nothing. He would donate the Monte Carlo tomorrow, since he wasn't supposed to drive for fear of suffering a stroke at the wheel.

People like Sam Fletcher probably thought he wasn't interested enough to listen to the stories. But Mallory kept his ears open, and he'd heard plenty about the miracles visited upon Ridley, an ongoing topic of conversation at the local barber shop.

People had been snatched from Death's doorway. Sick babies were healed. Lula Jasper didn't have arthritis anymore, and now she was walking all over town. Wasn't it a kind of miracle that people were getting rich off the land developers even while they whittled down their needs to nearly nothing?

The people in Ridley had been filled with love and the Holy Spirit. Lots of them had started giving half their yearly incomes to Aaron's church. The land was being sold out from under their feet, but they didn't seem to notice. Mallory had even heard that Aaron was truly Christ Returned, and the last conversion of the multitudes was scheduled to take place with Ridley as home base, the site of the Rapture before the end of the world.

Just like Elsie used to say, Mallory was a born-again skeptic. Plenty of times he had cursed Aaron for making monkeys out of his old friends and neighbors. But they all seemed so happy and choked with joy. Even Sam Fletcher, with his college education, had taken his mother over to the Church of Mystery and Miracles so she could get rid of her palsy.

Where two or three are gathered in My Name, I am there. But Aaron had a durned sight more than two or three, or even two or three hundred, and the number was growing.

The car bucked and wavered almost out of his control. He played with the brake pedal while turning the steering wheel in the direction it wanted to go. In a few anxious seconds that felt like hours, Mallory managed to steer the Monte Carlo to the narrow shoulder of the road. He snapped off the ignition, fell back against the seat, and clutched his chest. He breathed slowly, in and out, his heart in flames.

When he felt strong enough to get out of the car, he walked around to take a gander at the right front tire. Flat as a hotcake. His temples were pounding. He wanted to grab the jack out of the trunk and beat the car to a rusty pulp for doing this to him. Instead, he got the jack, a flashlight, and the spare tire, and set to the task.

The wind at the back of his neck was an icy knife. By the time he had changed the tire, leaving the flat in a bed of brambles at the side of the road, he was shivering so hard his dentures chattered. Vaguely he hoped he wouldn't get the pneumonia.

Well, he wouldn't have time to go home to freshen up and put on his suit. But maybe that didn't matter. Where did it say in the Bible the Lord gave a hoot how a man decorated himself to come to church? Suit or no suit, he'd be there, because he had to see what was going on up at that church, he had to see it for himself.

If you think you'll be around for a long time, then what you do from one day to the next doesn't seem so important. A young man can always tell himself he has plenty of time to spare. But when you start feeling your days are numbered…

He rehearsed what to say, should anyone ask why it had taken so long for Mallory to show up at church.

He started the engine, crawled back onto the road. And he knew his decision to let things simmer for a little while was the right one, when the second part of his request for a miracle came to him.

He was going to ask for no pain when dying, first off. But the meat of his miracle was to have a talk with Elsie. Barnett Shiloh claimed he'd spoken with his dear departed Daddy. If Mallory could just hear her voice…

For that, Mallory would have gladly donated the car and his house, the house after he died. If he wanted to come out to his land, he could hitch a ride with Hawke or Timpkins or catch the bus to Overton and walk the rest of the way. The exercise would do him good, what with his bum ticker and all.

He wished more than anything that Elsie was riding along with him tonight. She would have loved going to Aaron's church to hear him preach. She'd always believed in the boy, and she thought the different thing setting him apart was a holy thing. Mallory had argued her down, believing it was pure evil. For the first time he hoped he was wrong, and he'd only had the scales of the world coating his eyes.

He couldn't remember feeling fresh and raw as a newborn babe, as he made the promise he'd be open to anything Aaron had to say. The tables seemed to have turned, because Aaron was the shepherd and Mallory was eager to be accepted as one of his sheep. Even if Aaron remembered those lickings out by the tool shed, surely he also believed the Bible's teachings as Mallory did: when you spared the rod, you spoiled the boy.

He turned left instead of taking the main street through Ridley, thinking of saving a little time. This road circled the abandoned arsenic and gypsum mines, went through the colored part of town, and on to the Church of Mystery and Miracles perched high on a hilltop.

A searchlight slashed through the black sky. He couldn't find a place to park, driving in and out of rows of cars. Leaving the keys in the ignition, thinking that after tonight he wouldn't be needing them anymore, he left the Monte Carlo at the end of a long line of cars and trucks, beside a Trailways bus that said <u>Charter</u>.

Mallory climbed from the car, resting his hand on the hood for a minute as if preparing to say goodbye to an old friend who had served him well. Droves of people hurried to the main entrance of the church, and Mallory let himself get caught up in the crowd.

The church was new, a great square made of brick and cinderblock, two stained-glass windows shining like jewels in the night, a huge concrete cross to the left side of the entrance. When he walked up the front steps, Mallory paused, feeling out of place in his bibbed overalls, worn flannel shirt, and scuffed work boots.

On either side of him, people streamed through the doorway, most with happy smiles of anticipation. For a split second, Mallory nearly turned away with the thought of dashing back to his old car, ready to forget the whole thing, just chalk it off as a childish whim of a sick, lonely old man.

Feeling stiff with indecision, Mallory's eyes glanced heavenward. Written in stone over the arch of the doorway was *Let no one be a stranger here*. Tears came to his eyes, and he knew that only the Lord Himself could know how deeply Jenkins Mallory wanted to believe.

In the vestibule of the church, a red-haired woman in a long white robe stood beside a wooden box. The worshippers filed past, some saying a word or two to the woman before going into the church. Others lingered to talk for a longer time. Finally, it was Mallory's turn.

She had a sweet smile and eyes as gentle and blue as a summer sky. "Your name, Sir?" She wrote his name on a slip of paper. "Did you bring a request for a miracle tonight, Mister Mallory?"

"Oh, yes, I surely did." He explained what it was he had come for.

"You want the end to come painlessly, and you'd like to speak with your deceased wife, whose name is Elsie. Can you make a small donation to the Church of Mystery and Miracles?"

"I don't have much ready cash. But I do have a Monte Carlo. And a real nice house right here in Ridley. But I'd have to live in my house until... you know."

"On the death of the donor, then. And the car?"

"I'm prepared to donate the Monte Carlo right away."

"That's very generous of you, Sir. You may go inside now. I pray that your request is among those to be chosen."

He walked through red velvet curtains and stood at the edge of a huge auditorium. It hadn't once occurred to him that his request might not be answered. But then again, how many of these other folks were willing to give a house and a car? He had to smile as he felt the pent-up tension seeping from his body.

A young boy with a flashlight motioned him toward a spare seat. Mallory didn't argue. He'd sit where he was told, even if the view wasn't the best. Everything by the rules. If he'd decided to do this thing, he meant to do it right.

He closed his eyes and, for the first time in as long as he could remember, he prayed from his heart, asking Jesus to please help him be among the chosen. When he opened his eyes, he noticed people standing along both sides of the auditorium or sitting on boxes in the aisle.

From the ceiling, wheelchairs were suspended on hooks like worthless toys, canes and crutches, metal and canvas things that looked like braces for a back or leg. Mallory tried to count all the things hanging from the ceiling, realizing that for each item he counted there'd been a miracle. He felt his heart swell with an emotion he'd never experienced.

As he sat quietly, his mind racing to newly discovered satisfactions, a man walked onto the stage and stood before the microphone.

"Brothers and Sisters, welcome! Before we get started on our evening prayers, asking the Almighty Father God to fill this tabernacle with His Glorious Presence, I'm going to read off the names of the faithful selected for the miracle session tonight. These individuals are those whose hearts seem most, I repeat, *most* in need. Just because your name might not be called tonight, don't give up hope and don't despair. No, friends. I want you to come another time and make your request another night. Don't think for one little minute God doesn't love you, or you're not a cherished child of the Lord!"

The announcer paused to swab at his forehead with a white handkerchief. Then he flicked at the sheet of paper in his left hand. "All right, when I call your name, please stand up, and the nearest usher will accompany you to a room where you'll be shown how to sign some necessary documents."

The names were in alphabetical order. Four names, and then Mallory's. He hopped out of his chair to find an usher and was led down a hallway to a room that said <u>Conference</u> on the door. A plain room with a couple of card tables and metal folding chairs, a filing cabinet in one corner, a yellow wall phone close to the door.

A man came in with some papers. As requested, Mallory filled out a detailed description of his vehicle, right down to the license plate number, and the address and location of his house. He was asked to sign his name in three places. The man kept calling him Jenkins, as if they had known one another a long time.

"You understand, Jenkins," the man said pleasantly. "These documents are legal and binding. The donations must be payable before the miracles. You can understand why that is, I'm sure."

"Yes, Sir," Mallory said solemnly. Because he thought he understood without having to be told, knowing what he did about human nature, how people will try to squirm and wiggle their way out of a deal given the slightest chance.

"Return to your seat, Jenkins. When the time comes, you'll be called to the stage by the Messiah."

Mallory hurried to the auditorium to find someone sitting in his chair. He stood against the wall and watched as a group of people wearing red velvet robes walked out to the middle of the stage and sang *Stand Up for Jesus*, and the whole auditorium burst into song.

Mallory sang as loudly as he could. This had always been one of his favorite hymns, and he was pleased to the point of tears that Aaron started his service with it. Hadn't Mallory taught this very hymn to Aaron? Why, sure he did!

By the time they were at the second verse, Mallory's idea of his own positive influence on Aaron's destiny had grown considerably.

The second hymn was *Christ the Lord Is Risen Today*. He didn't know all the words, but he hummed along and did the Alleluias. Think of that! An Easter hymn being sung in Aaron's church in the month of November!

Well, if it was true what they said, and Aaron was Christ Come Again, Mallory thought the hymn could be sung any old time in the Church of Mystery and Miracles.

When a new man came to the microphone, the choir stopped singing and the organ stopped playing. Mallory listened, but he could scarcely keep his mind on the prayers. It seemed like an hour's worth of prayers.

He thought he'd have to sit on the floor for the grinding in his knee-caps. And his heart, when he focused on it, beat like a big bass drum. He had a terrible urge to go to his car and lie down in the back seat.

But he couldn't, because the Monte Carlo didn't belong to him any-more. But it had been a fair trade, yes it was.

"We're now ready to commence the making of miracles, Brothers and Sisters!" The man was answered by jubilant cries from every section of the auditorium.

Mallory's mouth fell open, from people shouting so loud in the House of the Lord, but then he opened his mouth wider and added a few whoops of his own. He couldn't remember when he'd last had such a fine time.

A name was called. A geezer older than Mallory shuffled up to the stage and had to be helped up the stairs. The announcer said that here was a man who had raised nine children, worked hard all his life, and was willing to donate his life savings of twenty-five-hundred dollars if the Messiah would restore his vision and let him see again.

Mallory saw Aaron step to the spotlights from behind a curtain. It was Aaron, all right, but he'd grown tall as a full-grown man. And his hair wasn't dark brown but blond, curved around his shoulders like in those oil-paint pictures of Jesus Christ.

He wore a long dress the color of oatmeal made of rough cloth like flour sacks, because it had no shine to it under the bright lights. He carried a long stick with a curved head. A staff, that's what it was, Mallory reminded himself.

Then Aaron came forward and said, "Before Abraham was, I am."

A hush fell over the audience. Aaron approached the old man, pointed the staff at his face and said, "Oh, Lord, let there be light."

In a few seconds the old man rubbed his eyes and started grinning. Then he leaped up and down and began pointing toward the audience, calling his grandchildren by name. All the grandchildren, there must have been thirty, ran up and hugged him.

The next miracle was for a great big fat woman in a wheelchair. When Aaron jabbed at her knees with the rod, the woman jumped out of the wheelchair and did a little jig. The woman's tiny husband came up on stage and yelled, "Praise the Lord!" Mallory wished Aaron had been able to cure Elsie like that.

Then there was a pair of twin boys who looked like a four-legged monster because they were joined together at the forehead. The lights were dimmed and a purple spotlight shone on the boys and on Aaron, who stood between them and slowly sliced right through their foreheads with the rod.

For the first time in their lives, the boys fell apart. They were about fourteen years old, and Mallory thought he'd just witnessed a mighty wondrous thing, something he could hardly believe even though he'd seen it with his own eyes. The audience went plum wild.

"Jenkins Mallory!"

Quivering with anticipation, he limped down the aisle and up the stairs to stand beside the announcer.

"Here's a man willing to give his car and his home! And we're here to tell you, Brothers and Sisters, that his miracle will, in time, be granted. So says the Messiah!" The announcer smiled while shaking Mallory's hand and patting him on the back.

"Uh, is that it?" Mallory watched as the announcer scurried off the stage. He turned around, and his voice trembled when he said, "Hello, Aaron."

"What will you give for proof of the existence of Heaven?" Aaron pointed the rod at Mallory.

"All I wanted was to see Elsie one last time." He felt as if he should sink to his knees in the presence of this young man whose eyes glowed like hot coals and seemed to burn right into Mallory's brain.

Placing his hand on his forehead, Aaron said, "You've donated your car. A Monte Carlo. Not a late model. Ten, twelve years old. Am I correct?" The audience made oohing noises at the Prophet Aaron's ability. "And a house. You've pledged your home."

"Yes, Sir," Mallory said quietly.

"The house is two-story, wood, painted white. Four rooms on the ground floor, three rooms on the second, bathroom on each level. In the backyard is a very large, very old oak tree. Also a tool shed. I see you, Mister Mallory, as a younger man, leading a small boy to the tool shed. The boy lies across your knees while you beat him savagely with a hickory stick."

"Why, Aaron, you ought to know, boy! It was you I gave a licking to. You already knew that!" But then Mallory feared, from the way Aaron was jerking, that he'd gone into some sort of trance. He almost looked like a chicken after its head was cut off, twitching and wobbling around, reeling across the stage as though somebody pulled him on a string like a marionette.

Aaron came to a dead stop in front of Mallory. "God has told His Son he wants your land!"

"My...my land?"

"My Father says your sixteen acres just past Overton will be the site for the new Center for Spiritual Health and Healing!" Aaron held up his arms to the audience for shrieks of approval.

"Well, you see, Aaron, I'd give it, but then there'd be nothing left, and I thought the house, the car, too, well...but the land, I don't.."

"What are you prepared to give for proof of the existence of Heaven?" Aaron seemed to have grown twenty feet tall. His deep voice roared with the power of thunder.

Mallory sank to his knees, his body feeling thin and fragile as paper. When he tried to speak, the words stuck in his throat. Tears streamed down his cheeks. With his hands clasped beneath his chin, he didn't know whether he was begging or praying, or both.

"Dear Lord, help me! Yes, yes, you can have my land. Just please let me go!"

Now he was prostrate on the floor like a vile, slithering thing. He sobbed, writhing from side to side. Some part of him knew that what he was doing was altogether shameful and, when it was over, if it ever was over, he'd die from the humiliation. But there was nothing in his feeble body to make him stop.

Whop! The rod smashed against his right temple. Whop! His back felt like it was breaking in two. The rod whistled through the air and landed on Mallory's legs, shoulders, the back of his head, his chest. When it smashed against his right wrist, he heard the bones crunch even before he felt the pain.

"Do you deny you're a sinner?" Whop! "Did you try to crucify a poor orphaned boy?" Whop! "Let go of those filthy demons infesting your soul!"

"Dear Lord, forgive me, whatever it was I done! Please, Lord, tell the Messiah here to spare a tired old man!" Mallory heard himself sobbing like an infant.

Aaron dangled the keys to the Monte Carlo above Mallory's face. "This is my downpayment on your miracle, Jenkins Mallory," he said, his voice soft as a woman's. "In the morning I'll come for the house. And by afternoon the Church of Mystery and Miracles will be richer by sixteen acres of prime-timbered land."

Afraid to move, Mallory felt the ache of every bone, joint, and muscle in his body. Somehow, he managed to scoop himself from the floor, bent over and bowing like a Chinese coolie. He staggered down the stairs, down the aisle and through the doors of the church into the freezing November night.

Bawling and gasping, he stood at the entrance and wondered how he was going to get home. Blindly, he hobbled through the parking lot to the main road, falling into the darkness as if pursued by the hounds of Hell. His left arm throbbed with shooting pains. His broken wrist was on fire. His chest pounded.

Nobody had to tell him he was headed for a heart attack. He thought it was a wonder he was still alive and able to move at all. He staggered into the shadows of a cluster of trees. On the far side was a horse-drawn cart.

Somebody, and only God Himself could imagine why, was singing.

"Hey!" Mallory limped forward as fast as he could to approach the driver of the cart.

"Hey, there, Mistuh Mall'ry," Old Claude said. "I see you can do for a ride."

Mallory nodded, tears cascading down his face. He held his right wrist, loose and crippled as a wounded bird. "I can't...I don't know how to climb up!"

"Jus' you hold on a minute," Claude said. He got down and helped

Mallory into the cart. Then he climbed up beside him and said Gaddyup to his horse.

When they were headed toward Ridley, Mallory said, "Oh, Lord God, Claude! I been robbed of all my earthly possessions. That boy, he liked to killed me. And I didn't get a miracle, no indeed. All I got was a heap of bruises." He began to sob loudly.

Claude said nothing. They drove through the colored section, past the winter wheat fields into town. Mallory pictured the two of them, two old codgers riding a junk wagon in the middle of the night.

He thought about what he had gone to church for, and he thought about what he'd received. And he couldn't understand why any of it had happened to him because, as far as he knew, Jenkins Mallory had never wronged another man in his life.

Except, maybe, for the Prophet Aaron.

Finally, he understood. It was finished, his frail hopes shattered like so many toothpicks. By the time Claude parked the wagon in front of the house, Mallory felt a strange calm.

Claude came over to his side of the cart and helped him down. "I swan, but if you don't look like you seed yo'self a ghost! You get to bed now."

He just stared at the man.

"Mistuh Mall'ry? You g'wan be all right?" Claude took his arm and led him to the front door. "You want me to get you in, Suh? Old Claude, he be glad to."

Mallory shook his head, opened the door and stumbled inside. Taking the whiskey from the kitchen cupboard, with his good left hand he poured himself a drink. He drank the whiskey without tasting anything but the fire. He poured himself another and slugged it down. He could hear Doc Watkins telling him it was the worst thing he could do for his heart.

Briefly he thought about the kindness Old Claude had done him, and he was sorry he hadn't thanked him for it.

With bleary eyes, he looked around the kitchen. A thin layer of grime covered the walls. The stove was splattered with cooked-on grease. Mallory smiled. Well, Aaron was welcome to it. And to the beat-up Monte Carlo, too. And that little chicken-shit piece of land.

Mallory felt giddy. Yes, indeed, Jenkins Mallory was one mighty generous man. Still, it hurt way down deep, finding out the hard way how the Prophet Aaron was nothing but a phony. At least now he knew, because he'd followed Roy Litchfield's advice and learned the truth for himself.

The only thing Mallory really regretted was that he hadn't had a word with Elsie. He'd been a desperate old fool, even thinking such a thing might have been possible. But his heart had been set on it.

He took the whiskey bottle upstairs to his bedroom. Slowly, he lowered his body to the bed, expecting to hurt all over, and it surprised him not to feel a thing. He was just plain numb from head to toe.

He sat there in the quiet of darkness, taking swigs of whiskey. When his body fell backwards, when it collapsed, Mallory was up near the ceiling watching it happen. That poor old body of mine, he thought.

Right out loud, he said, "Look at them bruises and whelps!" Suddenly it seemed the most amazing thing, how he could peer down at his own body.

Then his attention was drawn to a vague reflection in the middle of the big bureau mirror. The mirror swirled in its center like colors in a puddle of motor oil. Something seemed to be calling out to Mallory, motioning him inside.

A woman was waving to him. She wore a baby-blue nightgown and held a bouquet of red flowers. "This way!" she said, her voice chiming like bells.

"Elsie?" Mallory floated to her side. "You *did* come! Why, I got my miracle! Don't that beat all, though? Praise the Lord! My sweet Elsie!"

"I been waitin', Jenkins. Waitin' such a terrible long time."

"Well, here I am!" He had to keep himself from squeezing her shoulder right then and there. But he knew they'd have time to spare, and then some. In the distance was a huge, shimmering light. "Where to now, honey?" Elsie looked up at him with a shy smile. She nestled her hand in his. Together they glided toward the light.

Chapter Four

"**G**ood God Almighty! Seventeen more months till my retirement. But do you figure I could get through it without a major incident? Hell, no!"

"I'll be right in, Ray," Deputy Wills said over his patrol car radio.

"Don't come to the office. Meet me at the church. And make it fast."

"Over and out, boss."

Already, Sheriff Hawke had radioed the hospital in Keyser for an ambulance, on the outside chance there might be a survivor. Driving past the town limits, he followed the billowing mushroom cloud on the horizon.

It looked like an atomic bomb had hit Ridley, West Virginia.

When he parked his vehicle a safe distance from the scene, he heard exploding bricks like a fusillade of gunshots. The stained-glass windows were long gone, gaping holes emitting a hellish blaze that reminded him of how brimstone might look.

The firetrucks arrived right behind him. Immediately, the volunteers went to work, hosing what remained of that damned heathen church Ray Hawke had never wanted built in Ridley in the first place, not that he'd had any say in the matter.

Miracles, my ass, he thought to himself.

For eleven years, this church of a false prophet had made a mockery of religion, as far as Hawke was concerned. But it wasn't against the law to milk people of their money, when they gave it so willingly and believed in their heart they were getting something better in return.

Faith, what it could do to people. Just a damned sorry shame.

The politicians could pass their legislation until Doomsday. Whatever wrangled its way into the State Code, Ray Hawke had taken a solemn oath to enforce it. But you couldn't pass a law to protect people from themselves.

Last year, he'd started hearing strange tales about the place. But when he tried to investigate, people clamped their lips shut, and seemed afraid to talk. How was he supposed to conduct an official investigation into the rumors, if nobody had the courage to step forward and be a witness?

Well, if nothing else came of this fire, at least he could hope all that foolishness was finally over and done with, and things around town might return to the way they used to be.

His next plan was to track down their leader, to press some trumped-up charges and run him out of town. Wasn't it convenient, though, how soon the word had gotten to the sheriff claiming the Prophet Aaron had perished in the flames?

What? Like a captain going down with his ship? Shoot.

The fire raged. Ray Hawke stood far enough away to avoid the intensity of the heat. He heard the wailing of a siren in the distance. Either the ambulance or Edgar, one.

The volunteer firemen shouted directions among themselves, while timbers splintered and bricks popped to punctuate the mighty roaring force of the blaze.

The wind shifted. Ray Hawke wouldn't know until his dying day whether he'd seen it, or whether it was a mirage thrown off by the heat-scorched streams of water from the firehoses. But he could have sworn something huge and black emerged from the flames, shrinking before his eyes only to disappear into the clouds.

Black, like the silhouette of a caped man, or a great crow with outstretched wings.

He was the only one who saw it, apparently, for when he mentioned it later to a few of the firemen, they looked at him as if he wasn't playing with a full deck.

His deputy parked behind Hawke's vehicle and jumped out of his patrol car. "I got here as quick as I could," Edgar huffed, out of breath.

"I swear, Edgar, you need to go on a damned diet."

"I know, I know. But with Angie big as she is…" The deputy's eyes were riveted to the fire. "How do you suppose this got started?"

"A problem for the fire marshal to figure out, not us."

"Maybe the furnace exploded, or something."

"Not likely in May. Besides, there wasn't a service here tonight. Not even a meeting of the deacons, far as I know."

A balmy evening wind blew over the hilltop, feeding the flames. Hawke's jacket was in the car, but he didn't need it, not with the fire giving off heat like an oven set at 500 degrees.

"Well, Ray, what are we going to do?"

"Why? You hungry?"

"Jeez, Ray. I sure wish you'd quit ribbing me about my weight."

"You want to be considered for the next sheriff after my retirement, or not? Fat sheriffs are only funny in the television comedies."

"Yeah, I know," Edgar said sheepishly. "Me and Angie, all we do is eat."

"Comes as no surprise, to look at the two of you." Even their ten-year-old son Waylon was a butterball, his thighs so fat the poor kid could hardly walk, but Ray didn't want to mention the boy.

"I know what I'd be more interested in than food, but she don't want no part of that."

Hawke felt almost tender toward Edgar Wills. He put his arm around the man and patted him on the shoulder. "Don't take it personal," he said. "Edith isn't much interested, either. If the truth be told, I think it's the same with most women, after they've been wives for a while."

"Wonder why?"

Hawke pondered the question for a few seconds before responding. "Well, you know, Edgar. If I knew the right answer, I wouldn't be sheriff. No, indeed. With such wisdom to my credit, I'd be something akin to that Prophet Aaron fellow, the one folks are already saying died in the fire."

"You hear the latest about poor Lula Jasper?"

"No. What this time?"

"Another one of them miracles gone bad, is what they're saying around town. Seems Miz Jasper got bone cancer in those old legs of hers the Messiah made work again from the arthritis she used to have."

"You might as well quit calling him the Messiah. If he was, I doubt his damned tabernacle would have been destroyed by flames. If you'll recall, I never believed he was anything but a charlatan, bilking good people out of their hard-earned money."

"Yeah, Ray. You always did say he was a fake."

Hawke sighed, wondering why he didn't feel vindicated. "Well, at least we can be glad the healing center he planned out on Jenk Mallory's land never did get built. Last I heard, the well they dug was about it."

Silently, the two men stood on the hill, watching until the fire was brought under control. The ambulance came and left. The firehoses continued to saturate the smoldering devastation. Great columns of black smoke had devoured the ragged flames.

"Do you really think he got away, Sheriff? Or would you say he got burned up?"

"Can't sift through this wreckage for bones, not for days yet," Hawke replied. "But if he did escape, you can bet he'll be long gone before we know one way or the other. Without his church, there's nothing to hold him here."

"With that escapee from the penitentiary being on the loose, I think we ought to concentrate on him." Edgar paused a minute before adding hopefully, "Don't you think so, Ray?"

Hawke snorted and began walking toward his vehicle, Edgar following along beside him with the eagerness of a faithful pup.

"If you ask me, the best we can hope for is, the Prophet Aaron runs smack into Lonnie Robinson, a sadistic serial murderer wanted by the FBI. Shoot, Edgar. You really think two small-town law enforcement officers would stand a chance against the likes of Lonnie Robinson?"

"I guess we would. The two of us together, I meant."

With a bitter laugh, Hawke climbed into his car and closed the door. He remembered the day he'd driven Robinson to Harrisonburg, Virginia, how much younger a man he'd been, with Robinson helpless in shackles and leg irons. Years had passed, Robinson had been released on parole, set free to murder and maim again and again. Before his death sentence in the electric chair had been carried out, he managed to kill a guard with his bare hands and escape from death row by hiding in a heating duct. And now he was on the run.

Edgar peered down at him through the open window. "I wasn't kidding. We could take him, the two of us."

"Dream on, Edgar. We couldn't even run a phony preacher out of town on a rail. How're you coming along with the grammar book I gave you to study?"

"I'm reading it, Ray." Edgar held up his fat hand. "Swear on a stack of Bibles."

"You'd better. Remember what I told you about how important it's going to be when you're campaigning for votes, if you can keep from using all those ain'ts and don'ts." When Hawke started his engine, Edgar backed away from the car and headed toward his own vehicle.

Sheriff Hawke drove past the steaming rubble. A pile of concrete bricks and charred timbers would serve as a constant reminder to anyone who drove past the ruins of the Church of Mystery and Miracles.

He knew there were people in Ridley who were going to be mighty disappointed. But Hawke gave thanks for the fire. At last, maybe things would settle down now, and Ridley would return to the friendly, sleepy town it was before those idiot revivals transformed the landscape with charter buses, campers, and RVs.

And Raymond Hawke could ride out the last few months of his career in public service and sail into a peaceful retirement. He and Edith had bought a little camper, to drive out West and see the Grand Canyon and the Painted Desert. Poker with Fletcher, Timpkins, and Crenshaw, fishing with Airlie Funge, skeet-shooting with Old Claude. He had good times yet to look forward to.

He sighed, braking at the foot of the hill to look for oncoming cars before making a left turn. After the many years he and Edgar had worked together, Hawke had almost come to regard the man as a son. But if there was any chance of Edgar replacing him as county sheriff, Hawke thought he'd probably have to throw the boy in a cell before the elections and feed him bread and water.

Which was what he'd been hoping to do with the likes of the Prophet Aaron, that smug, fraudulent bastard...

He didn't believe he'd ever despised a man as much in his life. Why in hell hadn't he left Lila's baby in the snowbank? He probably would have, had he known things were going to turn out this way, Christian charity be damned.

But Hawke thought that if such a level of pure hatred for another human being should drag his soul to Hell for all eternity, then brimstone it would be.

He parked his vehicle in his own driveway and walked into the kitchen. Edith greeted him with a kiss and the smell of warm cinnamon buns from the oven.

He poured himself a cup of decaf coffee and sat down at the kitchen table. Jingo, their elderly Jack Russell terrier, snuffled across the room to settle himself at Hawke's feet.

"You know, Edith," he said, reaching down to pet the dog. "There's an awful lot of damage can be done to folks in the name of the Lord."

"Just forget about it, dear," Edith said, shoving the plate of sticky buns in front of him to enjoy.

Looking at his wife, Hawke had a sudden, burning desire to slip his left hand under the skirt of her pink ruffled housedress. But for the past few months, she'd been feeling poorly. She couldn't sleep, and roamed the house at all hours. He'd wake to find her in the living room, reading her Bible. He had no idea what troubled her, because she wasn't talking.

But Ray Hawke would never share what he'd heard through the Ridley grapevine, how more than once Edith Hawke had been up to the Church of Mystery and Miracles, too.

Chapter Five

In a strangely benign, peaceful mood, he created an August day with warm sun and temperate breezes.

His latest conveyance was a plum-colored delivery van found last night with the keys left in the ignition, in a deserted alley behind a gay bar called the Hello, Dolly!

He'd crossed the bridge from downtown Detroit to a floating park known as Belle Isle. Far below, pleasure craft and sailboats fanned down the Detroit River. Insignificant specks, the people on the decks of yachts.

He was pleased to be back on American soil. Canada wasn't all it was cracked up to be. Toronto, especially. Too much French. He didn't speak French, and in a foreign environment, he stood out as an alien.

His strength, his advantage, was remaining anonymous. After too many years of limelight, he prided himself on the uncanny ability to blend in with his surroundings, a chameleon among ordinary men.

Coasting off the bridge onto a paved road that circled the island, he drove slowly past groups of people picnicking on Sunday afternoon. When the sun hovered low in the sky, they'd relinquish the beautiful day and return home.

But not just yet. First, there were a few things he needed to accomplish, while the Sunday crowds were at his disposal.

He made two loops around the perimeter of the island, observing the layout. Indoor aquarium, botanical gardens. Public restrooms. Snack bars, and a restaurant. An outdoor ice-skating rink closed for the season. He tucked away those locations for later.

But for now, the duck pond. Perfect.

Parking the van in a public lot, he got out and casually sauntered over to the pond, deeming himself invisible. A man in faded jeans and threadbare gabardine jacket over a black turtleneck, scuffed cowboy boots, a baseball cap with visor pulled low to protect his eyes from the bright sun. Nothing unusual about that. Who would notice him standing at the edge of small clusters of people enjoying a summer day? Not a soul.

As he made his way toward a cement bench near the pond, a woman in her early twenties glanced at him. When he trained his eyes on her in a slow, penetrating gaze, she looked away, as if embarrassed. But why shouldn't she be curious? Compared to the doughy man she was with, the stranger by the pond was an Adonis.

Momentarily he allowed himself to relax, feeling the sun warm the back of his good hand. His thoughts drifted toward a new identity.

Waylon Hawke was good enough for Canada, but since he was back in the States, that persona must vanish. Besides, by now they'd be looking for him, and it was only a matter of time until they narrowed the trail.

Catch up to Waylon, he said to himself with an ironic grin. But Waylon had disappeared.

His attention focused on three little boys in bathing trunks wading in the shallow end of the pond, floating small plastic boats on the water. Two women sat in plastic lawn chairs, sipping their drinks through straws, talking, keeping an eye on the children. As his mind wandered in search of an invented self, he concentrated on the three boys.

Six or seven years old, two of them looked to be. The third boy may be four, possibly five. One of the bigger boys, the one with bright yellow hair, was the ringleader, the bully, the kind of kid he'd never had any use for. He told the other two what to do, critical of the youngest child, a quiet boy with dark hair.

"Not that way, Curtie!" The bossy blond boy soon presented himself as a likely target. But he wasn't ready, not quite, not yet.

Thinking of himself an Adonis compared to the young woman's plump, pasty-faced companion in plaid Bermuda shorts and an alligator polo shirt, he settled on a new identity.

Adrian. Adrian Lightfoot. A Choctaw Indian from Montana.

For a while he continued to observe the three boys, how the blond bully tormented the smallest boy, barked orders, snatched the child's boat from his hands and made him cry.

"Jimmy, take care of your brother and Curtie," one of the women called to the blond boy. "We're going to the refreshment stand for sodas. Be right back."

As the women walked across the rolling lawn to a cedar-shingled building, the sun moved behind a bank of dark clouds, plunging the children into shadows, causing them to shiver against the sudden wind. The small boy named Curtie climbed from the pond and ran to sit on one of the lawn chairs, wrapping a towel around his bare shoulders.

Then the blond Jimmy began to scuffle with his younger brother, wrenching the boy's arm behind his back until he shrieked in pain—the red and white plastic boat he clutched in his hand fell into the water, where it bobbed on little wavelets pushed by the wind across the surface of the pond.

Adrian Lightfoot tilted his head toward the sky to gulp ozone from the air.

Whimpering, the boy who had lost his boat got out of the water to sit beside Curtie in the lawn chairs.

But Jimmy still coveted the red and white boat, splashing after it as the waves carried the fragile toy toward the middle of the pond, farther and farther toward the center and in the direction of Adrian Lightfoot.

The sky grew dark. A violent wind lashed out at the people who glanced fearfully at the scudding black clouds and began packing their things to hurry away. Lightning rent the clouds, followed by the sound of thunder from a northerly direction. On a perfect summer day, a surprise thunderstorm threatened.

He sat on the concrete bench, his arms folded across his chest, watching as Jimmy flailed his arms and cried out for help. He was in over his head now, the boat forgotten, so far out of reach.

The turbulent waves buffeted the boy, tossing him about like a rubber doll. As he sucked in water, his yelling subsided, and became the feeble sound of gurgling.

Curtie was screaming at the edge of the pond. The two women ran down the grassy incline toward the water. One of the women dove into the pond from the deep end and swam against the current toward the blond boy.

Adrian reached out to grab the boy's hand, and pulled him, gagging and choking, to the sloping berm. He let the red and white boat fall from his good hand, where it landed beside the boy's head, before leaving the pond.

He was almost to the parking lot when he heard one of the women call out to thank him for saving her son's life.

But he did not look back. He walked to the plum-colored van, climbed in, turned the ignition and drove away. Once more around the island, and then he stopped at the botanical gardens, parked the van and went inside.

An oversized clock face with Roman numerals for numbers read 5:20 pm . The building closed at 6 pm . An impatient security guard at the entrance was checking his wristwatch. Less than an hour before closing on an August Sunday, there were few visitors to admire the indoor palm trees,

46

to inhale the humid, cloying steam of a simulated tropical climate, which is what he'd been counting on.

He meandered off on a side trail past the birds-of-Paradise, large and bright as parrots, delicate orchids, blood-red bougainvillea, jacaranda. A baobab tree. Tarnished brass plaques identified the popular and botanical names of plants, trees, shrubs, and flowers.

In the hot fecundity, the profusion of colors and textures, he began to feel as though the blood pounding through his veins had turned to molasses, making him feel lethargic. He realized how much he missed the pine trees and crisp mountain air of his boyhood home.

But that was years ago, a home lost and forever gone to him now. His travels had taken him all over the country, time on the road moving relentlessly from one strange town to the next, running from the past.

And reading, hours turning into months and then years spent in public libraries reading the Great Books of the Western World, avidly storing away knowledge and information like food for a starving man.

He might have been born into ignorance, held captive by simple country women named Alma and Elsie, but thanks to Granny Altizer, he'd been given the power to create a self, to make himself new.

Not just in name only, but in substance. Even his West Virginia diphthongs had been expunged, so that he could not be instantly identified by his speech. With time, he had transformed himself into a citizen of the world, fitting into any social milieu.

Botanical names, popular names, native habitat, favored climate. For a moment Adrian yearned to sink his feet into the soft vermiculite loam and disappear among the trees and flowers. If he could have snapped his fingers and created a genuine miracle, he'd have chosen the miracle of physical dissolution, complete annihilation.

What a colossal waste of money this place was, when there were hungry people willing to kill for a slice of bread...

At one end of the arboretum was a wishing well, with pennies, dimes, even a few silver dollars nestled in the green algae along the bottom. Goldfish swam mindlessly, oblivious to the tawdry treasure shining beneath their bellies.

He stood in front of the orchid display and stared hard and long at the delicate blossoms until they began to quiver, shrink, turn brown.

"What a crime! Such gorgeous blossoms, so delicate, and now they've died."

With no need to confront the woman standing behind his left shoulder, studying her reflection in the glass case, Adrian had found his mark.

She had come to him, as he'd known she would, as he had willed it to be.

Fortyish, henna hair, too much make-up, dressed in white tennis clothes, the handle of her racket sticking out of the tote bag she'd slung over her left shoulder.

Slowly, he removed his baseball cap and turned to look into her eyes. "Variation in the temperature," he said. "I'll mention it to the guard on the way out."

"Yes, we should! I chose orchids for my bridal bouquet. I'm very fond of orchids."

Her name was Sarah Marchand, and she lived in Bloomfield Hills, a Detroit suburb. After several moments of neutral conversation, she learned that he was Adrian Lightfoot, a Choctaw Indian from Montana who had traveled to Michigan to visit relatives. The information seemed to please her immensely, and she invited him to be her guest for dinner at the Detroit Yacht Club near the entrance to Belle Isle.

"I appreciate the invitation, Mrs. Marchand," Adrian said. "But I'm afraid I'm not dressed appropriately for dinner at a yacht club."

"Nonsense. Look at me in tennis clothes. Why, I absolutely insist!"

She and her husband were members of the Club, she said as they walked to Adrian's van, though presently her husband was out of town on business. She had spent the afternoon playing a foursome of tennis with friends.

Sarah soon revealed the truth, the essence of her life. She'd married for money, and now she was lonely. Her hands fluttered through the air as she talked incessantly about her unhappy life, the jeweled fingers with long nails painted scarlet.

He ate a T-bone with a chef salad, watching as she picked at her jumbo shrimp, as she had too much to drink. She paid for the meal with a credit card. Afterward, he walked her to her vintage Spitfire, white with red-leather upholstery.

Gently, he closed her car door, gazing down into her eyes at twilight.

"Do you have a place in town to stay tonight, Adrian?"

"No, Sarah. I don't," he said with a smile, expecting yet a second invitation, to take the woman to bed.

"Well, we can't have that, can we? Here." She dug through her tennis tote bag and gave him all the cash she could find in her wallet.

"You're very kind, Sarah. It was a pleasure meeting you." He was glad she hadn't invited him home, because then she'd have had to die to be born again.

With a gallant bow, he watched her drive away before walking to his van. He spent the night sleeping on a stained cot in the back until he was roused at dawn by a park policeman, who beat on the van with his cudgel and ordered Adrian Lightfoot to hit the road.

Across the bridge, he stopped at a White Tower for coffee and a donut, used the bathroom to wash up and comb his hair. Then he pulled out the map from the glove compartment of the stolen van and decided to drive north, straight up the center of the Michigan mitt.

The Ontario police wouldn't be looking for him in Michigan. Only a fool would stick so close to the border, a fugitive from the law.

As he drove along the congested Chrysler Freeway, he couldn't seem to remember, not exactly, what it was he had done in Canada. With so many offenses, one crime seemed to collide with the next and merge into a continuous blur.

But on second thought, Adrian Lightfoot hadn't done anything. It was Waylon Hawke they were tracking across the border. And Waylon Hawke was a phantom, he didn't exist.

At dusk he used a stolen credit card to stay in a Super Eight Motel. In the parking lot under cover of night, he traded license plates with a late-model Caravan parked some distance from the motel.

In the morning he stopped at a factory outlet in Cadillac and bought new clothes. Tourist clothes, white chinos and pastel shirts, a crisp pair of jeans, a lightweight jacket, clothes for a vacation. Here he was, a thirty-year-old Choctaw Indian from Montana planning the first vacation of his new life. Adrian Lightfoot, a man with no past who lived only in the present, with little use for a future.

For a long time after he healed them, they went away. He never saw them again. What was in it for him? A moment of fleeting thanks, a small donation offered as a simpering gratuity?

Still, there was money in it, lots of money. But so many others depended upon him for food and shelter. The utility bills for the tabernacle, the cost of the deluxe searchlight alone. He had surrounded himself with apostolic leeches, obsequious bloodsuckers for the Lord.

The constant bills, expenses, made him feel weary. Sometimes he'd look around at the adoring faces of his disciples and focus on dozens of mouths needing to be fed.

One thing, and one thing only, he had learned. You cannot mend a broken body or fix a tortured spirit, not when your will to invoke healing powers emanates from a corrosive hatred for humanity.

Like battery acid, the old resentment began to fill his veins. The miracles began to backfire. And suddenly some of the faces on the stage night after night were familiar to him. He'd seen them before, he'd healed them, and now they were back for more.

In those days he began to weave accusation and recrimination into his message. He scolded the repeat customers, calling them backsliders.

"When you were healed, what did you do? Were you worthy? This new sign of tribulation visited upon you is the wrath of the Great God Jehovah!"

For surely it was their fault, not his. After all, he was the Prophet Aaron, the new Messiah, the hope for the new millennium. Weren't there ample passages in Revelation to prove it?

To the organ, trumpets, and tambourines, the church music director added kettle drums to flood the tabernacle with the pounding of the Lord's fury. If he couldn't truly heal them, he was content to strike the fear of God into their selfish hearts.

Complaints and muttered grievances turned into lawsuits. Articles appeared in the newspapers calling for a full investigation of the Prophet Aaron's Evangelical Corporation.

When the sheriff appeared after a Sunday night service, placing a temporary injunction on the continued operation of the tabernacle until certain questions had been answered to everyone's satisfaction, he was already well past twenty-one, subject to prosecution as an adult.

It was easier to shut it down himself.

The empty tabernacle, with its red velvet curtains and expensive organ, pews and baptismal font, exploded in showers of brick and cinder-block.

At dawn all they found was a mountain of ashes. They assumed the Prophet Aaron had perished with his church, and no one suggested taking on the expense of clearing the ruins of the Church of Mystery and Miracles, sifting through the rubble for evidence of his demise.

It was enough for them that he was gone.

As to what happened to the entourage of parasitic followers after his departure, the Prophet Aaron didn't know. Nor did he care.

But the Prophet Aaron was buried in the past, along with Waylon Hawke and the rest. Only his spirit remained, the Phoenix rising from the ashes, he who had died countless times to be reborn.

Adrian Lightfoot consulted the map. Northwest to Traverse City, and beyond.

Part II

The Magills

"Where we lay,
Our chimneys were blown down, and, as they say,
Lamentings heard i' the air, strange screams of death,
And prophesying with accents terrible..."

Macbeth, II:iii
Shakespeare

Chapter Six

They stopped for lunch in a Howard Johnson's restaurant due south from Grand Haven – clam rolls and cottage fries, salad bar, hot fudge sundaes for Philip and April, orange sherbet for Beth. But their cheerful holiday mood was instantly destroyed by a disastrous ending.

Beth Magill felt as though she was shrinking into herself, stuffed into an envelope like a letter hurriedly mailed. For the first time in memory, she was tempted to turn and walk away, pretending not to recognize her own daughter. Surely the curly-haired child writhing on the dirty clay tiles at Beth's feet couldn't belong to her, this raging, shrieking, red-faced monster.

"April! Get up from the floor, this instant," Beth ordered in her I-mean-business tone, focusing on the odd tangerine, cream, and turquoise décor of the restaurant's interior. She turned beseechingly to Philip, but one glance at his judgmental expression told Beth there'd be no help from that quarter. If anything, her husband's reaction only increased her anxiety.

They'd been married a short time but long enough for Beth to know she'd be sure to hear his opinion before the day was out, as if April's behavior for better or worse was entirely to her mother's credit. Or disgrace.

A well dressed, middle-aged woman waiting in line said, "If she were my child, I'd jerk her bald-headed."

Beth met her disapproving glance head-on. "Yes, I'll just bet you would."

She reached down for April's hand, dismayed by her daughter who was now kicking the heels of her white Mary Janes against the glazed terra-cotta tiles on the wall. Before their retreat into the women's bathroom, the undigested orange sherbet burned its way to her throat in an emulsion of bile. Her vision blurred and her temples were throbbing. She rushed into a vacant stall to vomit her lunch.

April continued to wail and stamp her feet. "I don't like Philip! I hate him! Why'd you have to marry him, anyway? Don't you even care what I think?"

Beth grabbed April and gave her a thorough shaking, astonished by an intense desire to slap the child's face, an urge exhuming horrible images from the distant past. "Stop it! Don't you dare say that. Philip's my husband, and he wants to be your new father, if you'll behave yourself for a change. But what can you expect him to think, when you've acted like a wild animal?"

The child whimpered, huge tears rolling down her flushed cheeks. Beth wet a paper towel and sponged off her face. Then, throwing her arms around her mother, April surrendered to a need stronger than anger.

Quietly, Beth held her until she'd calmed down. It wasn't the time for a lecture on proper behavior in public places. That would come later.

Added to the bathroom's odor of disinfectant, Beth tasted curdled orange sherbet. She was desperate for a cool sip of water. "Come on, honey. Let's get out of here." Starting to open the door to the hall, she looked down at April. "Do you need to use the bathroom before we leave?"

The child shook her head, the picture of repentance. "Are you mad at me?"

"What good would it do if I were, young lady? What's done is done. Promise me you'll mind your manners. You're not a baby. You're nine years old."

"I know, Mom. I'm really sorry. I couldn't help it."

"You'd better help it, April. I don't want this to ever happen again. Do you understand?"

"Yes, Mom."

"All right, then. We'll go out the back way. I can't face those people again."

"Can we stop at the gift shop where they sell stuff? You promised!"

As they drove through the center of a boulevard of towering pines on a breezy August afternoon, Beth struggled with her own sense of divided loyalties between her daughter and Philip Magill, her husband of seven months. Studying his handsome, chiseled profile, she reached for Philip's knee and gave it a squeeze.

"April needs to get used to the idea we're actually married," she said, though she was painfully aware of April's sulking presence in the back seat of the Blazer.

"I wanted this to be our special time together," he said. "Was that too much to ask?" When Philip turned to look at her, the quiet irritation telegraphed in his eyes, his prim lips, made her feel even more defensive about April's embarrassing tantrum.

"I apologize, darling."

"She must accept the fact we're a couple, and the three of us are a family. But she won't meet me halfway. If you have any suggestions on what more I can do to win her friendship and trust, I'd like to hear them."

Philip had billed the trip to Northport, at the tip of the little finger in the Michigan mitt, as a belated honeymoon and family vacation rolled into one. But the night before their departure, April had balked about coming. Philip wanted to leave her with Beth's parents, Frank and Winona Block, which in Beth's mind was not an option. Now she felt like a traitor to her little girl because she questioned the wisdom of bringing her along.

"You can't expect immediate acceptance from a child, Philip." She removed her hand from his knee and stared straight ahead through the windshield to the white stretch of two-lane highway cutting through the Northern Michigan forests.

"No, I suppose I can't." His curt tone of voice told her he was peeved and probably would be for some time to come.

Then she became annoyed with Philip. Who was to blame for April's scene in the restaurant? And who could have predicted it? Normally, when they were in unfamiliar surroundings, April was rather shy and introverted, looking to her mother for guidance and never caused a minute's trouble. Beth searched her memory for the moment when everything had seemed to go wrong.

Wanting to use the restroom, she'd asked April to wait with Philip. But the child had whined, begging to come with her mother. When Philip tried to take her by the hand, April screamed and kicked, causing other people who were waiting by the register to stare curiously at a pretty blond nine-year-old who was acting like a toddler.

To end the commotion and to remove her daughter from the wholesale disapproval of strangers, Beth had grabbed April's hand, yanked her to her feet, and hurried down the hallway toward the bathrooms.

When they returned to the car, Philip was sitting behind the wheel, his jaw set in concrete. Beth tried to make conversation, but as if he wanted to punish her with his silence, nearly half an hour passed before Philip would respond to her in more than monosyllabic grunts.

She stiffened when he looked over the seat. The new book with the magic pen on April's lap was not lost on her husband. Philip thought the child was spoiled. Well, if a diversion from the motel gift shop would smooth April's mood, Beth was not above a little bribery.

In an icy tone, he called over the seat, "Are we finished with the infantile behavior now?"

April chose not to respond, busily solving mysteries in her Mister Magoo Detective Workbook uncovering hidden clues with the magic pen.

"You say I can't expect instant acceptance. What do you call seven months? How long is it going to take, Beth? Seven years?" He gave one of his best theatrical sighs, the sort of fabricated drama that made Beth want to slap him. "I don't know why you refused to leave her with your parents."

"Please don't start harping on that again."

"It was only for a week. What's the big deal? Weren't we entitled to a week alone? She'd have been fine with Frank and Winona."

"You know how I feel about April being around my mother for long periods of time. Especially without me there. I can't allow it."

"Oh, yes, how could I be so callous as to forget your miserable, wretched childhood with dear old Mother? God, I'm tired of hearing about it." He slapped his palm against the steering wheel.

"Then I won't bore you with a recap, not again. In fact, never again."

A tense moment crackled in the air like a downed powerline neither of them was willing to cross.

In a low voice, Philip said, "She's already done it, hasn't she? We're not even at the cottage yet, and she's managed to wreck it for us."

Beth turned her head and stared out the passenger window, fighting back tears. He was right, of course. April, who had promised to be on her best behavior, was having things her way, as usual. But she had always had things her way, when it had been just Beth and April the past two years. Why should she be expected to make a seamless adjustment to her mother's second marriage?

Philip didn't know the real reasons she could never leave her daughter with Winona and Frank. She had scarcely glossed over a few of the high points of how it had been growing up in the Block house. Beth and her younger brother Ted skulked around the woodwork like cockroaches to escape the hysterical wrath of Winona Block, guilty for having ruined their mother's life.

Had there been any way to make him understand…but what was the point? It was ancient history. Beth had managed to grow up and move out, though poor Teddy was forever doomed to be only a stone's throw away. He would never escape.

But what did it matter to Philip, really? He could have cared less about Beth's memories regarding her own family. In his mind, Beth Block Warner had no past to speak of, before Philip Magill happened along and proposed marriage. All he cared about was now, today and tomorrow, not what might have happened in her life yesterday, before he had assumed what he obviously considered his rightful place at the center of her life.

"Mom! I solved it. Look!"

Dutifully, Beth turned around to glance at the workbook April was holding up for her approval. "Good for you, sweetheart. See if you have as much luck with the next mystery."

"The next one's called The Hanging Pirate."

"Yo-ho-ho," Philip said. His profile was trained on the highway as he grimly made his way north.

Perhaps she was being unfair to him, expecting Philip to have a saintly side compared to other men merely because he was a Presbyterian minister. She even suspected he was perfectly justified, pronouncing April a spoiled child.

She *was* spoiled, and it was Beth's fault. After the child's father was shot by a sniper while on Shore Patrol duty in Haiti when April was nearly seven years old, Beth had tried to compensate for the loss by heaping attention on her daughter. An effort to make her feel loved, wanted, and secure. To let her know that her mother would always be there for her, even if her father had gone to Heaven.

Far better to err on the side of too much love than to deprive April of maternal affection, as Winona had deprived her children. Beth didn't want anything to cause April to feel as she had felt as a child, guilty for having been born. Nor did she intend to give her daughter a reason to fear that, one day, she might wake up to find her mother gone, too.

Sometimes she caught herself, as now, comparing Philip to Randy. Well, perhaps there could never be another love like a first love, and she had been naïve to hope for a reasonable facsimile from Philip. She had to believe that, in time, she could make herself forget Randy's tender passion and learn to settle for Philip's infrequent, lukewarm touch.

There were other things to cherish in a good marriage besides sex. Weren't there?

She lowered the window on the passenger side and greedily sniffed at the pine-scented air. "It's lovely here," she said, a small attempt to alter their sour mood. "I'm so glad you insisted we get away for a while, Philip."

When he said nothing, Beth felt justified in having comforted herself with memories of her first husband. Philip might not be aware of it quite yet, but she was much stronger than he seemed to give her credit for, and there was only so much groveling she was willing to do. From the pulpit he preached about the finest steel being tempered in the flame. Hadn't she experienced her personal share of trial by fire?

Following Randy's stupid, pointless death, Beth moved their household goods from Fort Polk, Louisiana, to her parents' house in Warren, Michigan. She settled April in a new school and returned to teaching third grade, searching on the weekends for an affordable house to buy, a home they could call their own, without success.

But little more than a year later Philip came into their lives, or they had entered his, when they began attending church services at the First Presbyterian Church in Sterling Heights.

How often Beth had reminded herself of their magical first meeting. As she had filed past Reverend Magill, their eyes met, and she felt as if an odd predestination had brought her to his church. The words of his sermon touched her spirit as much as the human magnetism in his expression.

He greeted her warmly and invited her to return the following Sunday; she counted the days until she could see him again. A bachelor, some of the older women eagerly informed Beth as she walked April to their car.

Sometimes it seemed as if ensuing events had progressed at a whirlwind clip. Perhaps she and her daughter hadn't had a decent interval for mourning Randy's death, though she told herself that life is for the living, and Randy would have wanted her to move forward.

He had been a good husband and father, and she had loved him very much. But April was Randy's little princess. After his death, Beth suspected no man could ever fill the void in her daughter's heart. No, not even Philip.

Of course, it might help if Philip would try to be a little more sensitive and understanding.

"I'm sorry," he said all at once. "I really am. You shouldn't feel as if you have to make a choice between your daughter and the old preacher here."

Playfully, Beth slapped his knee. "You're not old! Would you get off that kick, once and for all?"

"Forty. Over the hill. You're too young and spry for me, you know."

"Oh, darling. This must be more difficult for you than I can imagine, marrying for the first time at forty to a woman with a ready-made family. Please know how much I love you, and how glad I am that you're my husband."

Her words elicited a genuine smile. "And I love you, Beth. I hope from human frailty I never do anything to make you doubt it."

Thinking the tension had been broken, she slid close to him and kissed his cheek, throwing a guilty glance over the seat. April had fallen asleep.

"She's napping, Philip. The emotional outburst must have exhausted her. I promise, I'll speak to her about it later. It won't happen a second time."

"Yes, it probably will. But we'll tough it out together. Heck, I'm a nice guy. Eventually she'll come around. At least I hope she will."

When he grinned at her, she realized all over again how handsome he was, with his clear blue eyes framed by long dark lashes, his full head of sandy hair. In fact, Philip was such an attractive man, he was almost pretty. She wanted to feel proud to be his wife.

This marriage must work, Beth thought to herself. Some nights, when she listened to him snoring as she tried to fall asleep aching for the safety of a man's arms, she wondered if marrying Philip Magill had been the easy way out.

But then she visualized the spacious house beside the church, a two-story clapboard with green shutters and a white picket fence, their new home, and Beth convinced herself she'd chosen well. A semblance of respectability she had yearned for all her life, an environment suitable for raising her daughter, a minister for April's stepfather...

She swallowed several times, fighting down a wave of nausea. She'd been savoring the prospect of telling Philip they were two months pregnant. Of course, he'd be overjoyed, delighted. Hopefully, the baby would be a son to carry on the Magill name.

Intent on not squelching Philip's truce, she tried not to worry. But there was so much to worry about: April's reaction to her mother's pregnancy and how she would feel when the new baby arrived, whether she herself would be torn between the daughter that she so loved and a new infant born to a thirty-year-old mother. The age Winona had been when Beth's younger brother Teddy arrived in the world.

"We're here!" Philip parked the Blazer in an overgrown driveway beside a quaint A-frame with a redwood deck overlooking the blue expanse of Grand Traverse Bay. "April, wake up, dear. Come and see your bedroom."

Sleepily, April sat up and looked out the window of the car toward the cottage. "I don't have a bedroom here."

"Suit yourself, then." Philip removed luggage from the rear hatch. "Beth? Are you coming?"

"In a second. You go ahead. We'll be right there."

She leaned over the seat and pleaded with her daughter to come inside. Glancing toward the cottage, she saw Philip standing on the deck with a suitcase in each hand, waiting.

"April, don't be a drag. Philip's been looking forward to showing us the cottage. Please don't do this, not now."

"I'm going to sleep in the car. I don't want to see anything. It's not his house, anyway." April folded her arms for emphasis, her lower lip settling into a decided pout. Oh, but this child could be so damned stubborn!

"No, it's his brother's. You remember Uncle Edward. He was Philip's best man at the wedding."

When there was no response from April, Beth straightened up, surprised by a glimpse of herself in the side mirror, her face creased with worry lines. It wasn't healthy to allow April to control her this way. Without another word, she slammed the car door and walked up the driveway to join her husband.

"I'd carry you over the threshold, but my hands are full." He flashed a smile conveying his pleasure that Beth had chosen to be with him rather than April. One of the first things she had learned about Philip Magill was his expectation of having things exactly his own way.

She pushed through the door and stepped into a charming chalet. A short hallway led to a peaked-roof great room, a small bedroom to the left, a bathroom on the right and a tidy kitchen beyond. Beth walked to the opposite end of the house, to a wall of windows and sliding glass doors overlooking another redwood deck, a sandy beach, and a tranquil bay.

Philip stood behind her. "Well, what's the verdict?"

"It couldn't be more perfect, darling." She turned to give him a hug and was surprised by a deep, lingering kiss. For some inexplicable reason, she felt awkward, even embarrassed, and turned away.

"Oh, a loft!" She escaped up the stairs. A double bed, nightstands, a bureau, a recliner chair and ottoman flanked by a floor lamp, a multi-colored round braided rug on the polished hardwood floor.

Leaning over the railing, she called down to Philip, "This is our room?"

"The small bedroom is for April." He walked upstairs with the suitcases and tossed them on the bed. "I'll carry in the rest. And while I'm out there, maybe I can talk some sense into April's head."

Beth started to follow but decided against it. She couldn't continue to act as a buffer between April and Philip, especially now, with the baby coming. They'd simply have to work it out themselves. God willing, they'd grope through the dark jungle of mutual resentment and find a way to become friends.

She released the latches on the overnight bag and began to unpack. Hanging things in a closet built in the eaves, she heard Philip's voice from below. She listened as he gave April a guided tour of the cottage.

In seconds, April came bounding up the stairs. "Neat! Can I have this room, Mom? It's cool!"

"No. Your room is downstairs. Didn't Philip show you?"

"Why can't I stay up here?"

Beth gave her a look. "You know the answer, don't you? Because Philip is staying with me."

"Just this once, just tonight, couldn't I stay with you? Please?"

Beth laughed. "You're a case today. I can't imagine what's gotten into you. Go on, I'll follow you down and we'll arrange your room. Then you can help me organize the kitchen and make a grocery list."

"What's for dinner?"

"Philip's cooking steaks on the outside grill. We're going to have a picnic on the deck."

"Can I put on my bathing suit and go swimming?"

"If you'll get the life jacket from the car, of course you may."

As April darted outside, Beth went downstairs to unpack April's suitcase and hung shorts and tops, a dress, and pants in the closet of her room. She smiled when she found the ragged but treasured scarecrow doll April had slept with since age two, propping Strawbaby against the pillow on the twin bed.

For the first time since they had left Sterling Heights at seven o'clock this morning, Beth dared to hope their vacation in Northport might turn out to be enjoyable, after all.

###

They sat on the back deck overlooking Grand Traverse Bay, a cool evening breeze, a half-moon sprinkling silvery beams on the water, classical Baroque music on the stereo from the great room.

Barefoot, Philip was dressed in white shorts and a light blue shirt. He looked like a rich man lounging on the deck of his cabin cruiser.

As he uncorked a bottle of wine and poured two glasses, Beth said, "What time is it?" She tried to stifle a yawn.

"Are you tired?" His piqued tone of voice verged on accusation.

"I hate to admit it, but I'm bushed."

Philip sighed. "I hoped we could enjoy a little alone time. Couldn't have a more romantic setting, could we?"

"Edward and Charlotte did a wonderful job decorating the cottage. It's like something from a fairytale."

"You know Charlotte. She's endlessly planning and arranging things in her mind. I suspect she had this place decorated before the architect finished the design."

Beth sampled her wine. "Incidentally, Philip, we need to talk about having the house painted. I'm anxious to make your house our home. But with the school year coming up so quickly, I don't know when."

She thought about dealing with a classroom of seven and eight-year-olds while three months pregnant, and the prospect exhausted her. She wouldn't be able to finish out the school year. The baby was due April fifteenth, providing the doctor's calculations were accurate.

"If you'd called someone like I asked you to, the house could have been painted this week, while we're here. I don't relish the thought of putting up with ladders and drop cloths. I despise anything that disrupts my routine."

"Too late now, though, isn't it? Guess I'll never be as efficient as Charlotte."

She wondered if the right moment had presented itself, whether she should tell him about the baby. At least her pregnancy was a legitimate explanation as to why she'd been feeling so tired and droopy in the past few weeks, and why she'd forgotten to call a painting contractor.

"To be honest, I've been wanting to ask you something, Beth."

"What, darling?"

He cleared his throat, an irritating habit Beth had learned often preceded some long-winded explanation or lecture – all right, then, call it a sermon – a discourse she generally didn't want to hear.

"Well, I wondered when you plan to take a more active role in my ministry."

"What am I not doing to your satisfaction, Philip?"

"As my wife, you need to be my partner in the church. There are all sorts of things a minister's wife is customarily responsible for. The congregation expects it."

She centered her full attention on him. "Such as? Laundering the curtains in the Fellowship Hall? Tending the marigolds in the flower garden? Pray tell, however did you manage before you married me?"

He laughed. "I didn't. Not very well, I'm afraid. The older gals filled in, you know, mothering me to death. Coordinating the refreshments and potlucks, church activities. I thought you'd be a natural for heading up children's Sunday school, recruiting and training the teachers, ordering materials, developing curricula, teaching at least one class yourself, of course. As the most obvious example."

She set down her wine glass, remembering the obstetrician's warning to curtail her intake of alcohol, and not to take so much as an aspirin if it could be avoided. "Frankly, I can't think of anything I'd rather do less. I work with children all week, don't forget. That's the last thing I'd want to do with my free time. Then there's April to consider."

"April. Always April."

"Philip, please don't start. Not now."

In reply, he made a great show of draining his glass of wine, got up from the deck chair and walked into the cottage through the sliding glass doors, leaving Beth alone.

She drew her sweater closed, noticing a chill wind. She thought Philip had some nerve, chastising her for benign neglect. It was all she could do to show up on Sunday mornings, smile and utter inanities to members of the congregation.

If he wanted the truth, were it not for his inspiring sermons, she'd have been bored to death by the whole scene. But perhaps she should have realized as much, before she so merrily married Philip Magill, imagining a minister would be the perfect husband.

And now she was pregnant with his child. There was no backing out of the marriage, however hasty. They'd all have to make the best of it, Beth included, though she hoped that he'd soften his demands on her time and energy after he learned of the pregnancy.

She got up from her chair and stuck her head through the open door. He was sitting in the far corner of the great room in a recliner beside a floor lamp, studying Scripture and jotting notes on a pad.

Retreating into his sermon, as usual, though at home he would vanish into his study for hours with his computer.

"Philip, would you come out here so we can talk? There's something I need to tell you."

"Sorry, Beth, but you weren't in a receptive mood, so now I'm busy with something else."

"Too busy for the minister's wife?" She walked across the room and stroked his hair, surprised when he flinched away from her touch. Well, she thought grimly, that was a first.

As if on cue, from the downstairs bedroom came a frightened cry. Philip's eyes locked with hers, and Beth was the one to look away.

"Excuse me. April's having a nightmare."

He reached for her hand and held her at his side. "If you really love me, you'll learn to not go to her every time she squeaks."

Beth studied the gray mortar between the flagstones of the fireplace.

Again, April cried out. "But she's having a bad dream! What's wrong with you?" When she tried to pull away, he tightened his grip.

"Ignore it. All children have bad dreams. But most mothers don't run to them as if they're still tied to an umbilical cord."

No, most mothers didn't. Beth's mother certainly hadn't, which gave her the single excuse she needed to shake loose from Philip and comfort her child.

But before she left the room, Beth said, "We're going to have a baby, Philip. Will you also let him cry alone in the night, with no one there to chase the goblins away?"

Only when she entered the dark bedroom and held April in her arms did Beth feel complete. An unwelcome, unexpected tear escaped from her eye as she soothed April and settled her back to sleep.

She was frightened by the sudden feeling of having been trapped in this cottage, knowing the last thing on earth she wanted to do in the next moment was to face Philip Magill's censure.

Everything had seemed fine, almost magical during their brief courtship. He'd been gallant, polite, and courteous to her daughter, parents and brother. He had given her ample reason to believe that marrying Philip Magill would be the best thing to happen for both Beth and April.

But in the past seven months, he had slowly revealed a different side of himself. She had fought against her growing suspicion that, to be a man of the cloth, Philip was sometimes the coldest and most insensitive man she'd ever met.

Due to his upbringing, no doubt, which could not have been more far removed from Beth's. Philip was the younger of two sons of an attaché to an ambassador to France. He had been schooled for many years by a private tutor named Victor whom he remembered with great fondness. Raised without fear or anxiety, his path through life was smoothed at every turn. Privileged and moneyed.

Silently closing the door of April's bedroom, Beth wondered if she quietly resented Philip's good fortune. Sometimes she caught herself imagining his reaction, if ever his metaphorical boat were to capsize in one of life's many storms.

To him, such an idea was not a remote possibility.

But what if Beth were to fall overboard? Would he reach out and pull her to safety? Perhaps, since he'd learned she was carrying his child, he might consider it.

Her meager hope for a respite from her husband's self-righteousness was dashed when he didn't so much as look up from his notepad as she slowly climbed the stairs to the loft bedroom.

Though she told herself she was simply too tired to worry over his mood or his evident displeasure about the pregnancy, tears of despair gushed from her eyes. She'd been a fool to stop taking her birth control pills, in the vain hope that having a child by Philip would cement their marriage. But she was hardly the only woman who had ever made that mistake.

Shivering as she changed into her nightgown, she considered sinking to her knees at the side of the bed in prayer. But it was Philip who claimed a special pipeline to a Higher Power. Let him be the one to pray.

Dreading the morning, she pulled the bedcovers over her head to drown out the booming sounds of a Mahler symphony.

Chapter Seven

"**G**ood morning, Mary Sunshine."

Beth was awakened by Philip holding a tray with the apparent intention of serving her breakfast in bed. A sprig of wild honeysuckle was tucked into a bud vase.

"Oh, Philip, you really shouldn't have."

After her sleepless night, she knew how wretched she must look. She tried to turn her face away, so he wouldn't see the puffy bags under her eyes that always greeted her in the morning after she'd cried, not to mention the frizzy hair from the miserable permanent she'd suffered at the hands of an incompetent beautician at the salon last week. The solution was left in for much too long, burning the ends of her hair.

"Since you're eating for two, darling, we must be certain you're getting the proper nourishment." He set the tray on her lap, the very picture of a solicitous husband.

The sight of the runny poached egg, toast with orange marmalade, made her stomach roil. But the steaming mug of black coffee was inviting. Immediately, she reached for it.

"April and I have had our breakfast. She's outside, playing on the beach."

"Why, thank you, Philip." She sipped at the hot coffee, manna from Heaven. It was the only way she could wake up in the morning.

"You'll be limited to one cup of coffee per day, so make it last. Nira Woods told me her doctor advised against caffeine during pregnancy. We'll slowly wean you to decaf. After a while, you won't miss the caffeine."

Terrific. "What time is it?"

"Eightish. I'll leave you alone now, so you can enjoy your breakfast. But when you're feeling up to it, Beth, I have a big day planned for the three of us."

"Couldn't we stay at the cottage today? I really don't feel much like..."

"Nonsense! This is our vacation. There are places to go, things to do! You'll love it, you'll see." He planted a kiss on her forehead. "Beth, I'm so pleased about the baby."

She looked up at him skeptically. "You are? It didn't seem so last night."

"As for last night, I want to apologize. I'm sorry, really I am, for being an ass."

"Apology accepted," she said with a weak smile. She couldn't wait until he left the loft so she could sneak downstairs to flush her breakfast down the garbage disposal.

"I'll sit on the deck until you get dressed. It's an utterly gorgeous Northern Michigan summer morning. I'm anxious to share it with you."

Who cares? She watched while he did a few jumping jacks as if to demonstrate his expansive mood. She felt like slapping him.

After he had gone downstairs, she drank her one cup of coffee. Though he had decided to be contrite, even pleased by the news of Beth's pregnancy, she regarded him as increasingly annoying. She had needed him to express his joy at once, but he had failed her in that. Then he punished her yet again, and one time too many, for her attention to April's nightmares.

Though she had granted him the smile he seemed to regard as a sign everything between them was hunky-dory, in her heart she could not persuade herself to forgive him.

Wearily, she got out of bed where, had there been a choice, she'd have remained. For she knew it intuitively, in her bones, how last night and this morning were merely a gloomy prelude of things to come. Up again, down again, like being chained to one end of a seesaw.

Despite Beth's frequent protests, for the next three days he drove them sightseeing.

To Lighthouse Point to feed the seagulls.

A ride in a dune buggy along Sleeping Bear Dunes for hours in a scorching sun.

An afternoon at a magical, fragrant herb farm on the western edge of Michigan.

A magnificent, picture-postcard sunset over Lake Michigan that Philip had ordained the most panoramic of the Great Lakes.

"Look, girls!" Philip had appointed himself cruise director. "A flight of migrating Canada geese! If you listen carefully, you can hear them honking to one another. The one in the front is the alpha male, the leader."

But April would have none of it. She was frightened by the seagulls squawking for crusts of bread, terrified by the rapid descent down the sand dunes in the buggy, bored by the herb farm, and could have cared less about the Canada geese.

As the crimson globe sank into Lake Michigan, April was nagging Beth to rent a television set for entertainment at the A-frame. Several times Beth saw the look of disgust plainly etched on Philip's face.

April's only previous request was to see a real Indian, having been entranced by a few shabby wigwams along the roadside on their way to Northport, a request Philip refused.

"They're entitled to their privacy, April," Philip said pompously. "No doubt the last thing they want is for people like you to stare at them."

For once, Beth was glad when he was hesitant to touch her. She stayed well on her side of the double bed in the loft bedroom, waking periodically to hear him roaming through the cottage at odd hours. Over breakfast he complained that he hadn't slept well, a lament for which she felt no sympathy. After he darted out the door to clean out the grill, Beth brewed a second pot of coffee and helped herself to a second, then a third cup.

By the fourth day, Beth's prayer that April would call her own truce with Philip had been answered. Her daughter seemed to enjoy the collection of seashells, Petoskey stones, and interesting bits of driftwood gathered along the beach fronting the cottage, and she was particularly eager for the frequent dips into the bay. Her damp bathing suit hanging over the railing of the redwood deck had become part of the scenery.

On Saturday they would leave for the long drive home, and Beth was anxious to be in familiar surroundings, telling herself the nesting urge had happened early.

In idle moments she planned the nursery. Blue or canary-yellow? Mother Goose figures stenciled on the wall, or Beatrix Potter's Peter Rabbit decals she could purchase at the hardware store? A walnut cradle to begin, or a white bassinette for Baby's first three months before they decided on a crib? She could move the maple rocking chair from the living room to the nursery. Since she'd have the summer unencumbered, she planned to breastfeed.

And April's old toy box for later. She would soon be old enough for a hope chest, something Beth had always wanted for herself when she was young, a hope chest and a canopy bed.

Unfortunately, confined to Army bases during April's formative years with everyone on a limited military income, as a neighborly gesture Beth had given most of April's outgrown things to a young couple who had lived next door at Fort Bragg.

She and Randy had agreed to have one child anyway, as Randy's plan was to attend medical school after his discharge from military service. Beth hadn't believed she would ever need the old crib and changing table, nor April's infant and toddler clothes. For this baby, things would have to be purchased new.

If they should have a son, Beth planned to dress him in little sailor suits.

On Wednesday night they drove to Interlochen National Music Camp for a concert featuring Van Cliburn as guest artist. Philip parked the car some distance from the shell-auditorium. They had to hurry to reach the ticket office minutes before the concert began.

At some point during the second movement of the Tchaikovsky piano concerto, April told her mother she had to use the bathroom.

"We saw the signs when we came in," Beth whispered. "Remember, I showed you so you'd know where to go?"

"Will you come with me?"

"Not this time, April. I really want to hear this. Slip out quietly, go and come back right away so I don't have to wonder where you are. And don't forget to wash your hands with soap."

Obediently, April excused herself and eased in front of several people to the end of the aisle.

Beth lost herself in the music, appreciating Van Cliburn's understated performance and the way his full head of sandy hair reminded her of Philip's. When the final movement rolled to a dramatic finish and a standing ovation, with a jolt Beth noticed all at once that April's seat was empty.

"Philip, she's lost, I just know it. I should have gone with her."

"I'm sure she'll find her way. How much danger could there be here? Quit imagining predators behind every pine tree."

"That's not the point! I don't want her to be frightened."

She started to leave her seat when she saw April's blond head bobbing along the far aisle in their row. Beth stood up until April spotted her and came down from the opposite side.

"What took you so long, April?" Philip said. "Your mother was worried."

"They wouldn't let me come till he wasn't playing."

Of course; Beth should have realized. The young Interlochen students acting as ushers had been instructed to keep audience diversion to a minimum while a virtuoso artist was performing.

"Well, now she's back, and we don't have to worry anymore, do we, Philip?" As if he had been worried in the slightest, she thought to herself,

half believing April's welfare was the last item of concern on Philip's ego-
tistical agenda.

The final selection was listed on the program as an annual occur-
rence, a traditional performance by the student orchestra of the Interlochen theme. Then the lights came up and they were threading their way
through a crowd of several thousand people of all nationalities to the rustic
tree-lined path leading to their car.

April scrambled into the back seat, sticking her thumb in her mouth
and hugging Strawbaby. Before they were on the main highway for the trip
back to Northport and north to the cottage, Beth noticed that April had
dozed off. The digital clock on the dashboard read ten-fifty-five.

"We're out of food," she said. "I'll have to come into town tomorrow
and do some shopping for the next two days. I'd hoped to take care of it on
the way back, but it's so late, everything will be closed."

"I promised to make blueberry pancakes for breakfast," Philip said.
"We can drive to Northport afterward. I wish we had another week here,
but they're expecting me back for Sunday services, and my sermon's only
half finished."

"What's the topic?"

"New beginnings. Spiritual rebirth, the life cycle, summer-fall-win-
ter-spring. You know."

"Second marriages?"

He chuckled briefly. "Yes, I suppose so."

"Did you enjoy the concert as much as I did?"

"Every note." A comfortable silence enveloped them before Philip
said, "Beth, are you in love with me?"

His words took her completely by surprise. "What a strange question! Why did you ask me that?"

"I've been wondering lately, the way you look at me at times. As if
I crawled out from under a rock."

"Philip, you're imagining things. That's absurd. Of course, I love
you. I'd never have agreed to marry you if I didn't. Life's difficult enough,
without marrying someone you don't care for."

"Care for is different than love."

She let a few minutes go by as she tried to collect her thoughts,
wondering what she had done to make Philip ask if she loved him. But then
she understood.

"And now the obvious question to come is, do I love you as much as
I loved Randy Warner. Isn't it?" In the darkness she felt his palpable gaze.

"Naturally, I've wondered. What man wouldn't?"

"What I feel for you, Philip, well, it's different, a different kind of love. Randy and I fell in love at college, when we were both very young. Puppy love, maybe. But it matured during the few short years we had together, especially after April was born. Yes, I did love him ... very much. I suppose part of me always will."

"But you haven't answered the question to my satisfaction yet."

"Oh? And what answer would appease you? Tell me what to say, and I'll parrot it back."

"Why don't you just tell it like it is? You married me because you wanted a husband and a father for your daughter, and I needed a wife for professional reasons. It was a marriage of convenience, for both of us."

He said it so reasonably, so matter of fact and in such a pleasant conversational tone, almost in a jocular manner. Whether it had been his intention, suddenly Beth realized with a dull thud to her heart that he had spoken the unvarnished truth.

"I really don't know what to say, Philip. Is that the reason you married me, for convenience? Because if it is, then I ought to have an abortion. We shouldn't consider bringing a child into this world, if the only thing we have between us is convenience."

As she had suspected, her remark pushed all his buttons. In fact, she'd wanted her words to have precisely such an effect.

"How could you mention abortion, Beth? You know my feelings on the subject well enough. I can't believe you'd even suggest it."

But she was feeling reckless and decided to go for broke. If he wanted to be miffed with her, she'd give him more than enough reason, and with pleasure.

"If you were the one who had to be pregnant for nine months and deliver the baby and nurse it and care for it every day until it's eighteen, perhaps your opinion of abortion would be altered, aside from your theological views on the subject. Why do men lead the charge against abortion, I've always wanted to know. Would you be so kind as to explain it to me, Philip?"

Quietly, he said, "Don't you want this baby?"

"To be honest, I'm not sure whether I do or not. Your initial reaction to the news the other night didn't do much to tell me *you* want the baby, if you'll remember." She stopped momentarily, trying to control her angry feelings. "To be frank with you, Philip, I doubt you'd have time to be a conscientious parent. You can hardly be civil to April as it is. Let's face it, children are annoying and demanding and likely as not to have a tantrum in a public place. In a marriage of convenience, children are probably the ultimate inconvenience."

"Then I'll make more of an effort with April."

Exasperated, Beth said, "It shouldn't be something you have to plan, or set out to do. You should want to spend time with her, and not just to placate me. She's a wonderful, inventive, bright little girl, but you'll never know unless you…"

"Well, how does this sound? Tomorrow when we get back from shopping, I'll make lunch. While you take a nap, April and I will go hunting for Petoskey stones. Hell, I'll even pick up one of those rock-polishing kits when we're in Northport."

Carefully, Beth said, "Sounds as if it might be fun."

"And I'll put her bicycle in the back of the Blazer and let her ride in the park while you're shopping."

Since their arrival at the cottage, April had been whining to her mother about wanting to ride her bike, but Beth was afraid to let her ride on the graveled road because she might fall and injure herself. That Philip had latched onto an idea for April to safely ride her bike genuinely touched Beth.

"Thank you, Philip. She'll love it."

When they reached the A-frame, Philip helped the groggy child from the car to the house. As Beth got her ready for bed, for once he didn't hover or make her feel as though she had to hurry to meet his needs.

After she tucked April in with a story, she retreated to the bathroom for a hot shower and changed into her nightgown. When she went upstairs to the bedroom loft, Philip was already asleep.

Beth's sensation of relief to find him asleep came as a surprise. Perhaps she was just weary from the day, because she did acknowledge a new feeling of gratitude toward Philip for his words of understanding concerning April.

Gently, she eased into bed and beneath the comforter, taking care not to jiggle the mattress.

At last, she was able to release her jumbled emotions in a long, slow exhalation of breath. She hoped she could make it through the night without having to rush to the bathroom to vomit. As a precautionary measure, she'd drunk a half cup of warm milk before coming upstairs.

Philip's words whirled in her mind. A marriage of convenience: had he only said it to hurt her, or had he made a not-very-Freudian slip?

Thinking of the way the older ladies, many of them widows, fawned over Philip at church, Beth couldn't help but wonder what had prompted him to take a wife. Once he had joked about his congregation probably beginning to think he was gay.

Well, he wasn't, was he? Gay? Hardly. She wouldn't be pregnant with his child if Philip were gay.

Which didn't necessarily rule out bi-sexual, did it? He'd never spoken of his past other than to remark about a woman named Mary Hannah from his youth, a girl who hadn't wanted to be a minister's wife.

Still, when she remembered her sex life with Randy, it was impossible for Beth not to compare those years of sensual pleasure against her few bloodless months with Philip Magill. Randy had been spontaneous and energetic, lovemaking his delight, his right as her husband. He had pursued her hungrily, and Beth had felt pretty and desirable and loved.

Philip seemed to regard intercourse as his husbandly duty, to be meted out in small doses. His technique was mechanical, making Beth think he had an hourglass in his mind with which he was forced to comply. Several minutes of tediously predictable foreplay, no affection after the act...

Did she love him? Or did she only *want* to love him?

She punched her pillow, trying to arrange herself in a comfortable posture for sleeping. Security and convenience were lousy reasons to get married a second time at age thirty. She gave herself more credit than...

But if security was not her primary motive for marrying Philip, why hadn't she been able to assure him of her love in answer to his question as they returned from the concert?

She could only hope the plans for tomorrow Philip had devised for quality time with April worked out to his expectations. If the child continued to resist him at every turn, he would never grow to love her.

And Beth might never be able to answer, even to her own satisfaction, whether she truly loved Philip Magill.

Chapter Eight

"The sun god's been with us," Philip said with a smile before unloading April's mauve-metallic Schwinn from the back of the Blazer with a series of unconvincing grunts and groans.

Beth and April climbed from the car and watched as Philip wheeled the bicycle over the curb to set it on the asphalt walkway of Northport Municipal Park. He held the bike until April straddled it and happily pedaled down the sidewalk. Beth stretched to give her husband a well-deserved kiss on the cheek.

"Well, there's one cheerful child," she said. "I shouldn't be long, darling. Did you bring something to read?"

"The ubiquitous, unfinished sermon. I thought the good weather experienced in the grandeur of the great outdoors might inspire the last few finishing touches." He bent down to return the kiss. "Don't worry about us. I'll keep an eye on April. Go ahead and take your time. I remember shopping in strange grocery stores, when you don't know where things are. Personally, I always hated it."

"Anything special you'd like for dinner?"

"Anything that strikes your fancy. But don't overbuy. Remember, we're leaving Saturday, in less than two days."

"I'll get something to grill on the beach, and marshmallows for April to roast. If this weather holds up through tonight, we should take advantage of it." Checking to make sure the grocery list was in her purse, she said, "Well, I'm off."

She crossed the tree-shaded street. A steady stream of out-of-state vehicles and tourists dressed for a holiday flowed down the main street of Northport. Beth stole a last backward glance, comforted by the blended-family scene of April on her bicycle and Philip reclining on a park bench under a shade tree.

What a contrast from the incident at breakfast, with Philip's snide criticism of April's table manners reducing the child to tears.

With a sigh, Beth entered the supermarket, found a cart, and started down the grocery aisles toward the dairy section.

She couldn't permit herself to worry about a recurrence of the morning's nasty confrontation between Philip and April. After all, he had solemnly pledged to leave the child alone, to refrain from making mountains out of molehills about niggling things that didn't matter.

Her own words came back to her, when she'd told Philip that April's childish ploys for attention didn't amount to a hill of beans. "If she can't get you to notice her any other way, she'll continue her bratty behavior."

"What are you? The expert child psychologist?"

"No, Philip. April's mother."

Nastily, he said, "How could I forget?"

He'd stomped out of the cottage to take a solitary walk on the beach. But when he returned, he apologized to April for sometimes being an old stuffed shirt.

"Sorry, April," he'd said to her with a boyish grin. "You're going to have to be patient with me. I'm trying to learn to be a good father, but I haven't had much practice. Guess it's up to you to teach me how."

Afterward, the tension had seemed to melt away, much to Beth's relief.

Choosing a quart of dark-maroon cherries, a head of lettuce, a bell pepper, and a package of locally grown hydroponic tomatoes, Beth paused at the meat counter and nervously looked out through the plate-glass windows toward the park.

Off in the distance, she spotted the metallic gleam of April's bike. Good, she wasn't bored yet.

Philip was sitting on the park bench, his sandy head bent over the sermon.

Beth proceeded down the next few aisles, pondering several choices. If they didn't eat the entire half gallon of ice cream, it would go to waste. She opted for a quart of rum-raisin, one of Philip's favorites.

The next time she checked through the front windows of the store, Philip stood by the park bench engaged in conversation with a young man, early twenties perhaps, with auburn hair, wearing a dark-blue jacket with orange or red stripes on the sleeves, a letter jacket from college or...

Apparently, their dialogue was rather intense, probably an impromptu philosophical discussion. She smiled. Young people did seem to be drawn to Philip.

She was almost finished with her shopping. She pushed the cart up the next aisle, pleased to find all was well.

Philip Magill felt as if he'd been trapped in the middle of a repetitious nightmare. "What the hell are you doing here? You've got some crust, showing up like this."

"You promised to keep in touch. To write. To call. You haven't."

"I did! But then there was no point to it. Don't you see? It's finished. And there wasn't much to begin with. You have your whole life ahead of you. Why can't you get on with it and forget about me?"

"That's not what you used to say, Philip."

"Look, Bruce. You've got to get this through your head. Everything's changed. I'm married. My wife is in the market across the street. My stepdaughter is riding her bike in the park. I don't have any...space for you in my life anymore. You're going to have to understand."

"Oh, I understand, all right. I understand exactly what you did to me. I'll never let you forget it. To you, I was a game, an evil little diversion. And because of you, I can't make love to a woman. Yes, you did this to me, Philip. How many other young boys have you done it to, I wonder?"

Philip's mind was racing. His first impulse was to walk away, to leave him standing alone in the park. But he couldn't. There were witnesses, not to speak of April, and Beth.

"Walk with me a minute," he said, placing his hand on the young man's shoulder.

When Bruce fell into step beside him, Philip's confidence was restored. He could handle this if he measured his words, if he was especially careful.

He fumbled in the pocket of his trousers for his wallet.

#

April's legs were getting tired from pedaling the bike. But she had promised her mother she wouldn't complain, because bringing her bike to the park while her mother did the shopping was Philip's idea.

She rode past some small children playing in a sandbox, then past a man and woman walking a cute little white dog on a leash. The dog yipped and tugged at the leash, trying to nip at April's back wheel, making her grin.

She wished her Dad was still alive, because then her mother wouldn't be married to Philip.

She couldn't help it, but her mother's new husband gave April the creeps. She didn't like it when he touched her, and she tried not to get close enough to him so he could ever touch her again.

She wondered how her mother could stand it, because she knew what people did when they were married, and how babies came. Julie Englebreit and Rachel Harris, April's best friends in third grade, told her all about it.

Thinking of her mother with Philip that way, it made her feel sick to her stomach.

She had *tried* to get along with Philip, really she had! But it was just so hard, when she couldn't make herself like him even a little bit. Not even pretend.

And then this morning, he yelled at her for slopping milk from the cereal bowl onto the table. *Anybody* could have done it. Just an accident, no big deal.

But Philip liked to make a federal case out of everything. She had to bite her tongue to keep from saying what was on her mind: *Who died and made YOU king?*

If she'd said it out loud, she might have gotten a spanking. Philip would have hated her even more than he already did, and then her mother would be sad. April didn't want to make her mother unhappy. She loved her mother, and sometimes she stayed awake at night in bed, praying for a long time to God, asking Him not to let anything terrible happen to her mother, like it did to Dad.

At the far end of the park, April decided to see how fast she could ride her bike to the park bench where Philip was. Maybe, by then, her mother would be finished with the grocery shopping.

One...two...three...Go!

But when she got there, she screeched her brakes to a stop. Philip was talking to some guy, and April could tell by his face that he was plenty mad about something. The only good thing about Philip being mad this time was, she wasn't the one he was mad at for a change.

He was so mad that his arm flew out and pushed the other guy's shoulder. And he hadn't even noticed April straddling her bike, hiding behind a tree, watching. She didn't want him to see her, either.

Slowly, April turned the bike around and began to pedal as fast as she could to the opposite end of the park.

Maybe her mother would be finished with shopping soon, and they could go back to the cottage. April had three things to look forward to: swimming after she helped her mother unpack the groceries, corn-on-the-cob with lots of butter, and roasted marshmallows on a stick.

76

###

While a teenage boy loaded the groceries in the back of the Blazer, Beth checked her watch: 11:40. She'd make tuna salad and lemonade to serve with cherries for a light lunch, so April could take her promised dip in the bay.

For dinner they'd have steaks on the grill, roasted corn-on-the-cob, salad, and marshmallows stuck on the twigs she'd ask April to gather as a pleasant chore. Then Beth and Philip could sip wine on the deck, beside the glowing embers from the fireplace in the great room.

A romantic evening, or at least she hoped for as much.

Thanking the boy and tipping him seventy-five cents, Beth crossed the street to the park and stealthily walked up behind Philip for a kiss on the back of his neck, making him jump a foot.

"You startled me!" He stood up from the park bench, a confused expression on his face.

"Sorry," Beth said with a laugh. "You seemed so lost in thought, I couldn't resist." She glanced around the park, shading her eyes with her hand. "Where's April?"

"Believe it or not, still riding her bike."

"But where? I can't see her."

"At the far end, probably. She's been practicing speed-biking. With all this exercise, she'll probably sleep like a rock tonight, and maybe we'll have a little time for ourselves." He gathered his notes in a bundle and tucked them into his shirt pocket. Taking her hand, he said, "Let's stroll down the walk and find her."

"We'd better hurry. There's a quart of ice cream in the car."

For such a lovely day, the park was sparsely populated. They passed an elderly couple walking a dog.

"Have you seen a little girl on a lavender bike?" Beth asked.

"A while back," the man said.

"Our dog tried to chase her," his wife replied with a smile. "Pretty child."

"Thank you," Beth said, dragging Philip away as a combined sensation of nausea and anxiety began to envelop her. *Don't over-react,* she told herself firmly.

As if he had instantly picked up on her mood, Philip said, "Don't worry, Beth. She couldn't have gotten far."

Together they searched for a sign of the Schwinn glinting in the sunlight. Beth had a sinking feeling of having gone to a certain drawer to find an earring or a brooch, or to a certain shelf or cupboard for some familiar object, only to discover it wasn't there.

An hour later, after they'd circled the park twice, first together and then separately, each going in the opposite direction, Beth found the bicycle lying on its side on the strip of graveled beach overlooking Grand Traverse Bay, but no sign of April.

"Philip! Over here!" Then Beth called her daughter's name repeatedly, so loudly that her voice began to crackle with hysteria. Helplessly, she staggered into the water until it rose halfway up the legs of her white slacks, shrieking April's name.

Philip reached out for her arm and pulled her back to the shoreline. "We'll have to get help," he said, his arms folded as he stared grimly over the sun-sparkled water.

"Who? We don't know anyone here!"

"I meant the police."

"Oh, Philip, *don't!* I'm not leaving here. I can't, don't you see? She'll come looking for me. She's here somewhere. I have to be here!"

He turned away from her. "Then I'll be back. Don't move the bike. Don't even touch it. Fingerprints."

Numbly, Beth stood on the beach alone, and it seemed as though the world had been covered over with gauze. Her mind raced to safe conclusions.

April had taken a walk along the beach to gather shells. She'd become disoriented and lost her way.

Some children had come by. April had joined them in a game and had simply forgotten the time.

She'd gone to buy an ice cream bar.

She had to use the bathroom and went off to find one.

Beth tried to fight against the worry that had spiked fear into a sharp panic and then to a seeping, poisonous terror. She reasoned with herself that in another few minutes April would be riding with them in the Blazer and they'd be heading back to the A-frame for lunch and an afternoon of swimming...

When she saw Philip coming toward her accompanied by a policeman in a dark-blue uniform, Beth's legs failed her and she crumpled to the ground. Philip helped her up, and she held onto his arm for support.

In a daze, Beth heard the man ask her, "What was your daughter wearing, Mrs. Magill? Do you have a recent photograph?"

She would have to answer his questions, and if she answered all the questions, April would be with her as always. Someday, years from now, they would look back on this day and laugh about the time April had wandered off in the Northport Municipal Park and had given Beth such an awful fright.

She simply could not allow herself to imagine what life would be like if April were not here.

"Mr. Magill, did you notice any strange people in the park?"

"No."

"Anyone off by himself, who seemed to be observing your daughter?"

"No, I told you. I didn't see anyone."

Beth's hand gripped Philip's arm so tightly that he winced. "Philip, the young man you were talking to!"

He turned to her with a blank expression. "What?"

"I saw you talking to a man with reddish hair!"

"Oh, I remember now," Philip said smoothly. "He was a panhandler. I gave him a few dollars to get rid of him."

"Can you give me a description?" the policeman said.

Beth mentioned the letter jacket the man had been wearing, the fact that he appeared to be in his early twenties, seemed to be a few inches shorter than Philip, maybe five-ten.

"This is helpful," the policeman said, making notes on a pad. "Did he happen to mention his name, Mr. Magill?"

"No, of course not. He just wanted money. Not that my experience with panhandlers is extensive, but as a rule do they generally identify themselves when they beg for money?"

Wildly, Beth cried, "We need to check the public bathrooms! Where are they?"

"Mrs. Magill, I think you and your husband should follow me to the station."

"I'm not going anywhere! If I'm forced to sleep here tonight, I'll not leave until we've found her!"

Gently, Philip tried to lead her away in the direction of the Blazer parked on the main street. "I'm sorry, Officer. You can see how distraught my wife is, and she's pregnant, which doesn't help."

"Mrs. Magill, we'll form a search party," the officer assured her. "We'll find your little girl, don't worry."

Woodenly, she felt herself walking away. She tried to wrench free of Philip's grasp. "But the bicycle!"

"Leave it," Philip said. "It doesn't matter, Beth, don't you understand? The police will see to it."

And then, incredibly, she sat in the passenger seat of the Blazer, listening to Philip talk to the officer, overhearing such words as abduction, drowning, and foul play.

She covered her face with her hands and began to sob.

Chapter Nine

The spacious white house beside Philip's church in Sterling Heights, the house Beth had planned to transform into her daughter's new home, became Beth's sanctuary.

She remained cloistered from the world for three weeks under doctor's care. Because of the pregnancy, sedatives were not an option. Dr. Wallace Ramsey's prescription was a nutritious diet and simple bed rest which Beth surrendered to willingly, shrouded by waves of endless sleep approaching a state of somnolent catatonia.

Dimly, Beth heard Dr. Ramsey speaking with Philip. "Some believe the mother's emotional and psychological state during pregnancy may influence the unborn child's lifelong physical condition and personality."

"We certainly don't want that, do we, Doctor," Philip replied. "She'll be back on her feet, up and around in no time flat. You have my word. I'm not one who has an unlimited amount of patience. This recuperation business has a deadline, believe me."

She crawled into bed and slept for days, getting up to use the bathroom or to take her vitamin capsules with a glass of water. When sleep eluded her, she moved about the house as a zombie, hoping she was trapped in a nightmare and would wake up to discover that the events in Northport had never happened.

At any moment April might come running into her bedroom with that special smile that lit up the world and made everything brighter and filled life itself with hope.

Although Philip was forced to arrange for a substitute minister for Sunday's service, they spent another six days in Northport, traveling back and forth from the cottage to the state police post in Traverse City. Beth would forever remember those frantic days as a heavy gray blur of constant disappointment and gloom.

Hundreds of people had combed the area for April, volunteers from a Search and Rescue Team, soldiers from the Michigan National Guard.

Helicopters with heat-sensor imaging devices scoured the park and surrounding miles, scuba divers plunged into the bay.

April's photograph was posted all over town, storekeepers were questioned. Had anyone seen a pretty nine-year-old girl with blond hair and blue eyes, wearing pink shorts and a white blouse, pink tennis shoes? As the police told Beth and Philip, it was a vague description to fit many children. They were not surprised when not a single volunteer stepped forward to reveal the information Beth was certain would be forthcoming.

On the fourth day, with April's whereabouts remaining a complete mystery, the police called in the FBI under the jurisdiction of the federal kidnapping law.

"The FBI?" Beth asked querulously.

"Whoever abducted her may have taken her over state lines, Mrs. Magill," the trooper explained.

At this admission, Beth broke down completely, leaving Philip to deal with the situation as best he could.

She had believed in some tiny corner of her brain that April was close by, in one of the houses dotting the shoreline, and all Beth needed was enough help to identify which house it was where someone was hiding her daughter.

A naughty game, a little lark!

It was the only way Beth had been able to endure the hours upon hours of questions that seemed, in the end, so fruitless. Pointless.

To think her child could be in a car riding through another state caused her to feel as helpless as if April were on a space shuttle to Mars.

Despite Philip's strenuous objections, Beth agreed to take on the expense of flying in a psychic from Maumee, Ohio.

The grandmotherly woman named Mrs. Rivers was escorted to the park by the police, to the exact place on the bay where Beth and Philip had found the bicycle.

The following report was delivered to the Magills by FBI Agent Stancil. The woman had said she felt waves of life energy, describing the park from April's viewpoint as if she herself were a little girl. Through her psychic child's eye, she claimed to have identified the culprit, a man with dark hair wearing blue jeans.

There, the psychic impressions ended.

"The man may not have used force," Agent Stancil said. "They often operate through trickery or what's known as inveiglement. But you need to remember. Less than one per cent of all missing children turn out to be stranger abductions. Is there anyone else, someone either of you might know, possibly a person with an ax to grind?"

No, Beth assured them, Randy had no relatives who might have come out of the woodwork to kidnap April. He had one sister who lived in New Jersey. His parents were deceased. Philip offered the unnecessary assurance that his older brother Edward would be the last person on anyone's agenda to consider a possible suspect.

"Obviously, we're ruled out parental abduction since the child's biological father is dead. But you're quite sure April simply didn't decide to run away?"

"Agent Stancil, she's nine years old. Why would she run away from home? Where would she go?" Beth was almost beside herself; such stupid, idiotic questions!

"Abuse? Mental, emotional, or physical?"

Alarmed, Beth stared at Philip. "No, of course not!"

"My best advice to you both," Agent Stancil said, addressing his remarks to Philip, the calm unruffled observer, "is to return home and wait by the phone. There might be a call for ransom."

"But what more can we do?" Again, Beth's tears obscured her vision. "I can't just sit by the phone and do nothing!"

"The search is being extended, and will continue, Mrs. Magill. Please trust us to do the best we can."

As if it were not enough, as though it could go on endlessly, there had been other horror stories, too. Some abductors kidnap young children to use as love slaves, and often kill them afterward. Beth was haunted by the story of little Adam Walsh, found dead two weeks after his disappearance, and by the terrifying evidence of John Wayne Gacy who had sexually molested and strangled over thirty young boys and buried them beneath his house in Chicago.

How could there be strange, savage people walking the earth undetected, capable of committing such heinous crimes? Why did God allow it to happen?

Surely those things would never happen to her April. No, it couldn't be possible!

But Agent Stancil had looked at Beth and said, "If we don't get a lead soon, you must prepare yourselves for the fact that sometimes a child simply vanishes and is never seen nor heard from again. No person is ever identified as the abductor, and no discernible motive is ever found."

Philip had said, "We can't think like that. We won't give up, whatever it takes."

"Well, you can always consider hiring a private investigator. But

I'll warn you from the start," the agent said gravely. "You might spend a lot of money and come up empty-handed. Some investigators have turned it into a ruthless enterprise, soaking bereaved parents for expense money and making not the slightest real effort to locate the child. Quite a joy ride for the unscrupulous. I can tell you from personal observation."

But there was one thing more they didn't warn Beth about, perhaps they didn't have the heart. Yet she was to learn soon enough for herself that, as April's mother, she could never stop thinking, twenty-four hours a day. Even when she was asleep, there were dreams.

She was so grateful for Philip, her rock of strength, her anchor to a belief that, eventually, April would be found and returned to them, and their life as a family would resume. Whenever Beth verged on impotent hysteria, Philip reeled her back to his side not only with his cool logic, but with his unswerving faith in April's return.

Certain helpful arrangements had to be made, to help Beth ease back into life. A substitute teacher was to fill in for Beth's third grade class for the first two weeks of the school year. Philip concurred with Dr. Ramsey, that the sooner Beth involved herself in a semblance of normalcy, the better her coping skills, not only with the reality of April's disappearance but with the advancing pregnancy.

A pregnancy that seemed unreal. Beth had to remind herself from time to time: incredibly, another child was growing in her womb.

With April missing, how could another unborn, separate life be asserting its unseen influence on her body, preparing to change Beth's entire life?

The Women's Altar Guild had been supportive, with casseroles, cakes, fresh flowers, and a domestic to look after Philip and the house during Beth's convalescence. The older women of the church, so fond of Philip, hovered discreetly at a distance, looking in on Beth, inquiring as to any special requests they might fulfill.

Rather than consider such solicitousness an intrusion, Beth was astonished by the kindness. There was no one else to do for her, not in a selfless maternal way. At the news of April's disappearance, Winona Block had taken to her bed. Frank Block announced that there was no consoling her.

Funny, Beth thought to herself, when she'd never believed April's grandmother cared much more for April than she cared for Beth. She'd known no succor would be received from the Blocks. Since Beth had never been able to depend on her mother for anything, she'd learned to expect nothing.

Sometimes she dreamed she was still trapped in the Block house, subject to her mother's tyranny and ruthless domination. As a child, her emotions were jerked between need and fear, and as though they were caught up in some fiendish fairytale, she and her brother Teddy interpreted Winona's erratic moods and behavior as Good Mother, Bad Mother.

Had her mother been insane, Beth thought her own childhood might have made some sort of deranged metaphysical sense. Perhaps then the chaos reflected in the schizophrenic disarray of the Block family's life could have been understood in a primitively justified if inexcusable way.

From the outside looking in, no one else had suspected Winona Block's duality. She functioned in the external world as a registered nurse, only to close the drapes in her house against inquisitive eyes and other points of view. In her own home, she reigned supreme, unchallenged, even deified.

Beth would always remember when the Queen in *Alice's Adventures in Wonderland* turned crimson with rage and shrieked, "Off with her head!"

But Beth was a good mother! In her dreams she screamed for April, begging the gods to return her beloved child. She had wanted only a perfect life for her daughter. Why was she being punished? Why not Winona Block? *She* was the Bad Mother, not Beth!

Not Beth!

When she'd recognized the horror contained within the Block house and began to live in fear of being permanently trapped and overwhelmed, she lost hope of ever molding the life of her family into an imitation of a normal home.

She held her younger brother and gently rocked him when he sobbed, while their mother wept.

"Someday, Teddy, we will grow up and move away," Beth would say. "And we won't ever have to come here again."

People had always made allowances for Winona, first her parents, then her husband, and finally Beth. As an adult, she believed she'd been forever altered by her memories of the years growing up under her mother's thumb, and she understood from her passionate study of psychology that, at very least, Winona was a narcissist and emotionally immature.

She learned about the concept of a toxic family, the nuclear unit that poisoned the minds of its members, often making healthy social relationships impossible without aggressive psychiatric intervention.

When Beth had fallen in love with Randy Warner, she thought their perfect union had broken the curse of the Block family. But then Randy died.

No, Winona Block was not mentally ill in a psychotic sense, but certainly neurotic, spoiled, and totally self-absorbed. Winona had always anticipated the world to pause in admiration as she passed by. Like Blanche Dubois in *A Streetcar Named Desire*, she depended upon if not the kindness, then the largesse of strangers.

Sometimes Winona would stare at Beth as if she silently wondered how the child had entered her life. "You little bitch, don't you *dare* look at me that way. What do *you* know about life? Not a goddamned thing! Oh, but you'll learn, just like I did, the hard way."

"I didn't say anything, Mother," Beth pleaded, trying to avoid becoming the focus of her mother's nebulous rage.

"You don't have to! It's in your eyes, judging me, always judging me. As if you have a right, you little slut."

Beth had tried so hard to understand, but then she tried even harder to turn off her own feelings, as if total numbness were preferable to being victimized by her turbulent emotions. Under abnormal circumstances, wasn't it the normal way to survive?

Oh, yes, she had heard from Winona about what Beth could expect to receive in this life: next to nothing.

But Winona was fond of Little Teddy, the son, the child she enjoyed calling her Little King. She could treat her children as she wished, depriving them of all maternal attention one moment and lashing out at them the next, but she would allow no criticism of Teddy.

Beth pitied her brother, for as he continued to trip and fall and fail, she suspected Teddy would never be free of Winona. He'd always require his mother's strange cloak of protection, just as he'd been conditioned.

But Beth had convinced herself that, if she could suffer her mother's wrath and endure, one day she would be free.

You little fool! I told you! I TOLD you how it would be. Didn't I?

She couldn't bear harsh words, arguments, not even mild disagreements. She winced from the sound of a sharp, angry voice. Only Randy had seemed to understand.

The nightmare continued unabated, with Beth dreaming she was trapped in a child's body, a frightened little girl running through the schizophrenic mazes in the House of Insanity.

But at last, by her mother's negative example, Beth resolved to regain her own emotional fortitude, to gradually become strong for April's sake even in her absence.

A superstition began to take shape at the edges of her mind. If she succumbed to the temptation of flying apart, she would never see April again.

Stumbling through the house, less bed-ridden, trying to handle mindless chores, scenes flashed through her mind, unwinding in painful slow motion, detailed, brilliant, and sharply etched in her memory.

The bicycle lying on its side in the bright sun...

...returning to the cottage to find April's damp bathing suit hanging on the railing of the deck...

...ice cream melted all over the hatch of the Blazer, the stench of spoiled Porterhouse steak...

...the police scuba diver emerging from the bay on the strip of graveled beach in the park, shaking his head in bewilderment...

...the pages of mug shots at the state police post in Traverse City...

"No! I didn't see any of these people!" Beth cried in frustration. "Why are you showing us these pictures?"

"Mrs. Magill, you said on the way to Northport you stopped at a Howard Johnson's for lunch. Think hard. Do you remember seeing anyone who..."

...Philip making a vain attempt to identify the panhandler, the red-haired man being the only possible lead in the case so far...

...April's Strawbaby doll carelessly tossed on the sofa in the great room...

...Philip unloading the Schwinn from the Blazer and slowly rolling it into the garage behind their house in Sterling Heights.

The words of apprehension, caution, discouragement from the state troopers and then from several FBI agents, wound on a spindle in her skull to play repeatedly.

Beth in her bathrobe, barefoot, dragging a wet cloth over the kitchen counters, heard the doorbell one Friday morning. Because Philip was away at a synod conference in Toledo for the day, she went to answer.

Mickey Carruthers, Philip's church secretary, divorced with two grown children. She was some years older than Philip, a rather plain, slightly overweight shapeless woman with a shy manner and sad brown eyes, her dark hair worn in a shaggy pixie cut.

Her husband had committed suicide when Mickey's children were still of school age. She had remarried a year later, but when her second husband proved abusive, Mickey paid handsomely for a fast divorce. In unctuous tones, Philip had related for Beth the unfortunate details of Mickey Carruthers' life.

Beth tried to greet the woman with a smile. "Please come in for coffee.”

“Oh, no! I don’t mean to interfere. I know you need time to yourself.” Standing on the door-stoop, the woman seemed confused, or embarrassed. “It’s just that...well, I know so well about...loss. And I brought this book. It meant such a great deal to me when...my...when my husband died.”

She looked down at the woman’s plump hands and reached out to accept the book, examining the spine. “An Anglican prayer book?”

“I...we were Episcopalian, in those days. I’ve marked some of the devotions for you. I hope it’s helpful.”

“How thoughtful,” Beth said sincerely. “Mickey, I’m very touched. Thank you. I’ll return it one of these days.”

“I’d best be going now,” Mickey Carruthers said quickly. “Philip left me a mountain of work to winnow through. Such a slavedriver, that husband of yours!”

“Thank you again.” She watched the woman walk down the steps to the sidewalk and cut across the lawn to the side entrance of the church office. Closing the door, she opened the book. Inside was an ornate bookplate. The name of a church in Columbia, Maryland. Idly, Beth wondered why it seemed to ring a dull bell.

But what could such a thing matter?

What an odd woman Mickey was. Though she joked about Philip’s perfectionist demands, she was obviously devoted to her employer. Beth sometimes suspected the church secretary might even be infatuated with Philip. There was an unspoken bond between the two, as if they had known...

And then it came to her. The name of the Presbyterian Church in Columbia on the bookplate was the church where Philip had once been pastor. Before or after he’d moved to Florida? She couldn’t remember.

But why would an Anglican prayer book have come from a Presbyterian church? Unless it had been given as a thoughtful gesture from the pastor’s private collection of theological works.

Had Philip been acquainted with Mickey Carruthers in Columbia? He’d never mentioned it, nor had anyone in the congregation.

She’d have to ask him.

###

Toward the end of September, Beth had begun her new routine. She enjoyed teaching, she liked her students, and the rote pattern of her days was becoming established.

Only Chuck Arzoni, her principal, knew of Beth's internal dilemma. She hadn't wanted to begin her new school year with misplaced sympathy from her colleagues, or to be regarded from afar as a victim. If any of the other teachers knew April was missing, they were kind enough to keep their questions to themselves, at least in Beth's presence.

Five days a week, she rose at six-thirty, prepared breakfast, exchanged pleasantries with Philip, each avoiding any mention of April. Then she dressed and drove to the elementary school to arrive at eight o'clock, to be immersed in classes, recess, lunch duty, bus line monitoring, and after-school faculty meetings.

Home by four-thirty or five to prepare dinner. After a few household chores and personal tasks – ironing a blouse, taking a bath, washing her hair – there were lesson plans, marking essays and grading tests at the table in the dining room.

With a glass of warm milk, Beth was in bed by nine o'clock for her weekly Scripture readings and a chapter or two of a current novel she'd buy from the racks of the grocery store.

Sometimes it was impossible for her to believe she was nearly four months pregnant.

But the dreams! In a state of unconsciousness there was no escape from the nightmarish scenes that flickered through her vulnerable brain. The relentless dreams were her only link to April, as haunting and hideous as those dreams might be. And though sometimes she would wake in the night with a tear-soaked pillow, drenched in despair, because the night images were of her daughter, Beth almost welcomed them.

On a Saturday morning when she was changing the sheets in their upstairs bedroom, Beth happened to hear the faint sound of voices. She paused with a pillow tucked beneath her chin, half free of its pillow slip, and looked down through the window into the front yard.

Philip was talking to a young man and, as she watched, they walked together around the corner of the house to the church. The boy was shorter than Philip, dressed in jeans and a baseball cap and a dark poplin jacket. When they turned toward the sidewalk leading to the door of the church office, Beth noticed some markings on the sleeve.

The same jacket! The one she had described to the police!

Beth dropped the pillow to the bed, tripped over the heap of rumpled sheets on the bedroom floor, rushed downstairs and down the hall to the front door. She hurried outside to retrace Philip's steps, only to find him in the church office, alone.

Mickey Carruthers sometimes worked on Saturdays, but not today. Today Mickey's accustomed place was vacant, not a paper on the gleaming surface of her desk.

She flung open the door to Philip's study and breathlessly asked, "Who was that man, Philip?"

"Who?" Philip glanced up placidly from the letters neatly arranged for signature on his desk.

"The man you were talking to in the front yard!"

"Beth..."

"It's the same person from the park. I recognized the jacket. Did he tell you where April is? Does he want money?"

Calmly, Philip got up from his chair, walked around the desk and placed his hands on her shoulders. "Beth, you must stop this. You're imagining things again."

"I *didn't* imagine it! Don't treat me as if I'm losing my mind, Philip! Don't you dare! You were talking to him!"

"That was Bruce Fielding. He's visiting relatives here and stopped by to say hello. Bruce and his parents were part of my parish family at the church in Florida. A fine young man. I've invited him to services tomorrow. You'll meet him then."

"But he's the one you were talking to when April..."

"No, Beth. I haven't seen Bruce in almost four years. You're mistaken."

"But I saw him, Philip! Through the windows of the grocery store!"

She looked up at her husband, her mouth trying to form words. She stared into Philip's face, desperate for any shred of confirmation of the suspicions she knew in her heart to be real and irrefutable.

Finally, she turned away from him. "I'm calling the police." She reached for the doorknob, intent on fulfilling her mission, angry at Philip without quite knowing why.

But Philip grabbed her arm and sat her down in the wingchair beside his impressive walnut desk. "You've got to get hold of yourself. How much longer do you think I can tolerate these crazy notions of yours? You're wrong, Beth. What if you led the police to believe Bruce Fielding might be responsible for April's abduction? You could ruin the man's life, with unfounded accusations. Then how would you feel?"

"How would I *feel*? This is my daughter we're talking about. My *child*. Do you think I give a damn about making somebody's life uncomfortable?" She was so furious with Philip that drops of saliva flew from her mouth as she literally spit the words.

The impact of his hand slapping her face jolted her from the vortex of a spiraling sense of panic. Breathing hard, she tried to get her tangled emotions under control. She felt light-headed, as if she might hyperventilate.

For the first time, there was a fluttering in her abdomen as her baby moved. "Oh, God," she said. "I felt the baby."

Philip sank to his knees beside her. "I'm sorry I slapped you, Beth," he said softly, his handsome face reflecting genuine concern. "I didn't know what else to do. You seemed to be verging on…"

"I know, I know," she said weakly. "I can't seem to stop myself. But, Philip, there's one thing I must know."

"What, darling?"

"Does Bruce Fielding have red hair?"

"Why, yes. As a matter of fact, he does."

She gazed into Philip's blue eyes. It was impossible to tell what he was feeling beneath his calm, pastoral surface.

Then he looked away and got to his feet. "You'll meet him tomorrow at church, Beth. I hope I can trust you to rid yourself of the insane idea that an innocent young man like Bruce could have had anything at all to do with April's disappearance."

Beth placed her hands on her belly and rubbed gently. The curious, furtive movements in her womb had seemed to take her thoughts into a subtle, quieter realm. Slowly, she rose from the chair.

"Beth, can I count on you not to make an embarrassing scene at church tomorrow? After everything that's happened, I can't afford another emotional outburst from my wife, not in front of the parishioners." Philip was now behind his desk, his tone of voice officious and slightly patronizing.

"Don't worry, Philip," she said as she began to leave the office. "I won't embarrass you. I wouldn't dream of it."

Chapter Ten

Philip considered himself an excellent chess player. And though he realized he was no match for the cosmic forces that threatened to overwhelm him, he gritted his teeth in acknowledgement of the contest.

There was little doubt about it now. He'd been pitted against a particularly formidable opponent, a chess game with Fate, and Philip Magill could not afford to lose.

Yes, a chess match with Fate, a game he had no intention of losing. There was simply too much riding on it.

On the one hand, he had much to be grateful for. Despite the long months stretching into nearly two years since April had gone missing, his wife had insisted on following up on any leads provided by the authorities, bits of information that flowed to them infrequently.

But somehow Beth managed to keep the details of her incessant search compartmentalized, separate from their life together as husband and wife and parents of a small son.

A son! A child with Philip's genes, to carry on the Magill name into infinity.

Peter Magill the Third, now fourteen months old and the very image of Philip. A beautiful son, precisely what he had always dreamed of but never imagined he would someday father.

When he watched Petey toddle around the house on his sturdy little legs, Philip felt as if his heart would melt with a tender feeling almost unbearable in its intensity. He loved Beth for giving him a son. Nothing would ever change that.

He had been at her side in the delivery room, as he witnessed the long hours of her sweating, painful labor and then the difficult delivery. He had seen the radiance in his wife's face as a nurse placed their tiny son in her arms for the first time.

And yet there were moments Philip studied her eyes as she went through the motions of their life – caring for Petey, doing housework, preparing a meal, directing the children's Sunday school. And he understood from her vacant expression, with a sick feeling in the pit of his stomach, how little pleasure she took from life, not even from their perfect son.

It was as if she had been shrouded in a twilight existence, a stasis, a world with neither moon nor sun. Grief without end.

Bruce Fielding had left Philip's life only to return time and again. He'd insinuated himself into the family, and now he was more than a guest in their home.

Beth seemed fond of him, having relinquished her prior belief that Bruce was the man in the Northport Park on the day April disappeared. For a while Bruce had been living with them, with the excuse he was trying to get back on his feet.

"From what?" Beth had asked Philip in the privacy of their bedroom. "He's only twenty-one. What could it be he seems to be running from?"

"He's had a major altercation with his father, apparently," Philip said, a convenient lie. "It came to blows. A rift only time will heal. Bruce isn't a burden to you, is he, Beth?"

"Not at all. He's very good with Petey."

But Bruce was a burden to Philip. Had he known any feasible way of excising Bruce from their life, he'd have already done so. He didn't want Bruce around Petey, not if either he or Beth were not in the same room.

To complicate matters, Kerry, Philip's nephew, his brother Edward's boy, had arrived to spend a few weeks with them over the summer. Kerry was considering going into the seminary and wanted to talk at some length with the Jesuits at the University of Detroit.

But Philip suspected Kerry's visit was an elaborate ruse. Charlotte had revealed to Beth over the phone that she and Edward were having marital difficulties and needed time alone to work things out between them.

Philip resented the friendship developing between his nephew and Bruce Fielding. Since Kerry's arrival, the two had become thick as thieves, and Philip couldn't do a damned thing about it.

Though he had tried. Two weeks ago he'd taken Bruce into his church study, in a misguided attempt to reason with him.

"How much do you need to open that door and walk out of here?"

Bruce gave him a greasy smile. Obviously, the young man believed he had Philip right where he wanted him.

"What's the going rate of compensation for being turned into a eunuch, Philip?"

"Don't give me that crap. I was a friend to you. I treated you well. You confided things to me you'd never have shared with anyone else. Don't deny it."

"Might as well put the checkbook away, Phil old boy. I got a look at your computer the other night. There's more to this incarnation of Philip Magill than meets the eye."

A slow sense of dread oozed through Philip as he watched Bruce stroll around the office as though he owned it. "What were you doing at my computer? You knew damned well it's off limits. Yet you violated my privacy!"

Bruce laughed. "No more than you violated mine, some years ago. Fascinating stuff, all those entries on your computer. You can bet the police would be enthralled."

"Look. This has got to stop. I can't live under the threat of your intimidation. What's done is done, don't you realize that?" In sheer frustration, Philip ran his hands through his hair. "I wish to God I'd never touched you!"

"Since you now have a son of your own, you mean."

Philip looked up quickly. "Don't threaten Petey. Not if you value your life."

With an ugly snort, Bruce said, "What are you gonna do, you old pansy? Shoot me?"

"Get out," Philip said quietly. "Get the hell out of my life, or I'll break every bone in your body."

"Can't do it," Bruce replied with a sneer. "Not at any price."

Somehow Philip managed to collect himself, with a silent reminder of how, at one time, this young man had idolized Philip Magill. Surely, with the right words, he could persuade Bruce to listen to reason.

"I'm prepared to give you a large sum of money, Bruce. I've talked with my financial advisor. There are certain assets I possess that Beth doesn't know about, assets I can liquidate in a matter of days, a week at the most. You'd have a good start. You could return to college, build a new life for yourself. What do you say?"

"How much?"

"Before we settle on a sum, you need to know and agree to the terms," Philip went on, in the same business-like tone of voice.

Bruce's smile could only have been described as snide or perhaps mocking. "So, Philip. What are the terms?"

"The first is, you never come here again or attempt to contact me in any way. The second, you sever ties with my nephew. Then the last, and the most important."

"Which is?"

"You conveniently forget the fact that I have a son. I don't want the worry of having you contaminate Petey's life, either now or at some inopportune time in the future."

"Fuck you, Philip. I advise you to quit trying to buy me off. It's insulting, and it's starting to piss me off."

Jesus! The boy was enjoying this!

Philip shot across the room to grab Bruce and slam him against the wall. "Listen, you little son of a bitch. Go ahead and try to discredit me. Go right ahead and give it your best shot. Who'd believe you? You're a nothing, a nobody. Which is all you'll ever be, if you persist in this insane little game of vengeance. So help me God, I'd like to throttle you!"

Uneasily, he released his grip on Bruce and backed away, taking refuge behind his desk, donning his cloak of respectable minister, community pillar, God's servant.

"Don't forget, Philip. I know what you've been up to," Bruce warned. "I wonder how Kerry would feel about his uncle, after a few hints about your unsavory past. Or your wife. I'll bet you put your filthy hands on that little girl of hers. Confess, Philip. You did, didn't you?"

Philip emitted a ragged sigh. With his frustration, he felt close to the point of tears. "If you'd spent enough time snooping at my computer, you'd have found out that pedophilia is an illness. I've spent hours with therapists, a fortune. I'm trying to get all of it behind me. And then you show up! What am I supposed to do? I can't undo the past, Bruce, much as I'd like to. Can't you leave me alone?"

In a sly, insidious tone of voice, half in and half out the door leading to the outer office, Bruce said, "Did you touch April, Philip? Yes or no. If you tell me the truth, maybe I'll go away. Did you?"

With a strangled cry, Philip hurled his Oxford English Dictionary at the door just as Bruce slammed it.

But in the end Bruce had capitulated. Next week a cashier's check in the amount of twenty thousand dollars would arrive, with Bruce Fielding's promise to disappear.

And with Bruce's final departure, Philip's most fervent hope was that his dirty little secret could vanish forever.

But what he had become wasn't entirely his own doing. When Philip was a boy, his father was an aide to the American ambassador to France. While the family lived in Switzerland, they hired a tutor named Victor. For years Victor slowly, progressively indoctrinated Philip in the sensual delights that could occur between a child and a persuasive adult male.

Bruce may have discovered Philip's obsessions as evidenced on the computer, a world in which he'd imagined he had complete privacy to play out his fantasies with no harm done. But then Philip had been forced to erase the hard drive.

At least Bruce hadn't found the collection of kiddie porn, hidden in a wall safe behind a file cabinet in the closet of Philip's church study. Those secrets would remain sacrosanct, inviolate, now his greatest and most sublime pleasure.

Sitting alone in his study, Philip thought back to an incident that had occurred when Petey was eight months old.

Having told Beth so much time had passed in the search for April that the trail was cold, Philip urged her to concentrate on her life with him and with Petey. Then one day the phone rang at the house. Beth had been in the shower, Petey was napping. Philip answered.

Of course, he had known of her efforts to locate her daughter. Notebooks she'd painstakingly filled with information were always within easy reach.

The Vanished Children's Alliance, the National Runaway Switchboard, the Heidi Search Center, the National Center for Missing and Exploited Children: Beth knew people associated with every possible resource by first name. Their phone bills were astronomical.

The description of April disseminated nationwide by the AMBER Foundation for Missing Children was periodically updated: *Age nine at time of disappearance. Child as she might now appear, through computer age progression. Missing for nearly two years, now age eleven. Last seen at a park in Northport, Michigan. Blond hair, blue eyes, strawberry birthmark in crook of left elbow. Two dimples. Small scar on right foot. April was last seen riding her bicycle, which was later found abandoned in the park. At that time, she was wearing hot-pink shorts, ruffled sleeveless white blouse, pink tennis shoes. Suspicious red-haired man was seen in vicinity wearing dark jacket with red or orange trim. If you have any information about April Warner, please contact...*

But when the telephone rang and Philip picked up the receiver, he suddenly learned that without his knowledge Beth had gone so far as to hire a private detective.

"Yes, this is the Magill residence, Philip Magill speaking. Who's calling, please?"

"My name is Dan Keefer. Could I speak with your wife?"

"Where are you calling from?"

"Currently I'm in Kentucky, working on another case. But the authorities in Florida got an anonymous tip. A child matching April's current description was seen at a roadside stand close to Disney World. I'm calling to ask whether Mrs. Magill wants me to pursue the lead."

Philip was standing at the extension phone in Petey's nursery. As he listened to the stranger over the telephone, he looked at his son, *their* son, sleeping so innocently in his crib.

"What wonderful news! Could I have your number? My wife will call you back. Unfortunately, she's not here."

He took down the man's number and said he would give Beth the message. He was sure she would return the call as soon as possible.

Then Keefer said, "I'm at this number temporarily. Could you tell me what time it might be? I'll wait."

"A couple of hours. No longer. If Beth doesn't call in the next two hours, it will mean you shouldn't pursue the lead. We've talked about this, believe me. I'm afraid she's almost given up hope."

"I'm sorry to hear that. If I can be of help in the future, let me know."

And it became yet another of Philip's terrible little secrets, when he tore up the phone number and neglected to tell Beth about the call from Dan Keefer.

Several weeks later Philip learned through artful questioning of Beth's father, Frank Block, that Beth had received a sizable sum of money following Randy's accidental death while serving active military duty.

Money she had never mentioned to Philip Magill. Money she'd been saving and reinvesting for April's college education. Money she had used to hire Dan Keefer.

But he would never confront her with his knowledge of her deception, nor with his own subterfuge concerning the pay-off of Bruce Fielding.

Beth knew too much horror about what can happen to missing children, such terms as survival sex, dumpster diving, spare changing. He could not fault her. Had it been Petey, Philip would have done the same.

He prayed that someday, however long into the future, his wife would learn what had happened to April, so they could be done with it, putting it behind them. Perhaps she could then emerge from the limbo existence she had come to regard as a normal life.

Even more fervently, Philip prayed she would never learn all there was to know about Philip Magill.

When he married Beth, he was looking for a façade of marital respectability. But since Petey had come into the picture, Philip understood how his had been only a half-life until his little son was born.

He could never let anything take Petey away from him.

Part III

Haley Mae

"...of all the men alive
I never yet beheld that special face
Which I could fancy more than any other."

The Taming of the Shew, II:i
Shakespeare

Chapter Eleven

How many hours had he been driving, how long had they been on the road?

The monotony of the highway, the expressways and side streets seemed the same, one place they stayed overnight just like the last, dark and drab and depressing.

Boy, was she ever sick and tired of hamburgers and grilled cheese. She had to sit in the back of the smelly van and get grease all over her hands, because he wouldn't let her inside the restaurants.

When she had to use the bathroom, it was usually on the side of a road where nobody else was around, or late at night at a gas station. He pushed her into the john, waited outside the door until she was finished, and then he'd shove her back in the van.

There was no way to escape, no matter how hard she tried to think of a way.

She lost track of what day it was, sometimes even what month. Was it still August? She didn't know.

Because she never knew where they were, the names of the towns were another thing she quit asking him about. Sometimes he told her, and sometimes he wouldn't. But even when he did, it didn't make any difference because she still didn't know.

Days and nights blended into a long time that never finished but went on and on. Like the streetlights when they drove through a town at night: she lay on her back and counted one after another and sometimes fell asleep.

When she started to cry from missing her mother, she knew she had no one to blame but herself. It was her own fault for being stupid and forgetting what her mother had warned her about.

Don't talk to strangers, never accept a ride in an unfamiliar car no matter what, even if the driver offers candy or toys or dolls, no, not even if he says her mother was injured in a car wreck and taken to the hospital, and sent this person to pick up April so she could see her mother.

Adrian said there was nothing stupid about her. She was naïve and trusting, which was fine because she was still a child.

Stupid. She knew now how dumb it was in the first place, her dream of seeing a real Indian. It was the one thing her mother never said, about not believing somebody nice who promised to take her some place special.

He said he was a Choctaw Indian from out West, and she believed him. With his black eyes and straight black hair worn in a ponytail, he looked like the pictures of Indians she had seen in books and in the Western movies.

He promised to take her to see the wigwams and meet other Indians on the reservation. They'd only be gone a while, they'd be back before her mother finished grocery shopping. Philip would never know.

Their little secret, Adrian said. He seemed so friendly. She'd wrestled with herself, thinking it wasn't such a good idea, but then she wondered what the harm was. Besides, no one would know she'd been gone, and then she could tell the other girls at school about her adventure. She'd be the only one in her class who met real Indians on her vacation and got to see the inside of a wigwam.

He promised to give her a turquoise bracelet or a squash-blossom necklace. When she didn't know what that was and asked him to tell her what a squash-blossom necklace looked like, he laughed and said he wanted it to be a surprise.

He told her to leave her bike near the edge of the water, so she could find it easily when he dropped her off at the park later.

Lies, all a bunch of lies. Now he expected her to trust him. Get real.

She remembered the way the purple-colored van had smelled inside when she first got in, like something rotten. He wouldn't let her sit in the front seat in case someone like Philip should see her. He told her to lie down on a stinky mattress in the back of the van. She didn't want to, but she did.

They drove around and around. She began to feel a little sleepy, a handkerchief with a strong smell over her face. She struggled and tried to breathe, moving her head from side to side to escape, and started choking. Then she couldn't remember anything for a long time.

They drove all day and half the night, she thought later, when he finally woke her up. It was dark except for the lights of cars traveling on a fast highway, and she didn't know where they were.

But Adrian knew. He always knew everything. She had learned that about him almost from the start.

"You're not taking me back to my mother, are you?"

He didn't answer, telling her to trust him because he had her best interests at heart and something special in mind for her. He said one day he was going to make her famous.

She woke up and got out of the van. The door to a room was open. Adrian dragged her inside. A motel room. It smelled musty, like her grandmother's attic.

Outside she could hear the big trucks rushing by, so close it felt like they would crash into the room, right through the thin, scratched, no-color walls.

Boy, she thought to herself: what a dump.

She stared at two twin beds covered with faded salmon-colored bedspreads. On one bed was a cardboard box with clothes folded neatly inside.

"For you," Adrian said with a smile. "For you to try on, Haley."

"My name is April!" She tried to shout, but she was so groggy that her voice sounded dull from the long sleep.

"You have a new name for your new life. Now your name is Haley, Haley Mae Lightfoot. Say it."

When she refused, clamping her mouth shut stubbornly, folding her arms, stamping her foot, he pulled her arms apart and twisted her right arm behind her back, which surprised her and made her scream with pain.

"Haley Mae Lightfoot!" she cried, wrenching away from him to fall on the bed and break into tears, tears that came quietly, without sound.

Suddenly she was afraid. She couldn't remember ever feeling so afraid, not in her whole life. When he started to come near her, she scooted up to the edge of the bed, cowering against the headboard.

"You must be hungry," he said softly, as though he couldn't remember twisting her arm only a few seconds ago, as if it had never happened. "Wait here. I'll be back soon." He left the room, followed by the click of the door lock.

When she heard the van's tires crunch across gravel, she tried to open the door with an idea of running far away, trying to flag down one of the cars or trucks on the highway to stop and give her a ride home. But the door wouldn't open. There was no lever on the lock, nothing to push or turn.

While he was gone, she could call her mother!

She picked up the receiver of the telephone on the beat-up desk, but there was no dial tone because the cord had been ripped out of the wall. She held the cord in her hand and stared at the green and yellow and white wires, all frayed at the end. Tears of frustration leaked from her eyes. She kicked the leg of the desk until her foot hurt.

Oh, she thought she was so smart. But he'd fixed the lock on the door so she couldn't run away, and he'd made sure to mess up the phone so she couldn't call for help. He'd thought of everything.

When he returned with hamburgers and fries and ice cream in Styrofoam cups, milk for her and something different for him, she stuffed the food into her mouth like a wild animal, chewed fast and swallowed the soggy, tasteless chunks.

Why was she so hungry? She didn't think she'd ever been so hungry. She couldn't remember when she'd last eaten.

"I want to go home now," she said while eating her ice cream, strawberry with runny whipped cream and nuts on top.

The way he looked at her and smiled gave her a creepy feeling. "You *are* home."

She didn't know what to say at first. "You mean...this is where you live, in this crummy room?"

"The world is our home, Haley Mae. You'll find out. Soon you'll feel as I do, that anywhere and everywhere is home. As long as we're together."

"Who says I want to be with you, anyhow?"

"You don't have a choice."

She watched as he turned on the small television set. "It's broken," she said, but then the picture appeared in a sharp outline, black and white. She'd already tried the television when he'd gone for food, so she knew it didn't work. But now it did.

The late news, the weather forecast. The station from Detroit they watched at home! Then they couldn't have gotten too far from Sterling Heights! For the first time, her hopes began to rise.

Sitting beside her on the bed, he patted her back. "Sleepy?"

She shook her head, gathering the food wrappers from the bedspread without looking at him. Already she had learned not to look at his eyes, because something in his eyes made her think of evil witches and mean trolls who did weird things to kids in fairytales.

She darted to the bathroom to throw the trash in the wastebasket. When she came back into the room, her own face stared from the television screen, like she was looking in a mirror.

Police and the FBI continue a relentless search for April Warner, age nine, missing from a public park in Northport, Michigan for eight days. Anyone with information as to this child's whereabouts is asked to notify the Michigan State Police, at...

Eight days! But how could that be? Had she slept in the van for eight days?

He sat on the opposite bed, watching her. The bed covers were turned down on the nearest bed. Not knowing what else to do, she climbed beneath the covers still wearing her dirty pink shorts and filthy white blouse and lay quietly with her face turned away from him, toward the wall.

The bed was lumpy, the sheets smelled sour, the pillowcase was rough and scratchy against her cheek. Tears welled in her eyes and spilled onto the pillow.

She wished she had Strawbaby. She didn't know whether she could sleep without Strawberry, not now.

Then she thought, they had already started looking for her. Soon somebody was bound to see her, and they would call the police. And she could go home and be with her mother.

And Philip. She knew it was mean, but she wished Philip had been the one Adrian kidnapped, so he wouldn't be there when she finally went home to her mother. But as her mother said, Life brings the good and the bad, the bitter with the sweet.

In a whisper, she prayed, "Dear God, please let somebody recognize me and call the police."

When she woke up the next morning, sunlight scalded the room through the open drapes, making her blink against the brightness. He had brought fried eggs and toast and cinnamon rolls. Milk and coffee. Little packages of butter and grape jelly. On a tray beside her bed, a blue hyacinth in a glass of water.

The food was still warm. But he wasn't there. Where had he gone this time?

She turned on the television to *The Price Is Right*. So it was a week-day. At least she knew it was a weekday.

But where were they? How far away had they driven in eight days? She could have asked him, but she was afraid to. Besides, she knew she couldn't trust him to tell her the truth.

She had time to take a shower and change into a new pair of under-pants, blue shorts and a new white blouse patterned with blue sailboats. Price tags were still attached. There was a new toothbrush and tube of toothpaste in the bathroom, and a big comb wrapped in cellophane. She brushed her teeth and tried to comb the snarls from her hair, thinking how much she missed her hairbrush.

After the game show and half a soap opera, he came back. She was watching the second half of *The Young and the Restless* when he opened the door.

"Good morning, Haley. Did you enjoy your breakfast?"

"It was okay."

"Don't you look nice, though?"

"Thanks for the clothes."

"You're welcome." He turned off the television. "Wrap a towel around your neck. We're going to color your hair."

"I don't want to!"

He grabbed her head between his hands. "Haley, look at me."

She tried to resist, but when he said it again, hesitantly she met his dark eyes, which was a big mistake. Her head started hurting, as if an invisible giant hand was squeezing her head, but it wasn't his hands that made her feel the pain because he had stopped touching her. It was his eyes.

She ran toward the bathroom so she could slam the door and get away from him, but he was too fast. All at once he was pushing her head over the side of the bathtub and pouring chemical stuff on her hair causing her to choke. He told her to hold still.

"Ten minutes. Then we can rinse it out. What kind of Indian has blond hair?"

Whimpering, she did as she was told. Now nobody would ever recognize her, no one would call the police. And she understood that dying her hair was the whole point, because he didn't want anyone to know who she was, or where or to whom she belonged.

Looking at her new black hair in the mirror, streaks of dye running across her forehead and down her left cheek, she repeated the words he said to her. She was afraid not to.

"My name is Haley Mae Lightfoot. My father's name is Adrian Lightfoot. We are Choctaw Indians from Montana. I have a special gift."

He sounded like a teacher from school, drilling her for the correct answers to the multiplication tables. "What's your name?"

"Haley Mae Lightfoot."

"Again."

"Haley Mae Lightfoot."

In the days and months to come, she learned that her name really was Haley Mae Lightfoot, because she had left April Warner at the park. As soon as she'd stepped inside the purple van, she wasn't April Warner anymore.

Like the kids in the Narnia stories who hid in the wardrobe, she had entered another world. She would never be April Warner again. And Julie Englebreit wasn't her best friend, because she didn't have any friends.

Only Adrian.

They knew April Warner was missing, but they didn't know she was dead.

Even when Haley was frightened by something Adrian said, or by the crazy look he'd get in his eyes, she never stopped feeling sorry for her mother.

For once she hoped creepy Philip wouldn't turn out to be a washout for a husband, after all. But if Philip was the only person left for her mother to love, and the only one to love her back, well...

At least Adrian bought her nice clothes. They got to eat in restaurants since he'd dyed her hair black and had good food. It was fun to read the different menus and to decide what she wanted. They were seeing lots of sights, like Disney World.

At night he was teaching her passages from the Bible, until she knew them by heart. He said he loved her as much as her real father had loved her before he got killed, and he would always take care of her no matter what.

Gradually, she started to sort of believe him.

When he touched her, somehow it made her think of her real Dad, warm and nice. Her skin didn't crawl, like it did when Philip used to try and touch her.

But that was a long time ago, stuff that had happened to April Warner.

And she was Haley now.

Chapter Twelve

Seventeen states in less than two years, wintering in Florida during the months of forced inactivity, one cheap motel room after another.

To cut costs, he'd have stolen a camper. But even small, nondescript motor homes were too easily traced. And forget RVs. They stood out like malignant tumors against the landscape of the open road.

A Byzantine trail of fraud and extortion followed them, discarded credit cards replaced by new ones. Customers of motels always carried plastic, and Adrian Lightfoot enjoyed an endless supply.

While the rooms were empty, sometimes he posed as a television cable repairman with tools on his belt, slipping in to sift through luggage, out before either the tourists or the management had a clue.

Only money: small potatoes.

The nature of his offenses had been drastically altered since he'd found Haley. For the first time in his life he was intimately responsible for someone other than himself, an obligation he held sacred.

He loved her.

The unexpected miracle of Haley Mae had fallen into his lap. She had taught him the value of loving, a lesson he'd despaired of ever having the chance to learn for himself, as a former outcast, a leper to the race of man.

But since he'd found Haley, the past receded like a bad dream. He had changed. His life had changed. He never wanted to return to the way he was, to the way he had been.

Hatred and loathing, the desire to plunder and destroy had flown far away.

A gray morning in late May, a room at the Mountaintop Tour-o-tel in Romney, West Virginia. At seven o'clock, she was still sleeping. He didn't want to wake her. Last night was exhausting. She'd fallen asleep in the car while he drove non-stop from Bristol.

She had been on stage for hours, a never-ending stream of ragged, ignorant supplicants craving a touch from the girl prophet, Haley Mae. She fell into her trance and fooled them all into believing.

But they wanted to believe, they were dying to believe. Hadn't they once believed as fervently in the Prophet Aaron?

Cursed by failure and despair, the dregs of humanity ran to the shabby tents of the traveling revival circuit, eager to fork over their meager offerings for the hope of absolution and deliverance from their pitiful sins of the flesh.

As if everlasting salvation could be purchased for alms.

Beggars; he despised them. They deserved exactly what they received, cheap tricks and empty promises. A lot of nothing.

He sat at a round Formica table overlooking the natural sculpture of the distant, rolling hills, a local weekly newspaper unfolded on the table. He was looking for the ad for the next revival, to see how the promoters had billed Haley Mae, Girl Prophet.

Against a leaden sky, blackbirds lighting on the trees plumbed old memories.

An infant in a snowbank, a huge black bird swooping closer and closer, the flutter of feathers against his cheek, its beak touching the baby's lips, feeding him.

The bird had lifted the infant's perception, circling him into the clouds.

Something about fire, the flames of destruction and resurrection. The fire had melted the snow, brought him warmth, and soothed his anxiety.

The lovely, raging flames...

Nothing could be reborn until it had died.

Sipping at the tepid coffee he'd gotten from a vending machine in the motel lobby, he flipped open the thin newspaper.

An ad for Marshall Fletcher's Pharmacy in nearby Ridley. Adrian hadn't thought consciously about Ridley in years, yet he realized he had never forgotten it, nor the things that had happened to him there.

His birth. His death.

Until now, he'd chosen to skirt West Virginia. But a singular opportunity had presented itself. They would spend two weeks in Kirby, a regional evangelical charismatic revival, where Haley would be seen and remembered by thousands.

He hoped they could stay in one of the guest cottages on the fairgrounds, to save money.

So far, her ministry had provided little more than subsistence, what with expenses for food and lodging. It was a way of life that would last through her apprenticeship. Eventually, according to Adrian's master plan, she'd have a church of her own, with lucrative appearances at large Christian tabernacles throughout the United States and Europe.

He took pleasure in watching her sleep. Her gentle breathing, the curve of her cheek, the long lashes. The portrait of peace. Such purity, innocence.

She believed she had the power. He wanted her to believe it. Perhaps the day would never come when she learned the bitter truth, that Haley Mae Lightfoot was Adrian's latest well-executed hoax. As long as necessary, he would be there to protect her from that knowledge.

An obituary notice caught his eyes, slowly bringing a smile to his lips: *Jerushia Altizer, age 91, passed over to the Great Beyond on...*

An aged crone who lived in a tarpaper shack across the meadow and through a line of bull pines behind the Litchfield house. The children had been warned away from Granny Jerushia. She was said to cast spells, to have an evil eye.

A dabbler in black magic, she had taught the boy Aaron, her apt student, everything she knew. Packaging and how to market the product, mainly, Adrian thought to himself with a smirk, remembering how she had instructed him to bring small toads and mice for the cast-iron kettle suspended over her stone hearth.

Roy and Ernestine Litchfield had never once suspected that, for each word of every self-righteous, priggish sermon assailing Aaron's ears on Sunday, Granny Jerushia muttered a contrapuntal message about demons and haints and bending the elements of Nature to one's own will.

Though the people of the town reviled and ostracized her, she refused to be a victim, and he had learned to emulate her posture, pitted as she was against conventional society and civilized codes of conduct.

When she heard about the boy's strange ability to move inanimate objects with the power of his mind, she had summoned him to come, to be her disciple. Only Granny Jerushia regarded the boy Aaron as worthy of love and admiration. Only she had believed in his potential.

Even the Litchfields, despite their talk of loving him like a natural son, had harbored a secret fear of him, and he knew it and was gladdened by that awareness.

In his imagination he could still savor the scent of her prized flower and herb gardens, sniff the bizarre blend of odors in Granny's shack – disintegrating clothes piled in corners to stuff the cracks against the winter wind, an ammonia smell from dozens of stray cats, something made of roots and wild cressy and lemons boiling in a pot on the woodstove. Her health tonic, she called it. Once he had tasted the acrid brew and spat it out.

He could see the large black Bible with the crumbling leather cover resting on a stump table beside a pile of small animal bones and colored stones, feathers, dried mushrooms, and wild herbs.

Because she was a spinster, devoting her adult life as an outcast to the study of supernatural forces, she claimed to know things ordinary people could never imagine. She had said his memory of the black bird swooping down upon him when he was a baby meant he'd been touched with special magic, like other famous men throughout the history of the world.

Granny Jerushia had cultivated in the boy Aaron a secret, hidden identity, helped him to fashion a self only known to ghostly presences unseen by the naked eye. She had introduced him to the other dimension, reality's shadow, society's curse...

...will be visited by friends at the Eternal Life Chapel and Funeral Home in Ridley.

The flash of dumb luck to which Adrian had grown accustomed, had learned to anticipate: the viewing was this afternoon. But as fearsome an old woman as Jerushia Altizer had been to the townspeople, Adrian wondered who would bother to come to see her cadaver or bear witness to her internment.

Unlikely he'd meet anyone from his buried past. Nor would a soul know the man Adrian Lightfoot for the strange child he had once been, shuffled from house to house as a boy until, prematurely, he'd become a man to be reckoned with. He'd shown them all, taken their money and split.

He'd go and pay his respects. He owed it to the old woman, perhaps the only spiritual debt he'd ever incurred before Haley entered his life.

But he was pulled back to the present when Haley spoke to him.

"I'm hungry," she said with a yawn. "You eat yet?"

"Just coffee. I've been waiting for you. What do you have an appetite for?"

"Pancakes, maybe. Lots of syrup and butter. Coffee."

He watched as she shyly pulled on the fleece bathrobe lying at the foot of her bed. Obediently she came to him for a hug and kissed his cheek, then disappeared into the bathroom. With a sigh, he folded the newspaper, got up from the table and called out to her. "There's a café about a mile down the road. I'll be back."

Through the door she said, "My roots are showing."

"I'll pick up the Clairol."

"Don't be long, Adrian. There's nothing but preachers on TV on Sunday. I had enough of them to last me a lifetime."

"I'll bet you have. Be right back, honey."

"Bring plenty of coffee. And a beauty magazine from the drugstore! And a candy bar with nuts!"

As he walked outside to their gray Nissan, Adrian realized how much he felt like Haley's natural father. He knew she had grown to love him. It didn't matter that he had forged the bond between them by design. Now she only called out for her mother in dreams of a restless sleep.

She had learned to depend on Adrian for everything. He was the center of her life. Of course, she loved him. She had no choice but to love him wholly, completely.

Desperately. Precisely the way he had planned it.

After stopping at the drugstore in town for hair dye and a *Vogue* magazine, he drove to the restaurant, parked the car in the shade of a large beech, and went inside.

A middle-aged waitress in a soiled white uniform, fake-red hair, scarlet lipstick, and weary eyes that had seen too much of life and wished they hadn't, spoke "Yeah? What'll it be?" She slouched behind the counter with an order book and pencil at the ready.

"Pancakes, silver dollars, double order. Eggs scrambled hard. Sausage. A big cup of that chocolate gravy, and make sure the cook crumbles bacon in it. Four large black coffees. To go."

"That it?"

"Yes. About how long will it be?"

"How the hell would I know?" she snapped. "Depends on if the cook's getting over a bender. Take a load off. You want coffee for here?"

"Black, please."

Adrian sat on the stool at the counter. He glanced around at the other patrons, three old men in bibbed overalls sitting at a table near the front windows, a family with two small children. Plates were on the tables. He shouldn't have to wait long.

He didn't like to leave her alone. Though she had learned her lesson about talking to strangers...

In less than five minutes, the waitress plopped a white paper sack on the counter.

"Seven-forty," she said.

He checked the bag. "Could you sparc me a few more packs of jelly?" he said with an ingratiating smile, watching as the dead-codfish eyes glimmered with a faint spark of interest.

Tucking the packets into the bag, she said, "You're not from around here, are you?"

"My daughter and I are just traveling through." He handed over a ten-dollar bill.

"You married?"

"Was. Not any longer."

"Divorced, huh?" she said, as she made change at the register. "How'd you get stuck with the kid?"

"The wife died."

"Oh, jeez. Sorry. Here's your change."

"Thanks."

"Come again, why don't you?"

"May do that," he said with a grin, handing her a dollar before turning to leave. He felt the glance of the waitress follow him through the door.

Most women, sluts, every one of them, with few exceptions. They said men were like dogs, but it was the bitch in heat that lured them. Since Eve had misled Adam.

But Haley was different, because she'd been sanctified by his pristine love.

When she told him about her stepfather, Adrian had promised that no man would ever touch her again, not unless she welcomed it. She would remain inviolate, undefiled, until she gave herself to the man she loved, the one man she'd want to belong to for the rest of her life.

He returned to the room. She was dressed in a navy blue and white-striped shorts set, her dark hair in braids, sitting on the edge of the bed polishing her toenails with pink luminescent pearl.

He spread the food on the table beside the window with the   dreary view of the West Virginia landscape. He thought how even the land itself seemed scruffy, ignorant, and hopeless. The State motto was *Almost Heaven*. But he'd grown up here, and only he could know firsthand what a damned joke *that* was.

"Brought you a special treat," he said. "Ever had chocolate gravy before?"

"Never heard of it."

"People around here eat it a lot. My Grandma Alma...no, never mind."

They sat at the table.

"I never knew you had a Grandma Alma."

"I didn't. That's just what the neighborhood kids called her."

Haley ate ravenously.

"Polish off the gravy, honey"

"I don't know why we can't eat in restaurants here like everyplace else, like normal people," she said between bites of pancake dripping gravy. "How come we have to eat in our room again, just because we're in West Virginia?"

"What'd you do, get up on the wrong side of the bed this morning?" He caught himself staring at the buds of her nipples through the thin blouse. "Put on a warmer blouse, Haley."

"Why? It's too damned hot."

"Then put on your bathrobe. Do as I say."

"Don't feel like it." Defiantly, she met his eyes.

His thoughts centered on the advice about parenting he'd gleaned from books and magazine articles: say yes as often as you can, but when you say no you'd better mean it. He decided to let her small act of rebellion slide by.

"Suit yourself," he said. He glanced at his wristwatch. "In a couple of hours, I have to go into town."

"And you're planning to leave me here with nothing to do. Aren't you?"

"There's something for you to do. Your hair, for one thing. And I got the magazine like you wanted."

"Yeah, but you forgot the candy bar I asked you for. Besides, I want to ride into town and look around."

"Nothing's open on Sunday in a backwater town like this. Remember? I'm just lucky I found the drugstore open." He sipped coffee from a large paper cup.

Her arm flew across the table and knocked the cup from his hand, spilling lukewarm coffee over the soiled paper dishes, dribbling off the table to the dirty carpet. Adrian sat back in his chair with a sigh, and their eyes locked.

"You can't make my head hurt anymore, so don't even try."

"No, but you're not too big for a spanking."

"Don't try that, either." She pushed away from the table, rose from her chair, and stood there, glaring at him.

"What's the problem, Haley?" Suddenly he felt old, and close to the end of his rope.

"I'm the one who makes the money, don't forget. Where would you be without the girl prophet? When you go into town, what if I walk out to the highway and hitch a ride and you never see me again? I could, you know. Real easy, too. I'm not just a dumb little kid!"

Calmly, he continued to look at her, at her body taut as a coiled spring. Adrian knew she would not always be as easily controlled as he had first thought, now that she was getting older.

The hormones of puberty, inevitable but tiresome.

She was breathing heavily, filled with rage at Adrian Lightfoot and at what her young life had become.

Too well he remembered how it had felt when he'd been a few years older than Haley, the anonymous throngs night after night, the easy prayers and glib thanks, only to wake up the next morning completely forgotten and alone.

But Haley had Adrian to protect her, for which she should be eternally beholden. Someday she'd learn. In time. How much longer would she insist he prove his love?

Gently, he took her into his arms, feeling the warmth of her tense body against his chest. He smoothed her hair. "It won't always be like this, Haley, I promise. Someday soon there won't be greasy meals in strange motel rooms. One day we'll build you a church of your own. We'll have a nice house and..."

"I *had* a nice house! But you took me away!" Her fists pummeled his back. "I want to be with my mother! She needs me worse than you!"

She got like this sometimes, when her dreams of the previous night were especially vivid. Tightening his arms, he continued to hold her until her energy was spent and she began to cry, her face against his chest, his shirt drenched with tears.

He'd been wondering when it should happen, when he should tell her. Now was the right time. He would tell her now.

"Sit down, sweetheart," he said, easing her into a chair. "There's something I've been meaning to show you."

"What?" Her voice was tainted by the hostile, rebellious tone of adolescence.

As she watched, he took out his wallet and removed a newspaper clipping yellow with age. He handed it to her.

Another anticipated stroke of dumb luck, Adrian running into Bruce in the park that early August morning, heeding his fury, listening to his story, his connection to Philip Magill. How serendipitous, Magill having a young stepdaughter...

Over the past months the helpful secretary of Philip Magill's church had sent a few newspaper articles about the Magills' search for their missing daughter to a post office box in Detroit, as Bruce Fielding requested. This one he had also saved, one of several he had forwarded to Adrian at another post office box in Tampa, where Adrian could request the contents through a special form, to be sent to his current address.

Bruce said Mickey had been most cooperative, keeping him informed about Philip Magill, even leading Bruce to Northport where the Magills were taking their vacation. She was a vulnerable woman who had followed Magill from one church to the next. Bruce and his parents had known Mickey Carruthers as Magill's church secretary in Florida.

Bruce Fielding had convinced Mickey that, with Beth Magill and her daughter out of the way, Philip would come to love the woman who had cherished him for years.

Whatever Bruce Fielding managed to wheedle from Magill was to be split with Adrian fifty-fifty, since Bruce had become an accessory to April's abduction. He liked the idea and said he would have done it himself had he had the nerve.

And so, wherever they traveled, Adrian always kept tabs on Bruce. An occasional phone call served as a friendly reminder, as a hedge against Bruce happening to forget his obligations and commitments to Adrian Lightfoot.

Periodically, money was wired via the Western Union to a large city closest to Adrian's current location. Already, money was waiting in Charleston, West Virginia, to the tune of several thousand dollars.

Bruce had been honest about his agenda, as much as the dowdy church secretary who had played into their hands. But unlike Mickey Carruthers, it wasn't Philip Magill's love Bruce wanted. It was Bruce's own need for revenge.

Ah, sweet revenge!

Adrian thought back over the years, to the old man in bibbed overalls cowering on the stage of the Church of Mystery and Miracles, old man Mallory, the one on whom he'd taken his own revenge and beaten half to death with a thousand witnesses to say the Prophet Aaron was only carrying out divine instruction as an instrument of the Lord's will.

He'd lived with Mallory and his wife Elsie for four years. The old man was a cruel bastard, beating the boy Aaron with a hickory stick or a razor strop for infractions real or imagined. Once the stick had smashed the boy's left hand. It hadn't been the same since.

He'd bided his time, gone to live with the Litchfields. And the day had come when he'd exacted his price for Mallory's requested miracle, a white farmhouse, an old car, and sixteen acres of prime wooded land just past Overton. Wealth he'd never wanted, had walked away from.

Yes, Bruce Fielding was with him for the long haul. Unless and until

Adrian decided to quit tightening the screws.

Finally, she looked up at him, wide-eyed, totally defenseless, again under his complete control. "Where did you get this?"

"From the newspaper."

"But how did you get it? *How?*"

He eased the clipping from her fingers and returned it to his wallet. "That's not important, is it? But don't you see, Haley? Your mother doesn't need you, since she has a son with Philip. You've cried out in your sleep about your mother being lonely. But she isn't lonely, not with a new little boy to care for."

"I'm going to the john, to put the dye on my hair." Stiffly, Haley got up and moved toward the bathroom.

"Good. Then you can ride into town, after all. I've changed my mind. You don't have to stay here alone, not today. I want you to be with me."

"Where are you going?"

"To a funeral home. There's an old woman I once knew who died. I'd like to pay my respects."

She turned around to look at him, her shoulders slumped in defeat. "A funeral home. Maybe where I should go, too. Maybe someday you'll go to a funeral home to see me. What do you think?"

As she closed the door of the bathroom and he heard running water, Adrian wondered how much longer he could shield her from the ugliness of the world.

Since she knew she had a little half-brother, there was no need for her to go home.

He would choose, craft his words, and over the next few weeks, help her to discover seemingly on her own that Beth Magill now had a new child to love and care for, because her daughter April had disappeared. A son who had usurped the mother's love, a child who had taken April's place in the mother's heart.

But Adrian would never leave her. He would always be here, for as long as she needed him. It would make her love him even more.

She had just turned eleven. In two short years, depending, maybe less, Haley Mae Lightfoot would not be Adrian's daughter.

She would be his wife.

Chapter Thirteen

"**C**hurch services must be over," Haley said, noting the people in Sunday clothes gathered on the main street of Ridley.

Adrian glanced over at her. The blond streak along her center part had disappeared.

He remembered when the ordeal of dying her hair was a major battle. Now she could do it herself as easily as she'd touched up the roots this morning. Best of all, she'd become acclimated to seeing herself as a brunette when she looked in the mirror.

"How much farther?" she asked.

"Look for Sugargrove Lane."

In a few seconds, she said, "There it is. Turn right."

He made the right turn and found the funeral parlor, parking the Nissan a few feet away from a hearse in the adjoining parking lot.

Haley uttered a grunt. "Oh, this is real pleasant. Next to a meat wagon. How depressing."

"Remember how you pack 'em in, honey. 'Death knows no such thing as prejudice, but arrives in his own due time to all people regardless of race, creed, or...'"

"'Or how much money you have in the bank! Easier for a camel to pass through the eye of a needle than for a rich man to get through the Pearly Gates.' Maybe it's time I changed my tune. You'll have to write me some new words. The old ones are getting stale."

"If it ain't broke, don't fix it," he said. "You're doing fine with the old words."

"I didn't mean for them, I meant for *me!* I get tired of the same old stuff."

"Okay," he said, pulling up the emergency brake. "Let me think about it, and maybe tonight we can come up with a new angle."

"We could steal the hearse over there," she suggested mischievously. "That'd be something different. Bet it would scare the devil out of them, before Haley Mae even opens her mouth."

"You're right. You could say, 'Here we are, folks. Who wants to be the first to hop into the Everafter? Just step right up! We'll give you first class delivery!'" When she chuckled, he squeezed her hand affectionately, kissed her forehead. "I'll only be a few minutes."

"You owe me a banana split at that Tast-T-Frost, don't forget."

Already she had dismissed him for the magazine in her lap, absorbed in glossy color pages of gaunt women in stylish clothes. Ruefully, he chided himself for not buying *Seventeen*. She was too damned young for *Vogue*.

He chalked up a mental reminder to buy her a portable sewing machine. If she learned to sew her simple gowns for the performances, he'd save even more money. He was trying to save fifty per cent of everything collected, so they could build her church and settle down together and have a life. Every dollar earned was fifty cents squirreled away for their ultimate dream.

Besides, sewing would give her something constructive to do in the evenings in the motels, while watching the idiotic television comedies she was so fond of.

He walked toward the front entrance of the Eternal Life Chapel, a sad gray-wooden structure with peeling white columns. The early afternoon sunlight, the warmth of May, the haunting call of a mourning dove slowed his pace, making him almost dread his impetuous decision to come. In the car Haley Mae was life, but within this building lay the way of death.

For the wages of sin is death; Galatians.

He took a deep breath, reassured by his habitual black outfit as appropriate attire, opened the heavy door and went inside.

A sickly-sweet odor assaulted his nostrils. When his eye adjusted to the hushed darkness, he saw the large vase of giant peonies in the foyer. Pink peonies like Granny Jerushia had grown in her flower garden. He touched one of the blooms, only to notice the black ants swarming over the flower, lured by the sticky sap.

Surely this was a pauper's service, and perhaps on his way to pick up the body the mortician had plucked the flowers from Jerushia's garden to avoid the niggling expense of fresh flowers from a florist.

The registry was on a nearby podium. Its pages were blank.

The name Adrian Lightfoot would be meaningless, so why not? He took the quill pen and dashed off the name, thinking that at least there'd be one official mourner.

Opening the inner doors, Adrian stepped into the parlor, a room dimly lit by a weak spotlight shining on the side of the plain pine casket on a dais at the far end of the room surrounded on three sides by rows of metal folding chairs.

As he approached the coffin, he was startled by the sudden burst of music, *Amazing Grace* over loudspeakers. But he was disappointed to find the casket closed. He'd come for a final glance of the old woman who, in some ways, he'd grown to love, perhaps more in his memory over the years than he had felt as a child.

Running his hand across the lid, he was on the verge of sinking to his knees on the kneeling bench placed beside the coffin when he noticed the spidery man who'd sneaked over in complete silence.

Unctuous, pious, smelling faintly of formaldehyde mingled with a cheap after-shave. "And you, sir. Were you a friend or relative of the deceased?"

"My family knew Miss Altizer many years ago," Adrian said.

"How nice you've come to pay your respects. Poor lady, I'm afraid she outlived most of the people she'd known."

"As I said, I haven't seen her for years. Not that I knew her well."

He stared at the funeral director, sizing him up. In his early forties, receding hairline, shiny suit, obsequious and servile in his chosen profession. Another small-town failure.

"Tell me, why a closed casket?"

"Oh, that," the man said, slightly embarrassed. "Well, her cats, you know. She was dead a day or so before the man from the electricity company came to read her meter and noticed the...the, uh, odor. Seems the cats had no food. There wasn't much left of her face."

"Death knows no prejudice but arrives in his own due time."

The man looked at him strangely. "Yes. Well. I'll give you time alone with...the deceased." Then he scampered away, gangly arms and legs preposterous in old gabardine.

Adrian waited a few minutes before carefully lifting the lid. The face was covered with cheesecloth, a veil to conceal the mutilated face already ravaged by the decades. But even the cloying odor of the wilting calla lilies adorning the parlor could not hide the foul stench of death.

The cheap bastard hadn't bothered to embalm her.

It was too hot in the car, so Haley got out, looking for a place in the shade to read her magazine. But her curiosity got the better of her. She decided to follow Adrian into the funeral parlor.

She wondered who had died, someone he said he once knew. Odd, how he never mentioned a single name from his past. As if he had no memories to speak of.

Quietly, she opened the door to the foyer and saw his name written in the book. Then she eased apart the inner doors an inch at a time and slipped inside.

He was talking to a man. Haley sat on a chair near the entrance just as the man walked down a hallway.

As she watched, Adrian looked inside the casket. She heard him cry out, saw him sink to his knees as if he needed to pray.

Though he drilled her on what he called the choice, convincing passages of the Bible, she had never known him to pray. All at once she felt as if what she had done was wrong, spying on a private moment.

Quietly, she got up from the chair and began to back out of the room. Feeling with her hands for the doors, she turned the knob, holding her breath until she was in the foyer and had stumbled outside into fresh air.

Trembling, she ran to the car. She didn't want him to know she had seen him, nor heard him utter an anguished sob.

Whoever had died, he must have cared about her.

Haley felt bombarded with confused thoughts and questions, because she had seen Adrian in a different light. He, too, had people in his life, an old woman he had not been able to forget who died.

Perhaps she'd been somebody he loved.

Kneeling on the padded bench, holding the edge of the casket for support, he felt as though his skull might explode from the onslaught of memories, a deluge, a flood rolling over him from lost and buried years, from another life.

When he was nine years old, a professor from the state university came to Ridley, after the furniture in the Mallory home started moving around and it was Aaron they blamed. That asshole Sheriff Hawke had taken him away.

He'd gone to live with Reverend Litchfield's family. They'd been good to him, a lot better than Jenkins Mallory who took such pleasure in his hickory stick. He still remembered the kindness and love of Alma Lightfoot and Elsie Mallory. It was as though he'd had three mothers. He'd lost each of the mothers, first Alma, then Elsie, then...

But the memory of his real mother was faint, so vague that he'd often wondered whether he only imagined her as a figment from a dream. But he remembered the soft white globe of warmth, and the sweet taste of milk from her pink nipple.

One day he'd taken it into his head that he could preach a damned sight better than Daddy Roy. Granny Altizer had told him so.

"You, boy. You're the one they'll take for Christ Jesus. You'll be the prophet. Mark Granny's words, now. Don't let them treat you as a leper like Lazarus. Rise up from the grave! Make them fear you!"

With backing from rich investors including several land developers, he built his own church. He hired a bunch of phony carnival freaks and used them to perform his miracles. Shills, every one, at fifty bucks a pop.

But the people of Ridley believed, and the money started rolling in.

Suddenly he remembered it vividly, he remembered it all over again.

One night Jenkins Mallory had come to the church begging for miracles. And what he had done to the old man returned to haunt him, how he'd taken gleeful pleasure in humbling the old goat...

As a boy, he liked to feed the wild things so they'd depend on him, only him. Banging squirrels against the tree, he killed them. But once they were dead, he had to find something else.

Blood-soaked furry carcasses, gathered in a pile to burn, the smell of kerosene.

"What'd I tell you about the hatred, boy? Innocent animals, natural creatures. You should be ashamed."

He learned to gaze at the small living things as Granny Jerushia taught him to. He could make them run in circles and turn flips, crawl on their bellies to take food from his hand. He became their friend, only him.

"Corinthians Two, boy! 'I who died for you and was raised again.' Remember that well."

Nestled against Grandma Alma's soft chest, the smell of Clorox on her cotton print dress, the big bed in the old house, pillows all around him. He was her Baby Winston.

Stiff feathers brushing his cheek, his forehead, the black wings shielding his face...

"Sanctify yourselves, sinners!"

The deep boom of kettle drums...

Tongues of flame licking the night sky...

He sucked in the taste of putrefaction, backing away, his legs weak. Adrian stood in the funeral parlor, wildly clutching for his sanity, willing the split halves of his brain to fuse, to heal.

He'd almost forgotten how it felt to lose control.

Losing control was what he had once done for his livelihood, something he could never allow to happen again.

For the last time, he looked upon the open coffin containing the sorry remains of Jerushia Altizer before turning away forever from the last reminder of his past, knowing in his tormented soul there was no one, nothing left to hate. Only Haley now, and she needed, she deserved his purest love.

"Why, Mistuh Aaron! It be you, ain't it?"

In disbelief Adrian stared at the shriveled black man leaning on a twisted sweetgum cane.

"Why, you all growed up, I do declare!"

He continued to gape, his mouth working to form words, before shambling away.

But the man called after him. "It's Old Claude, Mistuh Aaron, Suh! Don' you remember me?"

He pushed through the doors to the sidewalk, where he bent over with hands on his knees and gulped the clean air. When he regained his composure, he walked to the car, calmly opened the door and got inside.

"What took you so long?" Haley said.

For some reason he could not explain to himself, he avoided meeting her eyes. Instead, he turned on the ignition, threw the car into reverse, and quickly backed out of the parking lot to the street.

"Banana split," she said petulantly, flipping through the pages of her magazine.

"Tomorrow we're driving to Charleston," he said quietly.

"Why? How come we can't take a couple of days off and have some fun, see the sights?"

"Because we have to drive to Charleston. There's something I need to pick up. Besides, have you seen any sights in this one-horse town you can't wait to see again?"

Suddenly, by focusing on the task at hand, he felt in charge again. Perpetual reward was the topic. The payoff embezzled from Philip Magill, evil child molester, was courtesy of one-time victim Bruce Fielding transformed into an avenging angel.

Chapter Fourteen

Ordinarily, Adrian did the few chores necessary to sustain their life on the road. But this morning, saying he had to leave to tend to urgent matters, he asked her to sort the dirty clothes so he could take them to the laundromat in town sometime this afternoon.

She could tell he was in a weird mood. When he woke her, he seemed distant, as if he had too much on his mind.

"Wake up, now!" he'd said, shaking her roughly. "I didn't want to be gone when you got up, so you wouldn't be frightened."

She groaned, saying he should have let her sleep. To his back, she made sure to remind him that if it weren't for the labors of the girl prophet, neither of them would have money for food, and she wanted her breakfast immediately.

It was the wrong thing to say, but she hadn't been able to keep her mouth shut.

"We'll get you something to eat later."

"I want breakfast now!"

"Get a Baby Ruth from the vending machine and a cup of coffee." He didn't look at her again before slamming the door on his way out.

He'd left her alone. She was hungry, and there was nothing to eat. He'd never let her go hungry before. Maybe he was trying to teach her another lesson.

The new sewing machine sat on the table by the windows, an end bolt of cloth she'd found on sale in a fabric store, two yards of tacky trim, a pattern and straight pins, thread, pinking shears. Since she wasn't in school, Adrian said she needed to learn a trade to fall back on, and sewing her own gowns would be a good start in that direction. Later she'd learn to cook.

"And clean your damned house, too?" she'd snarled. She didn't want to sew, and she refused to cook, but he hadn't asked her what she wanted. He didn't care.

They weren't getting along very well, and Haley knew it was because she...well, she couldn't help it because her thoughts had centered on the way her life had been with her mother. She hadn't known how lucky she was, having a normal life with best friends and school, piano lessons, fun things to do like going to the movies and slumber parties.

All at once she'd understood, like a lightning bolt had struck her. Her life with Adrian wasn't temporary, but permanent, and it would never change. He liked it the way things were. He liked it fine. And why shouldn't he?

Ever since he'd shown her the birth announcement from the newspaper, things had been different. *She'd* been different. She couldn't figure out how he'd gotten it, or why he'd waited so long to show it to her.

The baby, Peter Magill the Third, would be over a year old. Born last April. In all the time she'd been gone, she wondered if her mother even thought of her. Probably not, since she and Philip had the new baby.

She resented it, finding the soiled items scattered around the room. But she gathered them together into piles, anyway.

There were big stains on the underarms of her stage dresses. She'd have to find a stronger deodorant, since she'd started her period. Adrian said she wasn't a child, she was a young woman.

She had zits on her face, too, and had started wearing make-up. And needed a bra.

She piled their underwear and night clothes in a white heap, then went through the pockets of Adrian's jeans. Everything he wore was black; he always looked the same. But he was fastidious about his appearance, changing his clothes every day at least once. Seven pairs of jeans and seven shirts, exactly alike, didn't even look dirty.

She found a handful of change and decided to get a candy bar, coffee, and crackers from a vending machine in the motel lobby. The selection at the Ridley Inn wasn't nearly as good as the vending machines in Romney, but she was starving to death so it didn't much matter.

Last night her stomach was too upset to eat dinner, for dreading the tent show. All she'd had was a Dr. Pepper. She'd be glad when they left Kirby for good. The people here were so clinging, it nearly broke her heart.

She put on her bathrobe and slippers to walk down the hall to the snack machines. It was nine o'clock on a Friday morning, and she didn't see anyone. The parking lot was almost empty of the few cars from last night. She wondered how the kind plump lady who owned the Inn could make a living, whether many customers ever stayed here.

Staring at the offerings, Haley threw in some quarters and chose a peanut butter bar and a package of Cheese Nabs. The coffee machine was broken. She went back to the room and turned on the television to a game show.

Romney had been bad enough, but at least there'd been the ice cream place for banana splits and sundaes. She still didn't know why Adrian wanted to stay in Ridley while they played the show in Kirby. Ridley was a dead town. There wasn't even a decent place to eat. Adrian had been getting hamburgers from the soda fountain at the local drug store and bringing them back to the room.

In another week or so they'd be on their way to Mississippi for the Bible Revival Extravaganza. Not much to look forward to, as Haley knew from experience. Just more of the same old stuff, and she was getting so tired of it. Some of the people she lied to seemed sick and desperate, and it made her feel bad to get their hopes up or down for nothing.

She made a cup of instant cocoa with hot tap water and ate the crackers and candy bar while watching the contestants try to solve a crossword puzzle. Outside, the sun had gone behind the clouds, and it had started to rain.

She turned on the lamp and looked guiltily at the sewing machine. She'd already decided she had no intention of learning to sew, but this new machine was going to be a real problem. She could already see Adrian lugging it along from one motel room to another. It wasn't as if the sewing machine was going to just up and disappear.

But then it came to her, call it a genuine revelation. She could cut out the pattern wrong on purpose and sew the pieces together awful. Maybe Adrian would throw the damned thing away and go to a store and buy some dresses for her, like a normal person. She'd outgrown nearly everything she had to wear.

But he'd been so grumpy lately, she suspected he might make her wear the screwed-up dresses, anyway. Which would probably serve her right.

For all the trouble he'd gone to, she could at least give it a try. How hard could it be, sewing pieces of cloth together in a straight line?

Once her mother had made a sundress for Haley, and she remembered her mother saying that the important thing about sewing was to press the seams flat as you went along, for a polished look. So she could try that, with the portable iron they always carried with them to press Haley's gowns.

Then she remembered she'd forgotten to check the pockets of Adrian's shirts. In one of the pockets she found some papers. On a yellow piece of paper was a message to Adrian:

The church secretary gave up on Philip leaving his old lady and tried to off herself. This has gone on for too long. Count me out. High time you returned the kid, or we could both face prison terms. Don't contact me again. There's nothing more to be had, and I mean it. We've bled him dry. B.

Philip! And the secretary had to be Mickey Carruthers who worked at the church! Whoever *B* was, he knew that Adrian had kidnapped April Warner!

A cold sensation of dread assaulted her as she folded the paper and put it back in the pocket of the shirt. Instinctively, she knew she wasn't supposed to find this. And yet Adrian was never careless, not usually.

Mickey wanted Philip to leave her mother? But why? Did that also mean Mickey knew something about April's disappearance?

She had memorized the words on the yellow slip of paper, the way the letters had looked, written in black felt-tip pen.

Haley felt like a fool, realizing how many times Adrian had left her alone when she could have telephoned her mother, or even Mickey. Anyone at all. Even Philip. There had been ample opportunity, yet she hadn't.

And suddenly she was furious with Adrian. Had she been so terrified of him, of what he might do? But why?

Lately there didn't seem to be much reason to fear Adrian. Maybe it was because she'd started her period and was getting older, but lately she felt angry at him nearly all the time. Everything he said or did seemed to rattle her nerves. Even the way he looked at her got under her skin.

He hadn't been the same since they'd driven to Charleston last week, where he said he'd had to pick up something or other. He left her in a restaurant for twenty minutes and came back in a terrible mood that had never lifted. Could the note from *B* have been the reason?

One word kept popping up in her thoughts: prison. She hadn't really known for sure, but now she did. It didn't matter whether she'd gotten into the van willingly at Northport Park. Adrian had committed a crime.

When she stopped to think about it, the fact that Adrian Lightfoot had kidnapped April Warner, well, it *had* to be a crime. You couldn't just pick up somebody else's daughter, dye her hair and give her a new name, and get away with it. Not forever.

Prison. Carefully, she peeked through the Venetian blinds toward the parking lot for any sign of the Nissan, but it wasn't there. She locked the door before using the telephone to dial 911...

...and barely had time to drop the receiver back on its cradle when she heard of Adrian's key in the door.

"Hi!" she said brightly, adjusting the volume on the television. "Did you bring me something to eat?"

Chapter Fifteen

"**N**o such *thing* as luck, little sister! Luck comes from Lucifer, the fallen angel. Evil! *Eee-vil!*"

The obese man dressed in the bibbed denims of a farmer fell to his knees in the middle of the aisle, raising arms heavy as sides of beef toward the ceiling of the tent, sweat drops cascading from his forehead.

Adrian's hope that the bastard would die of a coronary on the spot was not to be.

Others joined in the refrain, lemmings that they were: *Eee-vil!*

Soon the chant filled the tent, the spectators whipped into an ecstatic frenzy by hours of calculated chicanery.

He felt sick to his stomach, as if he might wretch. The odor of sweat and mildew wafted in waves in the ninety-degree heat at ten o'clock at night. The tent flaps had been lifted and fans set up. But body temperatures of nearly a thousand of the faithful had simmered with the long procession of charlatans and their acts, stupefying, smothering, until now the tenuous, unpredictable mood of the audience, with the slightest provocation, had come to a boil.

They had no lives. They needed someone else, *anyone* else, to tell them what to think, how to behave, what was black and what was white. Ignorant fools. Adrian's lip curled in disgust, thinking these remnants of the human race had sunk to an all-time low.

By the time it was Haley's turn to appear at the microphone, they should have been ready to believe the moon was made of green cheese, the world was flat, and the Apocalypse galloped its way to Kirby, West Virginia. But even without the hours of build-up, Adrian suspected their dull, pinched lives had already persuaded their unfaltering belief in such corn-fed stupidity.

Haley was what he wanted them to believe in, for the gossamer length of an hour, just long enough to reach for the greenbacks lining their threadbare pockets.

But the fat man had presented an unexpected test. You never knew when a goon would emerge from the throng, and here he was.

This was one of her greatest challenges yet. From his perch on a stool at the end of the stage, Adrian monitored the method she would use tonight to squash the dumb rube and reclaim the audience.

He took pride in the way she stood center stage, as if she were completely in control, unruffled, even slightly amused, a lovely divine vision beneath the bright spotlights.

The sheen of her dark hair, her arms lifting and hands extended toward Heaven itself, and her head bowed over a microphone. Her stage presence, her persona almost took Adrian's breath away.

"Oh, Lord," she said softly, repeating the words with quiet fervency, a plaintive tone to pierce the heart of the mob's relentless chanting. "Oh, Lord, be with us in this humble place of worship, where we the faithful have gathered to praise your holy name. Hear our heartache! Be with us, my sweet Jesus!"

As Adrian watched, one by one the people turned their faces to Haley, succumbing to her spell. They scooped themselves from the aisles, sat down in their chairs, and gave her their undivided attention.

This young girl, this child: such power! Surely this innocent would speak divinely inspired words to soothe their broken spirits.

Her arms still lifted heavenward, Haley continued to pray aloud, softly, convincingly from the heart.

It had been quite a night, one of the best. Adrian sat with a notepad, jotting impressions of the performances for future reference. His was a scientific analysis of the tent-revival circuit, what played especially well, the ruses and swindles that had most successfully bilked the masses. The barometer of profit was measured by the intensity of crowd reaction.

A local preacher had welcomed them all on behalf of the area Ministerial Association, beginning the festivities at 7 p.m. with Communion, the body and blood of Christ, paper plates of Saltine crackers and grape juice in Dixie cups clumsily passed through the rows. Then a church choir marched up to sing several Bible-belt favorites, topping it off with *The Old Rugged Cross*.

Orville the Snake-Handler staggered onto the stage, rolling his fly-specked aquarium loaded with sickly copperheads and rattlers. This was followed by an appearance of the Jesus Boys Makin' Joyful Noise, a rag-tag collection of two old men with accordions, a prepubescent fat boy with a bass drum, and two middle-aged women, one with an annoyingly strident autoharp and the other clashing cymbals on every downbeat.

Next was Reuben Swope, Faith Healer. Haley and Adrian had

become well-acquainted with Reuben, as she often followed his act. A sad performance, every time, Adrian noted, and tonight was no exception. Reuben drank too much, pickled when he mounted the stage. Not that the audience seemed to notice nor to care.

When Reuben Swope finished his odious routine, pretending twice to have been lanced by poisonous fangs of Orville's sluggish reptiles only to be protected by Divine Love, the faithful went crazy. They broke into gibberish, babbling in tongues, tear-streaked faces gleaming, bodies writhing on the sawdust floor, overcome, smitten as they were by the Spirit, flattened by the Holy Ghost.

A few more musical selections, the choir accompanied by the weird collection of instruments of the Jesus Boys, and Haley was up.

He had billed her not as a faith healer, but as "The Girl Prophet Bringing the Lord's Luck into Sorry Lives." Generally, it fared well, looked good on the playbills and posters pasted around town for advanced publicity.

But tonight the fat bastard had come prepared, the man in the bibbed overalls with his own sermon about the concept of luck being from Lucifer.

Adrian had tried to warn her about bad apples, how just one could spoil it for her unless she grabbed control. Haley had her chance to demonstrate that she remembered what Adrian had taught her.

She had to do well. The act couldn't fail, no, not even once, for the rumors would precede them on the revival circuit.

She stood in the spotlights, her simple floor-length gown with the scooped neck and puffed sleeves she had sewn herself, a golden crucifix on a delicate chain around her throat that had set Adrian back forty dollars. When she heard the quiet fall upon them, she depended on a prolonged silence, letting the tension build. But when she spoke, her voice boomed from the speakers.

"Lord, help the poor man who said there's no such thing as luck! Though the unseen curse of cancer is eating up his belly, he's too unlucky to know it, Lord! Help us to pray for the poor soul who doesn't believe in Your Power, oh great and mighty Savior!"

The fat man's bony wife, a ready believer, took no convincing at all. At the news from the girl prophet, she leaped from her chair and delivered a blood-curdling shriek before collapsing on the floor. Now the fat man had more to do than carp at the girl prophet.

She had them right where she needed them to be, in the palm of her hand. Adrian smiled, admiring her obvious self-assurance, the bold confidence belying her tender years.

From one prophecy to the next, Haley dealt her blows to the inbred mongrels, an oracle like Sibyl or Cassandra, sometimes a ray of hope but often a terrible portent, some manufactured clue as to a bright or bleak future.

On his notepad he jotted *Time for a staff*. A small staff to give the illusion of extending her reach. She would appear as a little shepherd girl for the few years they had left to profitably milk her waning childhood. Perfect!

Like a Las Vegas performer, she yanked the microphone from its stand and worked the crowd, gliding from one end of the stage to the other, pointing from one grotesque person to the next, no discrimination here, no preferential treatment, for each member of the audience was equally vulgar and ignorant. Adrian knew that people with breeding, education, class wouldn't have been caught dead in such a place as this.

Before now, he'd never had an opportunity to watch the production as a member of the crowd. The Prophet Aaron had been cloistered in the wings, offstage, hidden from the audience until his appointed moment, blinded by the stage lights from the ravenous faces before him, except for the chosen few for whom he'd performed his tawdry miracles.

Those buried memories surfaced, careened into the present moment amplifying the effect, until suddenly he felt as if he himself were Haley, or Haley was a female version of the Prophet Aaron, as though his own past had never died or gone away. Yin-Yang...

And Adrian experienced a frightening physical reaction, making him feel suffocated, trapped, almost deranged. Flecks of color wavered and whirled, kaleidoscopic before his eyes, faces flickering into sparks of flame. His belly convulsed, as if he might spew forth the bile of hatred, gagging him.

He got to his feet, holding onto the stool for support while he dragged himself from the pit of his own internal hell. He watched as Haley captured their emotions and turned them back onto the audience like venomous demons.

How she enjoyed this! Her small face glowed like a beacon, brighter than the lights illuminating the stage.

Abruptly he saw that her complaints were as dust, for Haley was loving every minute of the show.

For how much longer, he wondered. She was ready for a larger, more dignified venue. Soon it would be time to abandon the sawdust floors and shabby tents, the ragged caravan of traveling dime-store tricksters, drunken prophets who, like Adrian and Haley, were homeless vagabonds, inhabitants of an alien world.

Like an evil portent, a harbinger of ill omen, Adrian saw the writing on the wall above Haley's head, the drab tent flaps like a vulture's wings. If he could not orchestrate a greater success for Haley Mae Lightfoot, she could be easily seduced by someone else who would.

He had trained her, created her. Yet the way of the world he had come to know so intimately served as a dark warning. In a blink of an eye, she could leave him.

Without looking back. Lot's wife she wasn't, not Haley Mae.

No pillar of salt in that girl's future.

When they began to surge over the sawhorse barriers to reach the stage and touch the hem of her gown, Adrian signaled to the Jesus Boys to start playing, hopped up on the stage and spirited her away.

Outside in the cool flush of night air, she turned to him, still caught up in her stage personality. "Why'd you stop me, Adrian? I was on a roll!"

And he realized the truth in a single moment: at age eleven, she no longer needed him at all.

"Enough of exorcising devils for one night," he said. "Let's go to the car. You wait for me there while I get our cut."

"Just don't be too damned generous with Reuben this time. He didn't earn it. *I* did."

His brain grabbed for a useful nugget, to bring her around. "Five dollars I can forecast tonight's take closer than you."

Safely in the car hidden behind a house trailer, Haley said, "I'll say eight hundred. What's your bet?"

"Yeah, you would. Talk about arrogance! You still have a lot to learn, little lady. I'll say five-fifty. You wait here, I'll be right back. And lock the doors."

"Okay. I'm eight, you're five-fifty. Don't forget. And don't try to cheat, because the girl prophet knows all."

As he cut through the stinking waves of people leaving the revival, Adrian estimated it would be close to a thousand. Long ago he'd figured it out. For each human body sweating under the tent, he could count on a dollar.

The least he could do was to please her in some small way and let her win.

Twelve more nights for this show, then they had a week off between engagements, the next in Tupelo, Mississippi.

He dreaded it. The farther south they traveled, the wilder the revivals, the more insane the crowds. Sometimes there was violence. It could be more than a little dangerous.

He ducked inside the tent, hoping Reuben Swope wasn't too drunk to be reasonable. Sometimes he could really be a pain in Adrian's ass, his grandiosity increasing with the amount of bourbon he'd consumed.

Not that Adrian couldn't handle Reuben Swope.

"Hey!" he said to the fat member of the Jesus Boys carrying the bass drum. "You see Swope around?"

"Back in the trailer outside," the boy said, easing the straps of the drum from his shoulders accompanied by an audible fart.

"Ease up on them beans, son," Adrian said with a grin.

No, he could handle the likes of Swope, no trouble there. The one thing gnawing at Adrian's gut was the surprising revelation about the depth of his love for Haley. He'd known he loved her. But until this night he hadn't quite understood that he was falling in love with her. The thought of losing her was like a fist hurled into his belly. It made him feel weak, fragile as a kitten.

Or like a defenseless squirrel held by its bushy tail, viciously banged against a tree.

The longer she was with him, the more human Adrian became. So strange, when he had convinced himself years ago that he was an anomaly among men, a human aberration, incapable of loving anything at all.

Finally, he knew the bottom line about love. To love was to become vulnerable. Well, he'd do whatever he had to do, to keep his hold on her.

He'd kill for her.

Without Haley, his life would have no meaning.

At the thought of a return to the dark void of his days before Haley, he knew he'd rather die.

Part IV

Adrian

"But I do love thee! And when I love thee not,
Chaos is come again."
Othello, II:iii
Shakespeare

Chapter Sixteen

Dan Keefer, portly, pushing sixty, bespectacled and balding, was not a man who stood out in crowds, a fact that had served him well in his chosen profession of private investigator.

For all he knew, he was unofficially off the case. But when he'd driven to Keyser, West Virginia, to visit with his daughter and grandchildren, a poster on an outside bulletin board at the paper mill caught his eye. Again, he was reminded of a perplexing mystery that for twenty-one months had remained unsolved.

To his sorrow, his daughter Melody, now thirty-five, had become a No person, always hanging crepe, seeing only the dark side. With three kids to raise alone and a job as secretary to the CEO of Keyser Paper and Box Company, she seemed to have lost hope, as though she'd despaired of life ever taking a turn for the better.

Melody rented a cramped, two-bedroom house with an overgrown yard and a dead lawn mower. Her old Chevy was perpetually on the fritz, now in the shop for repairs.

To make matters worse, as if the sadness of her life wasn't enough, the town reeked of the paper mill's effluvium – a rancid, decayed odor that hung over the place like a gray shroud and seemed to permeate even the faces of the downcast people walking along the streets. Dan found it more than a little ironic, how Keyser's major industry gave its citizens jobs and regular paychecks from one hand and took away the beauty of their town with the other. A nice town, with historic old homes, views of the mountains; but who would notice, with the stink in the air?

They had just finished a late dinner of homemade tacos, butter beans, and peach ice cream. Melody hustled the children – Butch, age eleven, Jenny age ten, and Robin, six – to their rooms for homework.

"Well, Dad," Melody said wearily. "How long can you stay this time?"

"Through Saturday, if it's okay, honey." He rescued the last of Robin's taco from a pool of congealed orange grease and crunched it down.

He set the plate on the kitchen floor for Lucky, the grateful cocker spaniel.

"You shouldn't spoil him, Dad," Melody said, stacking the plates for the dishwasher, Dan's Christmas present several years back. "I tell the kids not to feed him from the table."

"Why not? We always fed our pets off the plates, remember?"

Melody snorted. "Sure. After Mom died."

"We didn't do so badly, though, the two of us. Did we?"

"Only that I felt like a guilty bitch for years after I ran off with Andy and eloped, leaving you to fend for yourself."

He bit his tongue to refrain from commenting on the ill-fated marriage of her impulsive youth. The slime-ball had absconded with one of Melody's best friends, Butch's Cub Scout den mother, who'd also left an equally confused husband and two kids in her wake.

But what was the point in dredging up the past? She had enough on her mind in the present tense. He loved his daughter, who in Dan's mind was probably the one accomplishment he could regard with pride, and he wasn't about to add to her troubles.

"I'm sorry you're having such a hard time of it, kiddo," he said. "But I think you're doing a damned good job with the children, considering what all of you have been through."

Melody added soap to the machine, locked the handle and pressed the On button before bringing two cups of coffee to the table.

"Thanks," she said, kissing his cheek and fluffing up the few embarrassing strands of hair she called his banjo strings arranged across his bald pate. "It's not easy raising three kids alone. I worry about Butch going through adolescence without a father."

"Actually, I thought I'd take the kids off your hands for the day Saturday, give you a break, and get to know my grandkids again."

"Do you have something in mind?"

"A picnic by the river. They can take their swimsuits. Then dinner out and a night game of miniature golf. You think they'd like it?"

"Are you kidding? They'd love it!" She blew on the hot coffee. "So would I."

He slipped her a fifty-dollar bill. "Get your hair done or buy yourself something pretty to wear."

"Dad, you're already paying for the repairs on the Chevy."

"Take it. I insist."

"Thank you. I don't like wearing my hair like this, but I haven't been able to afford an appointment at the hair salon." When she glanced at him self-consciously, the expression in her eyes reminded Dan of his wife

Glenda, Melody's mother.

Dan looked at his daughter, at the lines in her face, the scarecrow-thin figure, the straggling mousey-brown hair pulled back at the nape of her neck with a barrette.

"You may feel old and used up, but there's a lot of mileage left in you yet. A woman needs to feel pretty. Someday your prince will come."

"So! Where are you headed when you leave here?" She was an expert at turning conversation away from the subject of herself. She was never a whiner, not even as a teenager. "Are you working on a case?"

He glanced around the kitchen, at the sheaves of kiddy artwork tacked to the door of the refrigerator, at the neat counters, the scrubbed floor. She wasn't suffering from a case of terminal depression, not yet. And for that Dan Keefer was eternally grateful.

"Always a case, honey. Several at a time, usually."

"Anything interesting you can tell me about?"

"Nothing current. Same old themes, you know. Does my husband have a girlfriend? Is he a bigamist? Can you find out whether my mother left me a fortune in buried treasure? Some I'm nearly embarrassed to take, but you have to pay the bills. I'm not proud."

"Yeah, but at least you're honest."

He finished off his coffee, stood up and poured another half cup before returning to the table. "But there was one case nearly two years ago. It still haunts me."

"Why? You couldn't solve it?"

"Wasn't given the chance. It involved the disappearance of a nine-year-old girl in Northern Michigan. The mother hired me, and then she up and refused to accept my calls. Never did understand it. Oh, but the child was never found, which is what puzzles me the most, I guess."

"What did she say when she fired you?"

"That's just it. She didn't terminate, not formally. Her husband said she'd call me back, but she didn't. It happened three times. I had to assume they wanted me off the case."

"You never spoke with the mother? Only the father?"

"A second husband. Not the child's natural father. He was deceased. Killed in military action or something like it, as I recall."

Melody's big brown eyes widened over the edge of her coffee cup, again exhuming Glenda's ghost.

"What?" he said.

"Dad, I do believe you're slipping."

"How so, honey?"

"Did it ever occur to you that the second husband might not have wanted the kid around? Maybe he never gave the messages to his wife. Maybe he even had some connection to the child's disappearance."

"What makes you think such a thing?"

"Dad, you're the P. I. I don't know. Being your daughter and all, some of the way you view things must have rubbed off. But can you imagine Andy wanting responsibility for any of his three children? If you ask me, the second husband might have accidentally on purpose neglected to mention your calls. Which could be why you never heard from the mother."

"Good point." Dan paused, wondering whether he should share his latest suspicion with Melody. "You know, something odd happened to me today after I let you off at the plant this morning. I got out to stretch my legs and have a cigar and saw a poster on the community bulletin board out front with the job listings and notices. Well, there was a line drawing of a child's face, artistically rendered, very nice. Somehow it reminded me of the little girl I was trying to find, but older now. Just a hunch, but in this racket strange things can fall into your lap, sometimes in ways you'd least expect."

Dan rocked his chair back, checking the wall clock against his wrist-watch.

"So, what are you planning?"

"I want to drive out to Kirby. There's a tent revival tonight. The girl's name is Haley Mae, and she's supposed to predict the future."

"You'd better be careful, Dad. I hear that junk can rot your brain. I work with a few people who really believe in that stuff. I try to avoid conversations with the born-agains at the coffee machine. Tedious, frightened people, if you ask me."

"A little faith never hurts."

"Dad. Believe me. These are not people who are well wired together. There's a desperate, vacant look in their eyes. It's chilling."

Dan Keefer leaned over to give his daughter a bear-hug. "I won't be late. Tell the kids goodnight from Grandpa, and I'll take them out to Hardee's for breakfast."

###

Melody and the children were asleep when he let himself into the house. Lucky, realizing the intruder was friend rather than foe, settled himself comfortably beneath the kitchen table with a whumph.

"Some watch dog *you* are, old friend." He bent down to give the dog

139

a pat on the rump.

He glanced around the kitchen, wishing Melody had something alcoholic in the house to drink. After tonight's shindig in the revival tent, he needed it.

A little before midnight, he placed the dreaded phone call to the Magill residence in Sterling Heights, Michigan.

"Hello?" A woman's voice, struggling up from the safe confines of sleep.

"I'm trying to reach Beth Magill."

"Who's calling?"

"Dan Keefer, from Keyser, West Virginia." Several moments of silence. "Is Beth Magill in, please?"

Quietly, "This is she."

"Sorry to call at this hour, but I...well, I'm not entirely certain, but I think I may have located your daughter."

After several seconds of a tense pause, in a whispered tone, the woman spoke in a rush. "Could you give me your number and let me call you back? From another phone."

Though he doubted whether she'd make good on her promise, he waited by the telephone in his daughter's kitchen for the return call from Michigan. He picked it up after the first ring.

Beth Magill didn't bother to identify herself. "Mr. Keefer, are you sure it's April? Where is she? Who is she with? Who *has* her?"

"I don't have all the answers yet, Mrs. Magill. Actually, I didn't know whether you'd accept my call, since you never returned the others."

"*What* others? When I didn't hear from you, I assumed you'd quit the case or moved to Australia or something."

Melody's words came tumbling back to him. He'd try to handle this delicately. "Your husband never told you I called?"

"When? How long ago? He never said a word."

Taking a deep breath, Dan Keefer said, "It won't be helpful to anyone concerned if...look, I don't have the right logbook with me, to tell you exact dates and places where I made the calls. And I'm only assuming the man I spoke with was your husband. But what I need to know now is, how do you want me to proceed with this latest bit of information?"

"Tell me my options, please." Suddenly she seemed like a woman who was in total control.

"I'll give it to you straight. I'm reasonably sure the girl in question is your daughter April. I saw her a little more than an hour ago. Tomorrow I'll go to the local authorities and process a criminal-records check on the girl's companion, one Adrian Lightfoot. At least that's the name he goes by. This will alert the FBI, who never closed the case and consider it unsolved and active."

"Please! You should."

"Secondly, you could come and see for yourself, whether Haley Mae is your daughter."

"Haley Mae?" she said incredulously. "But what if she's gone by the time I get there?"

"If we don't arouse suspicion on the part of this Lightfoot guy, they should be here through Saturday night. Three days away, but by asking around I found out that some of the performers leave a day early so they can travel to their next engagement, so we need to go Friday night. I can't give you all the details, and it wouldn't serve much purpose if I did. Suffice to say, the girl's hair isn't blond but dark brown, which isn't unusual when a child has been abducted. The kidnapper often disguises the child to prevent discovery, as you're aware."

"Dark hair? But how can you be sure if,,,"

"The face, Mrs. Magill. I saw a line drawing of her on a poster and went to see for myself. Of course, your daughter is now eleven, but this girl is a dead ringer for your daughter April, right down to the dimples. Believe me, with all you've suffered, if I weren't ninety per cent certain, I'd never have called you."

After a few minutes more, exchanging information as to Keefer's location and directions to Keyser, Keefer hung up.

Beth Magill will leave Michigan tomorrow as early as possible. She should arrive in Keyser sometime on Friday afternoon.

In the morning he'd have to corner Melody and let her in on the latest developments. The trip with the grandkids would have to be postponed until Sunday.

All he'd needed to tell Beth Magill toward the end of their brief conversation was that he, too, had a daughter he loved dearly, an offhand remark that had seemed to convince her he was serious as death.

Rarely was he wrong, and he didn't believe now would prove an exception to his almost flawless track record.

Oh, sure. There'd been cases he hadn't been able to close, but generally because there hadn't been much of a case to begin with. Which is what he'd tried to tell himself for more than twenty months about the case involving April Warner...

He stood at the kitchen sink, poured a glass of ice water and took an aspirin, fearing sleep would be elusive. With so much on his mind, he'd have to court that fickle woman of the night.

What he wouldn't have given for a stiff shot of Scotch.

When she hung up the phone in the den, surrounded by darkness broken only by the dim light coming from the top of the stairs, Beth felt herself go numb.

Dawn would break before she could gather the strength necessary to go upstairs, and then it was only because her maternal ear was attuned to the faint sounds of Petey fretting in his room. Recently she and Philip had exchanged the crib for a day bed, and she had to go to her son, worried he'd be disoriented and fall to the floor.

After she had rearranged Petey's little shape beneath the covers and rubbed his head until he settled back to sleep, Beth knew her plans had been structured.

She tiptoed from the room, quietly closing the door behind her. Then she went downstairs to the kitchen, pressed on the coffee machine, and sat at the table with paper and pen.

Since April's abduction, Beth had become an inveterate list maker. Philip teased her about her lists. But he'd never seemed to realize that, without an ongoing list, Beth feared she might spin out of control, the flimsy underpinnings of her life melting away like a spider's web in a driving rain.

In an instant she had learned how utterly meaningless and futile, to believe one could have control over the random forces of life. Any control at all. Any say about what might happen in the span of a sigh, when reckless circumstances could change everything you held dear beyond your imagining.

The way she viewed the world. Beth Magill, before and after. She was not the same woman she had once been, not after she'd lost April, seemingly forever.

But some small, buried, secret part of her had always held a spark of hope in reserve, privately breathing on the fragile ember to keep it bright and alive.

The network she'd developed for the past twenty-one months had sustained her. Other parents, people like herself, who had never found their children but somehow doggedly survived, were her only friends.

Carefully, she wrote on the pad of paper "Items 1 through 10:

"1 -- Get Philip off to conference. Ask about calls from Dan Keefer.
"2 -- Call for substitute for Thursday and Friday.
"3 -- Check on Mickey; send plant arrangement.
"4 -- Take station wagon for oil change.
"5 -- Get Philip's shirts from dry cleaners.
"6 -- Go to the bank for traveler's checks.
"7 -- Go to Triple-A for map."

She paused to pour a cup of coffee, adding an ice cube to cool it quickly before gulping it down and pouring a second cup. Like an automaton, she went to the left upper cabinet and took a tranquilizer and her blood pressure medication, then two aspirins to thwart the pounding headache she could feel at the base of her skull.

Reading over the list she had made, Beth picked up the pen to continue.

"8 – Pack Petey's clothes.
"9 – Pack my clothes.
"10 – Leave for West Virginia at one or two o'clock."

She'd forgotten something, but what? Beth almost laughed when she remembered the ploy she'd devised long ago to help identify her daughter from any child imposter.

"11 – Don't forget Strawbaby."

Only April Warner would know the significance of the scarecrow doll Beth had tucked away in her lingerie drawer, to save for the day when April came home.

That had been in the early months, when Beth could still believe in April's disappearance as a slight administrative glitch in Heaven's management of the world, a small error with astonishing repercussions that would be discovered during a Divine audit and corrected immediately.

Sipping the lukewarm coffee, tears burned at her eyes. She was terrified to let herself believe in Dan Keefer's words. Could the child with dark hair he had seen in West Virginia possibly be her own daughter April? But, if so, what was April doing in West Virginia? And who was this Adrian Lightfoot?

Beth couldn't bear to set herself up for another disappointment, but nothing had surfaced in such a long time to give her the slightest shred of hope.

Then she remembered something else, the psychic from Maumee, Ohio.

"12 – Call Susan Rivers and make appointment for tonight or tomorrow morning."

Whether or not Mrs. Rivers could be reached, much less be willing to spend an hour with Beth, would determine where she and Petey might stop for the night.

Surely her list now covered all the bases. If it didn't, Beth would be damned if she'd add an item thirteen.

Briefly she regretted not being able to visit Mickey Carruthers in the hospital where she'd been recuperating from the drug overdose for almost three weeks. Beth had been to see her several times, taking a floral arrangement, the Book of Common Prayer thoughtfully loaned to Beth following her own personal tragedy, a box of chocolates.

But Mickey refused to talk. She simply looked at Beth and wept copious tears, breaking into sobs when Beth conveyed Philip's regards and prayers for her recovery.

She chalked it off to Mickey's acute embarrassment, seeing as how Philip had been the one to find her unconscious on the floor of the church office.

She heard the music from the clock radio in the bedroom she shared with Philip, followed by Petey's steady stream of chatter.

Yawning, Beth got up from the table and put three eggs in a saucepan to boil. Then she walked out of the kitchen and down the hall and hurried upstairs to officially begin the day.

Chapter Seventeen

Damn it all to hell, but he'd had that nightmare again.

Philip was yanked from a disturbed sleep after becoming entangled in the top sheet, kicking and groaning as if he'd been fighting for his life. When he looked over to his wife for assurance, he was finally awake. Beth's side of the bed was empty.

The sheets were cool. How long had she been up? Had Petey gotten sick in the night?

He fell back against the bed, his right hand shading his eyes. A cool dawn breeze whispered through the open window. He breathed the moist air in gulps, trying to calm his nerves as he reminded himself it had been only a dream.

It hadn't happened. It *wouldn't* happen.

His subconscious must have admitted the thing he most feared as a real possibility. For in the dream his pulpit had been removed from the church and, nude, he stood at the front of the altar before his congregation in public disgrace accused of child molesting, with nothing to hide behind, nothing to shield him from humiliation.

Even while fully cognizant and in total control of his faculties, Philip did not do well with confrontation. His policy had always been to avoid unpleasantness at any price. But now it seemed as though even his own subconscious conspired to destroy him by sadistically chipping away at his armor.

Yet it wasn't entirely a dream, a construction of primitive, subliminal thought waves. Because he knew that in his actual ministry, there were those who were trying to persecute him, *him*, Philip Magill!

Uttering a deep sigh, his thoughts paraded back in time through the past weeks.

Erickson, one of the most powerful and respected members of the church and one of the largest contributors, appointed himself to break the news. A big, bulky Swede, an oncologist by trade, Erickson had seemed bewildered, even nervous.

Nira Woods had made a bald accusation, saying perhaps it would be best if Philip were not left alone with the children of the church.

"It's not *my* fault she lost an infant!" Philip protested. "What the hell does she have against me, anyhow? I've been nothing but kind and comforting to Nira and her husband."

"She didn't go into detail, Phil. I plan to meet her for lunch in a few days and explore it further. I'll let you know whether this can be resolved."

How he despised being called Phil! Almost as much as he despised the thought of Erickson and Nira Woods meeting for lunch to talk about Philip Magill behind his back.

Explore, Erickson had said. What? Like exploratory surgery, the oncologist digging for cancerous morsels to be used against Philip Magill, to seal his fate?

Jesus!

Who did they think they were, treating him like the hired help, with a veiled hint he could be dismissed with alacrity? Well, he'd just see about that!

And Bruce Fielding wasn't going to bow out gracefully, oh, no. Foolishly, Philip had believed he'd bought him off for twenty thousand dollars, but Bruce's most recent telegram last week demanded five thousand more. When would it ever end?

Had Bruce spilled his guts to Nira Woods after a church service over coffee and pastries in the fellowship hall? Why else would the woman be coming after him?

But it could have been Mickey Carruthers who dropped the hint, as Philip had learned to his chagrin. He'd prided himself on having Mickey's undivided loyalty. Now, he knew better. He'd been an idiot to think he could trust her with his secrets. She knew far too much about him.

He'd never forget the moment he returned to his church office after lunch on a bleak, rainy afternoon, to find Mickey crumpled on the floor behind his desk. Thank God he'd been alone when he tripped over her body.

And the note! Had anyone else seen it, Mickey's last words and testament could have ruined him. Still, he winced from those words – how Mickey accepted partial responsibility for April's abduction, how she couldn't live with her guilt any longer, how she would always be in love with Philip Magill.

The stupid, ugly *bitch!*

Philip, cool, methodical, had destroyed the note immediately and then ransacked Mickey's desk, finding an unmarked manila folder hidden beneath hanging files at the bottom of a drawer.

The folder contained copies of chronological communications she'd had with Bruce Fielding, a record of how Bruce had managed to keep tabs on Philip from any location, all the details of his life meticulously recorded by his in-house Judas.

With the buttresses of his roof caving in, Philip could find isolated moments of pleasure only in his son. Little Petey was the one bright spot in his father's crumbling existence. When he heard the cheerful sounds of Petey's vocalizing from across the hall, a fond smile came to his lips, momentarily erasing Philip's grim, furtive expression.

He sat up, throwing his legs over the side of the bed. An image assailed him, Mickey's fat body in the tent dress behind his desk, making him wonder how long she'd been lying there.

Checking for a pulse was one of the last things Philip thought to do, just after he called for an ambulance. By the time the paramedics arrived and lifted her hulk onto a gurney, Philip had transformed the energy of his unbridled fury into a semblance of anxious concern for his faithful employee and dear friend.

Why, he'd even followed the ambulance to the hospital.

He should have cut her loose years ago. But he'd been afraid to, since she knew what had happened at the churches in Maryland and Florida, the reasons Philip Magill had been forced to move on. And he'd made the naïve mistake of believing that, if he assured her a place of employment and his continued friendship, she'd keep her lips sealed.

When he left the hospital after admitting Mickey several weeks ago, Philip carried with him a fervent hope. If she regained consciousness, he prayed Mickey's brain would have disintegrated into mush, a vegetative state to match the lumpy bag of potatoes she lugged around for a body. How she'd ever believed he'd want to touch her...well, it was not only repulsive but absurd. But no more so than her apparent hope that, one day, he'd fall in love with her. She was insane!

Though Bruce harassed him periodically, Philip had not heard from him again since Mickey's aborted suicide attempt, which told him plenty about the way Bruce Fielding and his church secretary had delighted in conspiring against hm.

A chess game, that's all it was. Philip simply had to plan his next moves with extra cunning and skill.

He got up and pulled on his tan velour bathrobe, tying the belt while staring at his reflection in the mirror of Beth's vanity table. He smoothed a brush through his ruffled hair, dismayed by the expression on his own face, reminding him of a frightened, cornered rabbit.

Hearing Beth's quick steps, he decided to take a shower before going downstairs for his breakfast.

Waiting until she and Petey were out of the bathroom, Philip darted in for his shower. He stepped beneath jets of water nearly hot enough to scald him, vigorously scrubbing his body with a loofa as if to rid himself of the doubts that had seeped into his pores while he'd been asleep and defenseless.

He dried off, shaved, and applied deodorant and cologne. After he returned to the bedroom to dress in a fresh white shirt and a gray Brooks Brothers suit, black wingtips, and a burgundy tie, his flagging confidence was restored.

It was 7:15 am when he bounded down the stairs and into the kitchen to find his wife and son. "Good morning, all," Philip said heartily, pouring himself a cup of lukewarm coffee. Testing it, he said, "When did you brew this, Beth?"

She was spooning oatmeal into Petey's mouth. "I've been up for a while. Did you sleep well?"

"As a matter of fact, no, I didn't. Bad dreams I can't quite seem to remember, probably just as well."

"Daddy!" Oatmeal oozed down Petey's chin and onto the bib tied around his Smurf pajamas. His white-blond hair fluffed out around his perfect round head like a halo. He was an extraordinarily beautiful child.

"Hello, my little man." Philip remained by the counter, drinking the coffee. "Daddy can't give you a hug this morning, Petey. I'll get oatmeal on my conference suit."

Beth looked up at him for the first time. "Oh, you're dressed already. You look very nice, Philip. Very professional. Did you finish the speech last night?"

"Yes, but it was nearly midnight before I finally turned off the computer and fell into bed."

"Well, at least you're prepared. Next time don't wait so long. You don't procrastinate as a rule, not when it comes to your sermons, at least."

"Presentation, Beth. Not a sermon, not today. Aren't you going to ask what I decided to speak about?"

But her attention was diverted when Petey knocked over his orange juice. "Philip, hand me some paper towels, would you?"

As she was sponging up the mess, he said, "I suppose I'd best be off. Anything you need before I leave?"

She stared at him for several long seconds. "Would you call me sometime this morning, Philip?"

"I could, Beth. Between workshops, probably, but why?"

"Just do. Please."

"But then they'll have to page you to come to the principal's office, and I'll have to wait forever until you come to the phone. Why don't we talk now?" He glanced at his watch. "I have a few minutes to spare."

"I...can't go to school today, Philip. Call me here. But I can't talk now. I'll have to rush to get Petey to day care, as it is."

"Why can't you teach today?"

"I feel a migraine coming on. I'm not up to it."

"Poor Beth." Philip finished his coffee and set the cup in the kitchen sink. "Then I'll call around 10 am to see how you are; 10:30 at the outside."

"Fine. Thanks."

When he stooped to kiss her cheek, he felt her stiffen. Beth, too, then.

He straightened up to leave the kitchen accompanied by Petey's squeals for his father's attention, picked up his attaché from the sideboard in the front foyer, and left the house.

As Philip backed his forest-green Audi out of the driveway to the street, he remembered an important item of business. He'd neglected to ask Beth whether she still planned to stop off at the hospital to visit with Mickey. He'd been meaning to warn her against it. Without much success, Philip tried to expunge from his mind the things Mickey Carruthers might say to his wife.

Wouldn't it be the last nail in the coffin, to make his interminable torment complete?

The woman was just so damned needy! With physicians and nurses fawning over her, flowers and visitors from church, Mickey Carruthers hadn't had this much attention in her dreary life. Now she was expected to enjoy a full recovery, one of the worst pieces of news Philip had ever received.

Well, if she expected to resume her role as church secretary, she'd be sorely disappointed. He didn't owe the woman a goddamned thing.

He turned left to take the convoluted suburban route toward the expressway, realizing he'd begun the day with a lie. Last night he hadn't worked on his presentation. He'd exchanged fantasies with several fellow pedophiles from Cleveland via e-mail.

Philip's therapy.

He knew it was only a matter of time until he'd have to purge his secret collection of kiddie porn from the church's archival files in the closet of his church study. So far, he hadn't been able to force himself to get rid of it, a splendid collection requiring years of his life to amass. Irreplaceable.

Only the photographs of smooth, lithe children's bodies kept him sane.

But for now, he had a long day ahead of him, and a presentation to deliver to thousands of his peers. He tried to push his concerns into the background.

Shortly, Philip took the access road to the Chrysler Freeway and headed for the Renaissance Center in downtown Detroit.

"Hello, darling. How's the headache?"

Petey was in the den watching Mr. Rogers with the door closed when Beth picked up the telephone in the kitchen to hear her husband's voice. She was dressed and packed, ready to leave the house, waiting for Philip's call.

"A little better, thanks."

"Did you get Petey to day care?"

"Yes. I'd have kept him here with me, but I didn't want to upset his routine. Besides, he'd have missed his playmates."

"For the best, darling. Give you a chance to rest."

She took a deep breath to calm her nerves. "Philip, do you remember hearing from a man named Dan Keefer?"

"Keefer? Well, let me think. Uh, don't recall."

"You don't?"

"No. Should I know the name?"

"I heard from him, Philip. He told me he'd talked to you and left messages for me to return his calls."

"When, Beth?"

"You honestly don't remember? I find that hard to believe, since Keefer's the private investigator I hired to find April. I have no reason to doubt what he says."

There was an uncomfortable silence. "You hired an investigator without letting me know about it?"

He was so adept at righteous indignation. "Yes. I did."

"Well, you might have told me."

"Why? When I couldn't even rely on you to give me his messages?"

She could hear a bit of commotion from the other end. Then Philip said, "Someone else needs to use the telephone. Could this keep until I get home tonight?"

"No, it can't. I need you to search your memory. I'm asking you a simple question."

"Beth, if I did talk to anyone named Keefer, I probably wrote it off as another crank call. You remember all those people who got our phone number and kept telephoning with tips and clues because they wanted the reward. How could I be expected to know the man was on the level? Particularly since you hadn't seen fit to include me in some half-baked investigation. What did it cost? And what did you get for it? April was never found, I don't need to add, I'm sure."

She felt as if the two hemispheres of her brain were at odds. She wanted to believe in Philip's cool logic, and yet she could not allow herself to be taken in by his words, not if there was a remote possibility he was glossing over the truth.

Staring at the digital numbers of the clock on the microwave, she said, "You should have told me."

"What is this, Beth? The Spanish Inquisition? My God, didn't I just tell you I don't remember ever having spoken to a man named Keefer?"

"You didn't care, that's the truth of it, isn't it, Philip? You're cold as ice. Why did it take so long for me to understand how you are? You never cared about April. You couldn't make yourself *pretend* to care!"

"Look, if you want the plain unvarnished truth, even though April was your daughter, I was not especially fond of the child. She was a spoiled, nasty little girl, and..."

Beth hung up the phone. When it began to ring, she waited until the tenth ring to pick it up.

"Beth, I'm sorry! I didn't mean it, honestly I didn't. It's just that, well, you know how I am, darling. When I'm under a great deal of stress, sometimes I tend to lose my temper. Please forgive me, please try."

"Alright, Philip. Whatever you say."

"You're angry with me. I don't blame you.

"Why would I be angry?"

"Beth, don't put me through this now. Don't make me grovel. I have a presentation in front of thousands in a few minutes."

"Do well, Philip. I know how important it is to you to make a good impression on total strangers. Only the people closest to you seem to present the problem."

"Yes. Surely you don't expect me to get into a debate with you now."

"No, surely not."

"Oh, there was one thing more I meant to ask, Beth. With your headache and all, you're not planning to visit Mickey this afternoon, are you?"

"I'd considered going if I feel better. Why?"

"Perhaps it might be best if you didn't."

Something had begun to click in her brain. "Oh? Why?"

"Well, you know. She needs time to mend. You did say she's not been in the mood to talk, didn't you? Really, until she recovers, what's the point? You have more important things to do with your time, darling."

"Send flowers, then?"

"I think so. Yes, make it a lovely arrangement. Or perhaps a terrarium. One of those big globe things with plants and stones."

"I'll let you get back to your conference. Goodbye, Philip."

The second time she returned the receiver to its cradle, Beth knew she'd have to find time in her busy day to stop by Mickey's hospital room and deliver the flowers personally. An imbecile could have intuited there was some reason Philip wanted to keep the two women apart.

She consulted her list, changing item three to *Take plant arrangement to Mickey*.

Then Beth picked up the phone one last time to place a call to the psychic Susan Rivers in Maumee, Ohio.

With her son dressed in his crisp little sailor suit, Beth led Petey through the doors of the elevator onto the third floor of Beaumont Hospital in Royal Oak, a spectacular purple amaryllis in ceramic planter balanced in the crook of her left arm.

"Go see Mickey!"

Petey was fond of the church secretary and had asked where Mickey was during the weeks of her convalescence in the hospital. Beth had requested special permission at the desk to bring Petey with her in hopes of cheering the patient.

Carts of lunch trays were being wheeled down the corridor by orderlies.

"Doctor!" Petey shouted.

Approaching Mickey's room, Beth leaned down to her son. "We can't stay long, Petey. And you must be very quiet. This is a hospital, and there are lots of sick people here trying to get better."

"'kay!"

"But I know how glad Aunt Mickey will be to see you. Will you promise Mommy to give her a big hug?"

Wearing a peach-colored bed jacket, Mickey sat in the raised hospital bed, her salt-and-pepper hair combed in the short pixie style she'd worn since Beth had known her. In the past months, the woman had aged ten years, gaining at least fifty pounds, neglecting to color her hair as if she'd abandoned hope long before she attempted to take her own life.

But when Mickey saw Peter Magill the Third run through the open door, her face lit up. "Petey! Come give Aunt Mickey a kiss!"

"It's good to see you feeling so much better," Beth said. "I promise we won't stay long."

"What a gorgeous flower! Beth, you shouldn't have."
Beth set the amaryllis on a nearby table and, when she turned to see her son in Mickey's arms, she was startled by the expression in Mickey's eyes.

"Beth, we must talk," she said in a flat tone of voice. "I've been wanting to tell you, but I couldn't seem to find the courage."

Earlier, Susan Rivers had listened to Beth's story over the phone, about Dan Keefer calling from West Virginia to say he believed he might have located April.

"You say she's going by the name of Haley Mae?" the woman asked. "Haley Mae?"

"Yes, that's what he said. She's traveling with a man named Adrian Lightfoot."

"Hmm. I see Haley Mae as a sideshow attraction of sorts. I see a huge tent with many people inside. You know, Beth, it feels right. You should go. I would advise you not to delay."

No meeting is necessary, Mrs. Rivers had insisted. No detour to Maumee, Ohio would be required.

Already, Beth had asked herself how much more she could endure before she reached her breaking point, not merely from the strange occurrences of the past fourteen hours, but from the entire panorama of bizarre events in the last twenty-one months.

But now, when Mickey Carruthers began to speak, Beth felt as if a giant hand had stuffed itself down her esophagus, and her throbbing heart was in danger of being wrenched from her throat.

Chapter Eighteen

"**P**etey, please, sweetheart! Don't be stubborn. Mommy has to make some phone calls."

"Dog!"

Petey tugged at Beth's arm, lured by the sight of a large golden retriever obediently chasing a Frisbee, a family with three children and a grandmother having a picnic on the grass at the rest stop near Pittsburgh. When the teenage boy tossed the disc and the dog leaped into the air to catch it in his mouth, Petey clapped his chubby hands and squealed his encouragement.

"I promise, just as soon as I use the telephone, we'll come back and watch the dog."

Dragging his feet, Petey let himself be led into the gray limestone building which housed the restrooms, along with soft drinks and packaged refreshments available from vending machines. Four public telephone booths were adjacent to a You-are-here map of Pennsylvania.

Beth hurried for the one unoccupied booth, closed the door, and hoisted Petey onto her lap.

The first call was to Dan Keefer at his daughter's house in Keyser. An answering machine took Beth's message that she had been unavoidably delayed due to car trouble and should arrive by 5 pm that night.

Next she consulted a list of emergency numbers posted on the wall of the booth for 24-hour wrecker service. Dialing the number, she whispered a prayer. What would she and Petey do, if the steam billowing from beneath the hood of her old Plymouth station wagon was a sign of the vehicle's imminent death? Well, she'd have to rent a car.

But she was heartened by the sound of a deep male voice assuring her a truck would be dispatched immediately.

"Okay, Petey. Let's go watch the dog and wait for the garage man to come."

They stepped out of the shadows into the blinding sun. Somewhere Beth had lost her sunglasses – perhaps she'd left them in the motel room this morning – and her eyes felt raw. She'd meant to drive straight through, but because she'd had so little sleep and then their late start from seeing Mickey at the hospital, combined with her own exhaustion, they'd stopped for the night.

In a way, God had been looking after them. When she thought of what might have happened had the car acted up last night in the darkness along an Interstate, a woman and a small toddler...

She lifted Petey for a drink of water from a fountain, then took a sip of ice-cold relief for herself. She chose a nearby picnic table. Petey settled down beside her, laughing at the dog who was still pursuing the Frisbee.

"You know what?" she said to Petey. "I think that dog would chase the Frisbee all day, he loves it so much."

"Do it again!"

Small shadows on the grass; it was almost noon.

The smell of diesel fuel accompanied the roar of huge trucks pulling in and out of the rest area. Chemicals in the toilet bowl in the restroom, a whiff of a man's cologne reminding Beth of Philip.

They'd driven for miles through a gushing rain, but as they traveled farther south, the sun came out. It had been a hot, steamy trip in a car with no air conditioning. Maybe she'd simply pushed the old car too hard. Now she wished she'd stopped to rest more often, to allow the engine to cool, though uppermost in her mind had been the warning about time being of the essence, received not only from Dan Keefer but from Susan Rivers, as well.

Beth longed for a bath. Petey's grimy, sticky hands and face, the back of Beth's neck and the sweat trickling down between her breasts had made her short-tempered, impatient to be done with it.

Fifteen minutes went by as Beth watched wheels against pavement in the distance, moving on. The gray limestone of the building brought an image of Philip in his gray suit, of the neatly folded corners of his buttoned-down, conservative, carefully orchestrated life.

Whom had he been trying to fool? From what Mickey Carruthers had told her, Beth was able to fill in the subtext. Of course, loyal Mickey would try to protect Philip, despite the libelous knowledge she'd harbored about her employer for years.

For the first time, Beth had allowed herself to believe the impossible, that there might well have been some credibility to Nira Woods' suspicion that the good pastor should be kept apart from the children, a rumor she'd caught wind of through the reliable church grapevine.

Yes, Mickey had first met Philip Magill in Columbia, Maryland. He had facilitated a grief therapy group that Mickey attended after her short-lived second marriage and Las Vegas divorce.

He invited her to church services, learned she was financially strapped, and encouraged her to apply for a job in the church office.

The woman hinted they'd been more than friends, claiming Philip made promises he'd never intended to honor. After everything that had happened, Mickey admitted she finally knew he'd only been leading her on, manipulating her to serve his purposes, as he'd used so many people in the past.

When Philip lost his position at the church in Columbia under suspicious circumstances, Mickey said she'd been bereft. She couldn't bear the thought of being alone again. With Philip, she'd never felt alone. He had been her friend and confidant.

Despite the objections of her adult children, she sold her home, her only asset, and followed him to the new church in Florida. There, she met the Fieldings, lovely people, and their son Bruce. Such a fine boy, so close to Philip. But then Mickey began to suspect that there was more between Philip and Bruce than friendship.

As Mickey Carruthers' words pounded against her heart, Beth slowly understood that her marriage of convenience, as Philip had once called their union, was nothing but a hideous sham.

Philip Magill only loved himself. He was incapable of normal adult love.

No, Mickey had no idea where April was or who had taken her. Had she known, of course she'd have told Beth. She'd have gone to the authorities herself! She had three children of her own, please remember.

Though she had no proof, she also suspected Bruce Fielding was somehow involved

"Please believe me, Beth!" Mickey pleaded tearfully. "Don't hate me!" But Mickey's last words had remained in Beth's memory for hundreds of miles. "You don't know Philip like you think you do. No one does."

Her resistance worn to a nub, Beth opened the forbidden pack of Merit Lights purchased from a vending machine, removed a cigarette and lit it with a match, drawing in the sharp satisfaction of nicotine.

She hadn't smoked in years. The first draw made her slightly dizzy. Before she was finished, she saw the tow truck slide in off the Interstate and jumped up to meet it. "The garage man is here." She took Petey's sweaty hand, and they went to stand beside the station wagon.

Beth had thought to lift the hood. The billows of noxious smoke had dissipated.

"You're the lady who called?" The boy couldn't have been much more than eighteen. Beth said a silent prayer that he knew what he was about.

She nodded. "I hope it's nothing terribly serious."

"What was the problem exactly?"

"We were driving along, and smoke started coming out from the engine. A lot of smoke."

The boy bent under the hood for a closer inspection. "Looks like a busted radiator hose to me. If I'm right, we can have you back on the road in nothing flat."

"Oh, thank goodness! Do I have time to buy a cold drink for my son?"

"Sure do. This'll take about five, ten minutes." He went to his truck and opened the door to remove a toolbox.

Petey sipped his drink as they stood on the curb and watched the boy fasten the old clamps onto a new hose, brush his palms together and let the hood of the car fall with a resolute thud.

"All finished, Ma'am."

She paid the boy, loaded Petey into the car, fastened their seat belts, and cautiously turned on the ignition. As she started to back away from the curb, a dark blue Pennsylvania State Police car drove up beside her with its blue dome light flashing, much to Petey's delight.

The officer motioned her to stop. Beth cut off the ignition and waited, wondering what she had done. Had she been speeding before she limped off the Interstate to the rest stop? But she was certain she'd only been going forty miles an hour. Other drivers had honked impatiently, urging her to speed up.

"Well, Petey, what do you know?" she tried to say cheerfully. "How's this for an adventure? A real policeman!"

The tall, broad-shouldered trooper wore dark blue trousers and a form-fitting gray shirt with official epaulets, a gray Canadian Mounties hat. She noticed a holstered gun on his hip as he approached her open window. "May I see your license and registration?"

"Certainly." Beth took the license from her wallet and the plastic valise containing the car papers from the glove compartment and handed them over.

"Would you step out of the car, please?"

"Why, yes, but what seems to be the problem, officer?" Standing beside the car, Beth realized she was trembling.

"The vehicle is registered to a Philip Magill."

"Yes. My husband."

"This car was reported stolen, Ma'am."

"By whom?"

"Philip Magill. You say you're his wife?"

"Of course, I am. Do I look like someone who'd steal a car, much less this old heap? This is our son."

The officer was silent for a few moments. "If you're Mrs. Magill, would you mind telling me your husband's occupation?"

"He's a minister. Presbyterian. In Sterling Heights, Michigan."

The trooper nodded, returning the license and registration. "Why would he report the car stolen, if he knew you were driving it?"

"Because he wouldn't approve of my mission, I'm sorry to say."

"Which is? Are you leaving him? A domestic dispute?"

She took a deep breath, and the words tumbled from her mouth unchecked. "My daughter has been missing for nearly two years, you can check with the Michigan State Police if you don't believe me, her name is April Warner. She was nine years old when she was kidnapped, and she's just turned eleven, on May the second. I hired a private investigator, his name is Dan Keefer, and I'm going to West Virginia, Keyser's the name of the town, to see if the child Dan Keefer has found is truly my daughter."

"You can wait in your car now, Mrs. Magill. Let me check it out, to be on the safe side." Had the officer's tone softened, or did she only imagine it?

She watched the trooper get into his vehicle and speak on the radio through static. In a matter of minutes, he returned to stand beside Beth's car. "I radioed into headquarters to check the validity of what you said about your daughter's disappearance. Confirmed."

Beth laughed nervously. "Glad to hear it. I wonder who would invent such an awful story about her own child, if it weren't the truth."

"If you don't mind me saying so, you seem all right to me."

She stared up at him. "I do? Well, why wouldn't I seem all right?"

"Your husband said you'd suffered a psychotic breakdown, and he's afraid for his son."

"Officer, I never had a breakdown. That's a lie. I can't believe Philip would say such a thing. He must be furious with me, is all I can think."

"We'll report back that you and your son are safe and sound." For once, the trooper grinned. "A minister, eh? Guy ought to be ashamed of himself, coming up with a tale like that."

"Even the devil can cite Scripture for his purpose. Philip's no exception."

"I'll accompany you to the State line," he said. "Just to make sure you get out of Pennsylvania safely. Follow me."

"How kind you are. Thank you!"

Beth waited until the police car pulled off the exit ramp into traffic, flashing its gumball and siren wailing, and she cut in behind.

"Po-weece!" Petey yelled, bouncing around in his car seat.

She hadn't allowed herself to show anger, but now she felt her simmering emotions come to a rolling boil that couldn't be stirred down. The unmitigated gall! The sheer acrimony of the man! A psychotic breakdown!

She glanced over the seat at Petey's bright, innocent face, completely happy in his excitement about trailing the police car. Truly, the one soul Philip loved more than himself was Petey.

If her worst suspicions proved accurate, if Philip had willfully kept Beth from locating April much sooner, even from the possibility by withholding vital information from Dan Keefer, Beth knew she would fight to the death to deny Philip Magill further access to his precious little son. Just as he had kept her apart from her daughter...

She tried to place the quotation she had spoken to the trooper, about the devil citing Scripture. Oh, yes. *The Merchant of Venice.* Shakespeare. Was it Shylock?

And then, as she felt a new surge of courage strengthen her resolve to find April, another aphorism popped into her head.

Time and tide wait for no man.

Or woman.

#

He'd been awake all night, after coming home from his conference to find the station wagon gone. The house was empty, and there was no note from Beth. She'd left nothing to warm in the oven for his dinner.

A suspicion, an insidious fear, began to form in his mind. Over the hours, despite several Scotch on the rocks, he could no longer contain himself. He called Beth's father shortly before midnight, thinking Petey might have gotten hurt at day care and she'd taken him to the hospital.

No, the Blocks hadn't seen her, hadn't heard a word. Frank Block had no idea where she could be.

Philip didn't wait until daybreak to again involve the police.

On the first ring of the call-back, urgently, he grabbed the phone. He listened as the call from the Michigan State Police came in from their office in Pontiac.

"Mr. Magill, we wanted to let you know your wife and son are safe. They were seen at a rest stop in Pennsylvania. Apparently, they're on their way to Keyser, West Virginia. Do you have family there? Maybe your wife is…"

"No. No family at all in West Virginia."

"We're alerting the West Virginia authorities to be on the look-out for the Plymouth station wagon and license plate number. We'll keep you informed."

"Thank you. This has been very helpful. I'll handle it from here."

"Mr. Magill?"

But Philip slammed down the phone, seething with rage, his temples pounding.

The dumb bitch! Did she really believe she could drive off into the sunset with Petey, and not tell Philip Magill where she planned to go or when she planned to return?

In a pig's eye would he allow it. She'd pay for her impulsive little act. How *dare* she put him through this waiting, this agony?

It was that damned kid of hers again. April, the spoiled little princess who detested Philip and would like nothing better than to make his life a living hell.

He ran his hands through his hair. Normally, Beth was so compliant. An act of open defiance was out of character. Only the frail hope of finding April would have driven Beth to do such a thing. In time, perhaps he could bring himself to forgive her. But not at this moment.

Philip picked up the phone and punched out the number to reservations at Metropolitan Airport. He arranged to be on a flight to Roanoke, Virginia by way of Chicago, with four layovers in various cities, departing Detroit in two hours. On such short notice, it was the best he could do.

Running out to the Audi, he checked his credit cards. At the airport in Roanoke, he would rent a car and drive the rest of the way.

Chapter Nineteen

Jagged lightning ripped across the black sky.

As Beth rode with Dan Keefer in his brown, late-model Cavalier, an occasional violent gust of wind buffeted the car. She watched as the stranger she'd only recently met corrected the steering against the wind currents. A quiet, unassuming man, his appearance and gentle manner brought the word trustworthy to mind.

"Looks like an electrical storm," Dan said. "Probably won't amount to much, this time of year. These mountains are famous for their pyrotechnics, but I know this area of the country. Summer storms, likely as not, are much ado about nothing."

Much ado about nothing; Shakespeare, again.

She knew he was trying to make conversation so the trip to the revival would pass more quickly. Still, Beth's fingers massaged her forehead with slow, circular movements. He clicked on the radio for soothing French piano music. They heard the last few minutes of a selection by Debussy. Then it was something by Poulenc.

"How much longer to the fairgrounds, Dan?"

"A few miles. But to be completely honest with you, Mrs. Magill, it's possible you'll be disappointed once we get there."

"Why do you say that? How could I be disappointed, if the child is April?"

"But what if she's not your daughter? What then?"

Beth sighed. "I haven't thought that far ahead, Dan. It *must* be April."

"Even if the girl is April, she won't be the same little girl you remember. She may seem...well, you know. Different."

"I don't care! I just want my daughter back. We'll put the past behind us."

"She's been through an awful lot. Have you considered her experiences, Mrs. Magill?"

"Call me Beth, please. And to answer your question, of course the answer is no. April has been in my thoughts constantly, and I can only see her face as I know her. Knew her, I mean, before she vanished. But what mother on earth wouldn't recognize her own child?"

"Remembering the computer age-progression drawings might help. It certainly helped me to make a tentative identification, nearly two years later."

They rode in silence. Beth understood that Dan's thoughts were as private as her own. She tried to center on the drawings issued through the AMBER Foundation and other missing children networks that she had plied assiduously. But as she had told Dan, the face in her mind was April's face on the last day, at the park in Northport.

But April's voice, like wind chimes in a breeze on a summer day. There could be no mistaking April's voice.

Petey was safe with Melody and her children, last seen on Butch's lap at the kitchen table dipping fish sticks and French fries in pools of tartar sauce and catsup, food Philip wouldn't have allowed Petey to eat at home.

For some reason, Petey had taken to Butch instantly. When she slipped out the door, Petey hadn't seemed to notice. But if he started to miss his mother, with three children of her own, Melody could handle things until Beth returned.

"It was so kind of your daughter to take care of Petey," she said. "I can't imagine what I'd have done under the circumstances, with my son in tow."

Dan's sigh was audible over the crystalline strains of classical music. "Melody's a good person. I wish she'd meet the right fellow, some-body she could depend on who'd take the weight off her shoulders. She's having a rough time being both mother and dad to those three kids." He fiddled with the radio, finding a Beethoven symphony.

"I don't mean to sound heartless, Dan, but finding the right man can be an illusion. I thought I had, when I married Philip. But now I just don't know. He's not the man I thought he was, that's for sure."

"If he didn't relay my messages, I'd say something's wrong some-where. But it's your marriage. None of my business, really."

She wondered if she should ask, hating to put Dan Keefer on the spot after all he'd done for her. But then Beth said, "The man April's with. What should we do?"

"I've got that one figured. Once you've made a positive identifica-tion, I'll call the police to get him out of the picture until you have a chance to reconnect with April. There's always the danger he could become suspi-cious and take her into hiding, a prospect we can't allow to happen. We'll make sure it doesn't."

"Were you able to find out anything about him?"

"Nothing. They ran a crime trace, but with no fingerprints, Social Security or driver's license numbers, or anything else, it's as if he popped out of the middle of nowhere. An assumed identity he's using, probably, an alias. One of several, no doubt, generally the way it goes. When one gets too much mileage, he trades it in for another."

"Dear God, I can only pray he hasn't...hurt her."

"She's alive. And gainfully employed, even," Dan said in a droll tone. "No telling how much she hauls in each night. I suspect those skills she's learned may serve her well later in life. Sales. Marketing."

"I wonder," Beth said softly, thinking of how April had missed two years of school. If she hadn't been kidnapped, in September she'd have been a sixth grader.

April didn't even know she had a little brother. What else had she missed besides a mother's love? Her daughter's readjustment would be complicated, perhaps painful. But Beth knew she could face any test, any challenge, if only she could have April back with her again.

Please, God. Let it be April.

Concentrating on the sounds of violins from the car radio, Beth realized Dan was turning into the entrance of the fairgrounds. A few tall lights shone on a river of parked cars and trucks, the tent beyond.

Her pulse raced with anticipation. She felt as if her nerve endings jumped through her skin, exposed and tingling.

"We're here. Now, if I can find the right place to leave the car. Look for a space, Beth, something subtle, out of the way, where the car won't be noticed."

"But what does that matter?"

"I'm bringing you and April to the car, so you'll be safe and out of sight, while I settle with Lightfoot and the police. They'll take him in, you know, and charge him with abduction minutes after you've positively identified April. It's the only thing we need to put him behind bars, where he belongs."

They parked the Cavalier between two house trailers. As they climbed from the car, Dan reminded her to leave the door unlocked. Then they were swallowed up in the crowd pressing toward the revival. As Beth was jostled by countless anonymous bodies, she began to feel claustrophobic from the smell of human flesh. An unpleasant smell, like old clothing and filth.

Recorded hymns sung by the Mormon Tabernacle Choir blared from loudspeakers. When they entered the tent, Dan steered her toward the back rows and they both took a seat on folding chairs.

"From my attendance the past couple of nights, the back rows are taken before the thing begins. And with the latecomers, it's standing room only. We'll be unobtrusive here."

"But I can't see anything!"

"Only because people are milling around. Once the show starts, you'll have a good view of the stage."

Impatiently, she sat beside Dan Keefer in the rear of the tent. In desperation, her eyes searched the faces of the crowd for a glimpse of April. It seemed an eternity before the audience filed in to be seated and, as Dan predicted, began to line up in the aisles.

Abruptly, the medley of hymns stopped. A strange collection of musicians took the stage and sang in twangy voices to discordant accompaniment.

"The Jesus Boys is what they call themselves," Dan said. "Awful, isn't it?"

But Beth was staring at the misshapen faces in the audience, crossed eyes, visible facial tumors, gap-toothed or toothless grins. The faces seemed to shimmer and glow, radiating a nameless emotion Beth had never seen before.

Faith and surrender, a child-like vulnerability, belief. Such raw openness made her uncomfortable. There was no similarity here to religious services she'd attended in her life, but neither were the worshippers like any churchgoers in her limited experience.

A tall, gaunt man with a greasy black pompadour and sideburns, dressed in a shiny powder-blue suit and white ruffled shirt, came to the podium and tapped the microphone. The Jesus Boys stood quietly behind him, the faces of the band members as rapt as those in the audience. The man began to speak.

"Welcome to the next to final night of our revival, brothers and sisters in Jesus! Some of you have been here every night, and we appreciate your support and all the prayers that have made this event such a wonderful blessing!"

The audience clapped and whistled in response.

"I have a little bad news," the man continued. "Orville's under the weather, so he won't be joining us tonight, and neither will his reptiles. But he's hoping to be here tomorrow night for the grand finale. We're going to lead off with some more music from the Jesus Boys and start right in with Reuben Swope and his miracles of healing through the grace and power of The Almighty! While the Jesus Boys honor His Name with some old-timey favorites, please bring the sick in spirit and lame of body up here to the front so Reuben can..."

Beth was surprised when Dan Keefer took her right hand in his. She glanced over at him. "How long does this go on, Dan? I feel like I'm ready to jump out of my skin."

"We have to wait it out. It wouldn't hurt to offer up a few prayers of our own, I guess."

Outside, the thunder boomed, and the wind rippled the walls of the tent. Beth felt nauseated from the odor of sweating bodies melded with a strange reek of mold or mildew. She almost felt as though she were trapped in a damp, humid cave.

Then it was Reuben Swope who came to the microphone. "You know, friends, what it tells us in the Gospel of Mark. I'll refresh your memory. 'And these signs shall follow them that believe: In my name shall they cast out devils; they shall speak with new tongues; they shall take up serpents, and if they drink any deadly thing, it shall not hurt them!' The Word, ladies and gentlemen. Praise Jesus! Yessiree! Amen! And how's this, for a poison cocktail to test a man's faith?"

He made a great ritual of pouring Clorox into a glass tumbler and adding Prestone Antifreeze. Swope slugged the mixture down his throat.

Dan leaned over and said, "Looks like Alka-Seltzer mixed with Mountain Dew."

"Like what?"

"Mountain Dew. It's a popular soda around here, the same color as antifreeze, too."

During the faith healer's time on stage, Beth tried to tune out the shrieks and caterwauling of the spectators. Several rows ahead, an old woman squirmed and hopped, ran down the aisle in matron's shoes and up the stairs to the stage. She fell to the floor in convulsions, twitching like a trout on dry land.

Swope's voice held forth. "This sister is anointed in the Spirit! The demons are running for cover! Now she's speaking in a foreign tongue! Praise the Lord!"

"My God!" Beth whispered.

"Evidently, it's a show of extreme faith," Dan said.

"It's insane!"

"Anybody else in here would argue that point. They're believers, or they wouldn't be here."

"Well, *I* can't believe April has been exposed to this."

Silently, she wondered if her daughter's psyche had been permanently damaged by an association with the level of ignorance she had witnessed this night. Deprogramming was what they called it. If she had to, Beth would hire an expert to remove the remnants of cult worship from April's brain.

Her stomach roiled from the sour, stifling air, the whirling dervish antics of Reuben Swope, the wild shouts and hallelujahs of the audience...

The overhead lights dimmed as Reuben Swope moonwalked his way off the stage.

"What we've been waiting for," Dan said, squeezing her hand as a single spotlight illuminated the microphone.

A hush fell upon the crowd when a small, dark-haired girl in a long white dress glided from the shadows into the spotlight.

Beth sat with tears streaming down her cheeks. She held onto Dan's hand so tightly she was afraid her nails were digging into his palm, but she couldn't let go.

"Oh, Lord! Be with us tonight in this holy place of worship. Feel our pain and misery!" The girl jerked the microphone from its stand, raised her right arm above her head. "There are people here tonight looking for their long-lost loved ones, Lord. Have mercy upon them, Jesus. Give me the power, Lord, to heal their broken hearts with the precious balm of your mercy..."

"It's *April!* Her voice, Dan! I'd know it anywhere. It's April!"

"Are you a hundred per cent sure?"

Mutely, Beth nodded, then began to whimper softly as her tears continued to flow.

"Sit tight," he whispered. "Don't make a move. I'll be right back."

Again, she nodded. "Hurry! Please, Dan."

"Five minutes. Stay here and promise me you won't budge."

She was vaguely aware of his absence, and she focused on what he had told her in the car, that he had to slip away to notify the police to request back-up...

But she couldn't begin for a single moment to take her eyes from the child on stage.

"How much longer do you expect me to wait?"

With obvious irritation, the deputy at the desk in the Keyser Sheriff's Department looked at the tall, slender man in the gray pin-striped suit.

"We've got an APB out on the vehicle, Mr. Magill. Several units are working on it. Shouldn't be long."

"You should have done that hours ago!" Philip paced back and forth, jingling car keys in his hand. He glanced at his Rolex. "You've had half the day to find it. While I was on a plane and then driving to this god-forsaken hole, you could have located the station wagon. You could have it *impounded* by now!"

"Why don't you have a seat?" the deputy suggested. "I guess we must seem like a bunch of stupid goof-offs to you, but…"

Furiously, Philip leaned over the desk, thrusting his face a foot from the deputy's. "If you want the truth, officer, that's about the long and short of it. But jerk-offs are more like it!"

The deputy rose from his chair and walked around the desk. "I don't much care for your attitude, Mr. Magill. If you want help from bumpkins like us, you might try being a little more polite."

"Polite? You think I give a flying fig about *polite?*" Philip straightened up to his full height, pounded his fist on the surface of the desk. "It's my son we're talking about! My wife had a breakdown and she's taken my *son!* Can't you understand that? Don't you have children?"

"Yes, sir, I surely do. Why don't you take a seat in the outer office, and I'll radio my units for an update."

As the deputy nudged him through the open door, then closed the door behind him, Philip turned around in astonishment. What heavenly hiccup could allow a boring hick to treat Philip Magill so rudely?

He was too wired to sit, so he began to pace the lobby, catching the resentful glances of other officers passing through the room. Word certainly traveled fast, didn't it? No doubt everyone knew him now as a Northern troublemaker, a modern-day carpetbagger from Detroit.

Never mind that none of these corn-pone human jokes were worth the salt to blow them to Hell. Well, he didn't care what they thought of him. Perhaps he *did* seem arrogant, but he had every right to be. If they'd done their jobs as they were paid to do, Philip would have already found Petey.

The door opened. "Mr. Magill, they've spotted the car. It's parked in front of a private residence not far from the paper mill."

"Where? What location? Give me directions and I'll drive there at once."

"Take a left at the intersection up the street and you'll run into it. There's a big neon sign, Keyser Paper and Box. A few blocks ahead, you'll come to a modest housing development, and Mulberry is off to the right. Do you want me to dispatch a unit to follow along?"

But Philip ripped the slip of paper from the deputy's hand and dashed outside to his rental car. As he left the parking lot beside the sheriff's department and squealed around the corner, he reminded himself once again, as he had for the entire day.

For subjecting him to this trauma, Beth was going to pay.

Yes, she would pay dearly.

Dan Keefer hurried to his car and placed a call on his citizens-band radio to the Keyser authorities. He figured on an hour, tops, maybe not more than forty-five minutes.

That Lightfoot character had to be detained before the girl finished her performance. Tomorrow was the finale, then the tent folded and the show moved on.

By Sunday night, only an empty space would remain where the large circus tent had been erected, and the caravan of trailers would be gone.

For several seconds, all he could get was static. Some sort of interference. He tried a different frequency and then heard the now-familiar voice of the local sheriff.

"Hey, Ed, it's Dan Keefer. The mother identified the child. It's her daughter, all right. You need to send some men out here and pick up Lightfoot."

"I'm on my way, 10-4."

Dan had to trust in his own powers of description, that the sheriff and his deputies would be able to pick out Lightfoot without any trouble.

Six feet, black hair in a ponytail, black eyes, olive complexion, dressed in black, a disturbing, silent man always off by himself, never part of the crowd.

Of course, Dan Keefer's top priority was to reunite Beth Magill with her daughter. But equally important in his mind was to capture the perpetrator, take him off the street so he could never steal another child, an innocent little girl like his own granddaughter, Robin.

But the guy was slick, elusive as a snake. He'd avoided detection seemingly with no effort. Lightfoot had traveled the roads with a kidnapped child, unseen by denizens of law enforcement personnel in several states.

Until Dan Keefer accidentally stumbled on the poster of Haley Mae and a small flicker of recognition had clicked in his brain.

If they were going to apprehend the man who had abducted April Warner and held her captive for nearly two years, it would either happen tonight, or never.

Chapter Twenty

"**P**raise the Lord! Praise His Name!"

"Amen!"

"Help me, Jesus!"

To the maddening din of jangling tambourines, the girl prophet concluded her dramatic morality play to a standing ovation, a cacophony of shouts and whoops mingled with the plaintive cries of wailing infants.

Dan Keefer had sidled his way through the assembly, grabbed the stiff arm of a stunned Beth Magill, and maneuvered her down the aisle between the chairs to the left side of the stage, which the performers used for exit. They stood together at the foot of the stairs.

Under the bright lights the girl's face glistened with perspiration. Repeatedly, she bowed humbly before her adoring audience.

Only when she eased away from the spotlight and took a few tentative steps to the left did the applause gradually begin to subside. As she descended the stairs, the girl looked up expectantly.

Keefer knew she was searching for Adrian Lightfoot, her balm in Gilead, her companion. He had said nothing to Beth about what he'd observed at the performances on previous nights, how the girl seemed to idolize Lightfoot.

Though to be expected, Keefer knew, recalling the Stockholm syndrome, when the victim finally begins to identify with the kidnapper. If it had happened to a privileged, educated Patty Hearst, why shouldn't it happen even more easily to a little girl?

But the child's bright countenance turned apprehensive, then diffident, as she faced a burly, balding man in a beige sports jacket beside a woman in a red summer dress. Weeping, the woman reached out for the child, calling to her.

"April, it's Mommy. April!"

The girl seemed to freeze midway down the stairs, staring at Beth with an indecipherable expression. Keefer wanted to allow her time enough to process and react, but he couldn't risk the luxury. He mounted three steps, latched onto the girl's fragile forearm, and urged her down to Beth's side.

In a flash, Keefer looked at mother and daughter, opposite sides of the same coin. Haley was April Warner, there could be no doubt in his mind. The resemblance was striking.

Beth took the child in her arms, smoothed the damp strands of black hair from her face and cradled her cheek. The girl flinched, blinking her eyes as if emerging from a self-induced trance, or falling into a trance, Keefer didn't know which.

Glancing around to ensure that the path to the exit was clear, Keefer said, "Let's go. They're praying, but then it'll be wall-to-wall people and we'll never get out of here. Come on."

They left the tent without interference. So far, so good, Keefer said to himself, his hand on his revolver, his eyes scanning the misty night.

No sign of Lightfoot. Either he'd been picked up, or he was only now making his nightly pilgrimage to the foot of the stage to escort Haley Mae, girl prophet, to wherever it was they went after the nightly revival show ended.

Beth's arms were shielding her daughter. He pushed them along, circling the back of the tent to where the brown Cavalier was parked between two house trailers. He opened the door on the passenger side and flipped the seat forward. "Get in, Beth. Hurry!"

Beth and April climbed into the back seat, Beth with her daughter's head against her shoulder, gently rocking the girl and murmuring words he couldn't hear.

Gruffly, he said, "Lock the doors and wait here. I'll be back." He slammed the door and saw Beth's hand push down the lock.

Keefer retraced their steps to the main entrance where a multitude of weary, subdued people walked toward the parking lot beneath a steady drizzle.

Off in the distance, beyond the crowd, Keefer saw a whirling red arc, the flashing dome lights of two or three patrol cars. Ed and his men must have apprehended Lightfoot. Keefer's confidence in the obese sheriff with the slightly confused but kindly manner hadn't been misplaced. Good man!

His spirits lifting, he stared toward the lights, moving in the direction of the spiraling red circles.

He elbowed his way through the crowd but came upon a horse-drawn wagon filled with several black women and their small children parked between a charter bus and a late-model silver-gray Saturn.

Keefer was momentarily disoriented. The police cars were only now approaching, their flashing lights distorted by the rising mist. The authorities hadn't arrived, hadn't had time to locate Lightfoot, and...

A rough shove to his left shoulder made Keefer simultaneously wheel around and click off the safety on his revolver.

Not Lightfoot, but a well-dressed blond man in a suit..

"You're the only one I've seen who matches the description the police gave me. Are you Dan Keefer?"

Mutely, he nodded, his hand inching toward his gun.

"Then what the hell have you done with my wife and son?"

Dan Keefer's eyes were drawn to the ugly snout of the weapon in Magill's hand, a German Lugar. Immediately he thought of the women and children in the wagon behind him, whose lives were in danger as much as Keefer's own if the idiot accosting him were to get trigger-happy.

"If you've tracked us this far, then you must know we came to find April."

He was seriously considering a surprise move, charging into Magill's gut head-first. He'd never felt the disadvantage of his weight and age quite so intensely.

"I'll ask once, and one time only. Where is my son?"

The gun was pointed at Keefer's chest. One bullet, and he'd be history. "Your son is safe, Magill. He's at my daughter's house."

"You're a damned liar! I went to her house, and he wasn't there. She said Petey's with you and Beth!"

Cold chills ran up Dan Keefer's spine as he thought of a crazed man with a weapon loose in his daughter's home, and not only with Petey but with Keefer's own grandchildren.

Though he could hear the whimpers of the children in the wagon behind him, he suddenly felt as if the hundreds of people on the grounds had vanished.

When his attention was temporarily distracted from his likely assailant, he saw Lightfoot behind Magill, moving in silently from Keefer's left.

The voice was soft yet steely when it said, "Are you Haley's step-father?"

Now it was Magill's turn to pivot toward the unearthly voice that sounded to Keefer's ears as if it had left a reverberating echo, a thin pitch reminding him of a faint noise heard through a wind tunnel.

"Haley? I don't know what you're talking about!" Magill's aim faltered, as if he couldn't decide whether the man now before him was a threat. "Who are you? This is between Keefer and me. Mind your own goddamn business."

Keefer was preparing himself, on the verge of trying a body shot to Magill. But in the next instant the gun dropped from the would-be attacker's hand in a burst of flame, making him cry out in surprise and pain.

"What do you want from me?" he demanded. "Who *are* you?"

"Are you the piece of filth who tried to molest your stepdaughter?" That voice, so eerie, almost horrifying.

Terror was written all over Magill's face. "Who the hell…"

Then, by some unseen wizardry, the Lugar was in Lightfoot's hand, and now it was trained on Philip Magill. As Magill lunged at him, the gun cracked out a shot.

In apparent disbelief, Magill moved toward the stranger in black before staggering backward and falling to his knees. He clutched his stomach and pitched face-forward into the mud.

The children began to scream, along with their mothers.

Keefer stood his ground, his revolver drawn and trained on Lightfoot. He had no choice but to tough it out. Where in hell was Ed?

"I'm here to take you in, Lightfoot. Or whatever your name is. The girl you call Haley, April Warner, is with her mother."

Lightfoot uttered a peculiar laugh. "You can put your weapon down," he said. "No need for that now. We're done."

"Not over till the fat lady sings," Keefer said. "I'm placing you under arrest, Lightfoot. But that's not your name, is it? What *is* your name, if you don't mind telling me?"

Make pleasant, non-threatening, ironic, almost jovial conversation; maybe Lightfoot would forget he had Magill's firearm in his hand.

Fat chance.

Keefer's relief was considerable when he heard at his back, "Put the gun down, Mister. You're outnumbered."

The sheriff stood by Keefer's side, two deputies fanning out in front of the wagonload of children. Now it was four against one, but Lightfoot seemed unfazed, even amused, tossing the Lugar several feet away to the ground. One of the deputies unhooked a pair of handcuffs and started to approach the suspect.

"It's done," Lightfoot said. "I am Overman. I am Lucifer, bearer of light. I, who died for you and am raised again."

Confused, Keefer watched as a small circle of flames surrounded Lightfoot's boots, fire ignited spontaneously that began to feed upon itself, shooting higher, higher, beginning to rage, sending out a white-hot heat from a dense column of blue flame that was almost unendurable.

He and the others gaped from where they stood as if anchored to the earth. They witnessed the flames consuming the mystery man in his black clothing.

His arms were raised as if in supplication, and before their eyes he was burned alive, demonic peals of laughter flung from his lips until even the laughter was burned away.

For a long time later he would question himself, as Keefer stared in disbelief at a large black shadow issued forth from the flames on out-stretched wings, like a huge dark vulture rising into the night sky.

As suddenly as it had begun, the fire diminished by degrees and burned itself out, leaving no trace of flesh or bone as evidence that Adrian Lightfoot had been consumed but for an insignificant pyramid of ash.

Ed was the first to break the silence. "I think we've been boondoggled! Where'd that boy go?"

Keefer exhaled, clicking on the safety before holstering his weapon. "Did you see that shadow, Ed? Tell me you saw something."

"Shoot, yeah. Like a big black bird, a giant crow or a buzzard. Hey, you men see that bird-like thing come out of the fire? Jessie? You see it?"

"Yeah, boss. Sure did."

"Well, I swan, if it ain't the oddest damned thing I ever did see," the sheriff said. "In the morning we'll launch a full investigation of this incident." He turned to the black people in the wagon, still cowering in fear. "You folks okay? Hey, Ransom! Best be getting your family back home now."

Keefer watched the young black man jump up to the buckboard, hoist himself into the driver's seat, giddyap the horses and drive away. Ed turned to Keefer. "Least of all they're out of danger now. Bet those kids were scared to death. What we think we saw, they saw too."

"Yes. Well." Keefer felt every ounce of reserved energy melt from his body. He couldn't remember ever having felt so whipped.

As one, they suddenly remembered that Magill had been shot. Somehow the fact had seemed to escape them all, as if through mass hypnosis.

But from Keefer's brief exposure to Philip Magill, he thought it was more likely that nobody much cared whether the pompous ass lived or died.

"Jessie, go radio in for an ambulance, on the double." Ed rubbed his sizeable belly. "I feel sort of like somebody beat me with a stick, Keefer. How about you?"

"I don't know how I feel. But I do know one thing. I have to get back to my car and take my client and her daughter to a safe place for the night."

He looked down at Magill, who was groaning in a high voice. "Where will you be taking him?"

"It's a gut shot. Hospital or morgue, one. But before you go any place, you'll have to follow me back to the station. Can't wait till morning, Dan."

Dan sighed. "Okay. Since you just did me a favor I can't ever repay, I'll follow you into town, then. Maybe you can get with the hospital in the meantime, so I'll know what to tell his wife. One way or another."

For some inexplicable reason, though a man had been shot and nearly murdered in cold blood, Keefer felt nothing resembling remorse. Lightfoot's words clicked into the proper channels in Dan Keefer's brain, his accusation that Magill had tried to molest April Warner.

How would Lightfoot have known that, if the girl hadn't told him? And if there was truth to it, then Magill's decision not to relay Keefer's messages to his wife would make some kind of demented sense.

Ed had mentioned they'd do a full investigation.

For all the good *that* was going to do.

As he stumbled wearily back to the car, Keefer thought about how he'd prided himself on having been around the barn plenty of times, on having seen it all.

On this night, he came to the grim realization he'd been sorely mistaken.

Chapter Twenty-One

Dan Keefer checked his Timex against the wall clock in the Keyser Sheriff's Department as he watched Beth Magill and her daughter accompany a middle-aged female deputy into another room.

It was 10:45 pm, late, but not *that* late. Keefer knew he'd been exhausted by the ordeal at the fairgrounds. His adrenaline had been pumping overtime and now he was yawning, a sure sign he needed to collapse and restore his strength.

Pushing sixty in another couple of years, he wasn't a young man anymore. Tonight he'd had to behave with the dexterity and cunning of a man half his age.

He tried to recall his last blood-curdling, man-to-man altercation, but whatever happened was so long ago he couldn't seem to remember. But tonight's once-in-a-lifetime experience was unequalled by anything in his comparatively dull memories.

He hoped it wouldn't be long before they could get out of here, so he could drive to his daughter's house and try to crash on the living room sofa. Or, if not that, complete rest in a dark room would suffice, with soft music and the company of a pint of Scotch he'd picked up a few days ago.

The outer office was dimly lit, the air redolent of burned coffee. Keefer glanced around at the deputy dozing behind the counter beside a muffled dispatcher's board. He spotted the coffee maker in a corner and, his muscles aching like twisted rags, he got up to switch it off. A layer of brown sludge had baked to the bottom of the pot. He took the pot off the element and set it on a couple of folded napkins.

Since Glenda died, Keefer had grown accustomed to taking care of small annoyances. The little things in life bothered him, as if he'd vented his lingering grief for his wife by tending to the domestic environment in her absence. He guessed he'd been living alone for too long.

Waiting for the sheriff to come in from conferring with his night shift, Dan Keefer told himself to quit beefing about the stink of scorched java when he remembered the damp, putrid air that enveloped the town, air saturated with the stench of the paper mill.

Tonight, that ubiquitous stink mingled with the eerie light from scudding clouds playing tag with a full moon, the low clap of distant thunder. It had been a night he'd just as soon forget, should that have been an option.

The department was paneled in knotty pine. Limp, pea-green curtains streaked brown from rain through open windows, a sheaf of FBI Most Wanted posters. He could have flipped through the entire stack and found neither hide nor hair of Adrian Lightfoot.

The sheriff required information for the paperwork, but mostly he was hoping to extract some vital clues from April's statement, a few necessary details to facilitate the manhunt.

Good luck, Ed.

As for personal motives, Keefer was here to wind up loose ends. To him, the case was closed. Beth Magill had found her missing child. He tried to convince himself it was all he knew, and all he needed to know.

The sheriff pushed through the door, the light from a long, six-battery flashlight still shining. He pointed it at Keefer and said, "Beam me up, Scotty."

Dutifully, Keefer chuckled. Ed was a good, small-town cop, a nice man. How many men would try to ease the tensions of this night with a little comic relief? Ed was the rare type of guy who always worried about the feelings of others before he considered his own. Kind of the antithesis of Philip Magill, come to think of it.

"Let's go on back to my office, Dan," he said. "Hey, Stiles! Wake up. You're sleeping on the job again. Better consider giving up your day job if you want to keep this one."

The deputy on night duty tried to rouse himself, turning toward the coffee pot only to mutter under his breath. Keefer followed the sheriff through a door at the end of the corridor.

An American flag beside the flag of West Virginia decorated the wall behind a scarred wooden desk with a gooseneck lamp and framed photographs of Ed's overweight family. An open jumbo bag of circus peanuts candy was also on the desk.

Expansively, Ed said, "Have a seat, Dan."

"Thanks. Can I use your phone a minute ...to call Melody?"

"Sure. I'll give you some privacy." Before Keefer could tell him there was no need, Ed was already out the door. He dialed the number and was flooded with instantaneous relief when Melody said, "Hello? Dad? Is it you?"

"How'd you know it'd be me, honey?"

"Who else calls me at 11:00 at night? Are you alright?"

"Melody, what happened when Beth's husband got there? Did he threaten you, or harm you in any way?"

"I didn't know what to do. He barged into the house demanding to know where Beth and Petey were. Butch had Petey upstairs in the bathtub, so I lied. I said they were both with you. He wanted me to show him a photograph of you, Dad, but I told him I didn't have one. I really didn't have a choice but to lie, because I didn't want him to find you. I'm sorry I didn't handle things better."

"Then he twisted your arm as to where we'd gone."

"Right again. He didn't seem dangerous, just angry. I thought it would be okay, maybe, once he talked to Beth and understood, well, you know."

"For all his trouble, he got himself shot. He's in the hospital by now."

Melody sighed into the phone. "Well, thank Heaven you're okay. You *are*, aren't you?"

"Yes, honey. I'm fine. Bushwhacked, but okay."

"Did you find the daughter?"

"It was April Warner. She and Beth are with a deputy, making a statement. Soon as we're through here, I'll drop them off at a motel, then I'll be home. Petey's asleep?"

"He's been a little angel. Tell Beth. He'll be fine here. He was up so late playing with the kids he'll probably wake up late. We all will since it's Saturday, thank the Lord."

Before he said goodbye, Keefer added, "Thanks for not asking me how Magill got himself shot. I'll tell you about it in the morning."

"Love you, Dad."

Keefer hung up, thinking a telephone conversation wasn't exactly the appropriate means for telling his daughter he'd almost gotten himself canned, had there been an inclination to tell her. But he wouldn't go into details. Since Glenda's untimely death, Melody worried about him enough as it was.

Ed came in carrying two coffee mugs, a can of diet soda, and a fifth of Jack Daniels. "Everything okay on the home front?"

Keefer accepted a mug and watched as Ed split the soda and then poured in a generous dose of bourbon. "Melody's fine. Evidently Magill was more obnoxious than dangerous. Which reminds me. Have you called the hospital?"

"Broken ribs, punctured lung, bullet exit through the back, missed the spine. He'll live." Ed slugged down his drink. "But tell the wife he'll be a guest of Keyser Community Hospital for a while. Unless they decide to airlift him to Lewis-Gale in Salem, Virginia. You know, outside Roanoke."

"Ed, you need to know there may be an accomplice, someone else implicated in the kidnapping, a Bruce Fielding. The last Beth knew, he was in Florida."

"Don't worry. We'll find him, if Fielding's his real name."

"It is. He and his parents used to be members of a church Magill pastored in Florida, suburb of Orlando."

"Shouldn't be hard to track him down." The sheriff stared at the bottle as if considering another drink, then pushed the mug aside and reached for the circus peanuts. "Tell you the truth, Dan, I haven't been able to quit thinking about Lightfoot."

Keefer had an urge to tell Ed about the feeling in his own gut. He knew something was wrong, but he couldn't put his mental finger on it. He said nothing.

"I have a hunch as to who he was, but I'm probably wrong."

"I'm listening."

"Well, you saw what came up from the fire, same as me. Didn't you."

An image was engraved in Keefer's memory, he feared for life. "A shape that grew, looked like a big black bird." He didn't add the free associations he'd been mulling over: bird, take flight, escape, free. Vulture: carrion bird.

"One minute Lightfoot was there, and the next he wasn't. Where'd he go?"

"You tell me." Keefer didn't intend to wax philosophic, nor to share the strange thoughts going through his mind, emerging from the dark realms of his subconscious.

Ed sat back in his swivel chair, resting his small, stubby hands on his large belly. "I remember something happening maybe nine, ten years ago, in a little town right around here. A church burned to the ground, and there was a witness who swore he saw a huge black thing with wings fly right out of the blaze."

"Is that a fact?"

"I never knew whether there was any truth to it, or whether the man who claimed to see it was having one of them hallucinations. Now I'm wondering if it wasn't so."

Keefer nodded. "Go on."

"Sounds dumb, I know, but maybe there's a creature who makes an appearance around here in the Blue Ridge and Appalachian Mountains, like people here in West Virginia claim to see the Moth-man, or the Jersey Devil in New Jersey, or Bigfoot in other parts of the country."

Dan couldn't conceal his grin. "Or UFOs."

A knock at the door, and a deputy informed Ed that the statement was completed. Keefer stood up and put his hand out to the sheriff, who gave him a hearty handshake. "Good working with you, Dan," he said. "Hope we got our man."

"I do, too. Well, guess I'd better be taking the ladies to a motel. What's close by?"

"Econo-Lodge. Cheap, too. Stiles will give you directions, if he ain't asleep on the job again."

"You know where to reach me if you need to." Keefer turned toward the door. "I'll be in town for a few more days, visiting with my family and trying to be of some help to Beth Magill as she decides what to do next."

At 11:45, Dan Keefer unlocked the door of their motel room, gave Beth an awkward hug, and took his leave. Beth had promised to call him in the morning.

The room was decorated in beige and dusty-rose, with a mauve carpet. April switched on the television as Beth turned on the lamp between the two double beds.

"Honey, why don't you take a shower first?" she suggested to the girl.

Obediently, April got up from the foot of the bed, where she'd taken interest in some old movie, and slouched toward the bathroom. Soon Beth heard the shower. She opened her suitcase and found a robe, which she hung on the bathroom doorknob.

She sat down on the edge of the bed and lit a cigarette. The smoke seemed to cancel the smell of Windex and furniture polish permeating the room.

She thought of Philip in a hospital bed among strangers and was surprised by her own lack of sympathy. All she could seem to feel was fatigue. But now that she had April back, the next riddle to be solved was what to do about Philip.

Against the wall where she sat, muffled thuds and grunts from the next room suggested lovemaking. Annoyed, Beth got up to open the curtains and stared out at the rain pelting the glass. The window had a view of nothing, only a square of black.

Soon the sounds from the adjoining room ceased. Noticing the temperature in the room was overly warm, she turned up the air conditioning, thinking that it might remove the dampness in the room.

April came out of the bathroom in her slip, a towel wrapped around her head. She plopped down on the bed across from her mother as if to say *Now what?*

"You must be exhausted, sweetheart."

"Not really. After a show, sometimes I'm so revved up I can't sleep for hours."

"Well, those days are over, April. No more shows." She was stricken by the difference in April now, compared to her stage persona. It was as if the child had been drained of all emotion and affect.

"April, would you tell me..." But then her voice trailed off, for she didn't know where to begin.

"What do you want to know, Mother?"

She stubbed out her cigarette in the ashtray on the nightstand. "Never mind. It's too late to talk now, after everything you've been through. Tomorrow's soon enough."

"Whatever," April said with a shrug, her face drawn toward the television.

Beth reached over to turn off the set.

"Why'd you do that? I was going to watch it."

"It's too late."

"No it isn't. Sometimes I watch television all night and sleep in till noon."

"April, you need to get back to a normal life and live like other eleven-year-old girls."

"It's too late for that, Mother. I'll never be the same as other girls my age. Life on the road made me old."

Beth reached for another cigarette. "Honey, would you answer me honestly if I ask you a question?"

"I guess." She was slowly drying her dark hair with a towel.

"After I married Philip...before we...well, did Philip ever try to...I don't know quite how to put this...did Philip ever try to bother you? In a way he shouldn't have?"

April's blue eyes centered on Beth's when she nodded.

"But why didn't you *tell* me?"

"I didn't really know what he wanted, Mother. But I do now."

Pushed to her feet by a piece of information that she wished she'd never received, Beth walked to the window and gazed out at the night.

At her back, April said, "You asked, so I told you."

"Then Philip is out of our lives, April. Yours and mine and Petey's. Tomorrow I'll call his brother Edward, and he and Charlotte can handle Philip's hospitalization and whatever else. I wish I never had to see him again."

"I wondered if it was because of Philip, why you didn't find me a long time ago."

Beth whirled around with tears in her eyes. "Oh, April! There's no way you could ever know how hard I searched! I did everything I knew how to do, but..."

"It's all right, Mother. I'm okay. It wasn't so bad."

"Oh, honey!" Beth sat down next to April and gave her a hug. From the look in her daughter's eyes, she wondered if April might be in shock. Silently thanking God for giving her daughter back to her, Beth said, "Well, the first thing we're going to do when we get you home is to take that awful black dye out of your pretty blond hair, so you can look like yourself again."

"Where's home?"

Beth had no easy reply. "I don't know yet, April. There are some things I need to work through. I thought I might rent a house close to my elementary school."

With Philip seriously injured, she would have to remain in West Virginia for a few days from common decency, at least until Edward and Charlotte had time to drive from Birmingham, Michigan. But it was the last courtesy she'd ever extend to Philip Magill.

In a bright tone, she said, "Remember this?" She pulled Strawbaby from the bottom of her tote bag and handed it to April.

"You kept this?"

"Of course, I did!"

The grin dissolved from April's face as she gave the doll back to Beth. "But I don't need it anymore."

"Well, then, I'll keep it anyhow. But aren't you anxious to meet your little brother?"

But the child had distanced herself from Beth, suddenly strange and silent as if an invisible veil had fallen over her face, walling her off from her mother. When she looked at Beth, there was something resembling hatred in her eyes.

"Honey, what's wrong? What..." Beth felt at a loss.

"Now I have a question for you, Mother," April said, coldly. "Where's

Adrian?"

Beth flinched. "We don't know where he went."

Again, the girl shrugged. "Wherever he is, he'll find me."

"Oh, April! Sweetheart! You don't *want* him to find you, do you?"

April jumped up to turn on the television. Adjusting the volume, her back turned, she said, "Yes, Mother. Of course, I do."

A shudder coursed through her body as Beth weakly took off her clothes and got into bed. To the sound of voices from the television, she reached over to turn off the lamp, yanking the bedcovers over her eyes.

###

Waking to a diffuse glow in the east, Edgar Wills pulled on his red sweatsuit, a gift from his sons last Father's Day, and quietly left the house before his family stirred. Though he was dressed in fatigues, he got into his official vehicle. Even out of uniform, he was sheriff of Keyser twenty-four/seven, a responsibility he held sacred.

He'd tossed all night long, haunted by the puzzling events at the fairgrounds, compelled to return to scour the scene for a shred of evidence, if such a thing might be found.

Driving through the quiet residential neighborhood and on to the outskirts of town, Edgar rolled down his window. There was a warm, slight breeze. With the temperature rising so quickly, the day promised to be a scorcher.

Last night he promised Angie he'd be back to the house in plenty of time to get ready for church. After services, they planned to take the boys down to the river for a picnic lunch. Angie had made fried chicken, homemade potato salad, and deviled eggs.

He needed to search for answers. There had to be a plausible explanation for what had happened Friday night to turn the incident involving Lightfoot into trick photography. He remembered when he and Angie had gone down to Myrtle Beach for the weekend and had their pictures taken behind a billboard that made them look like they had donkey bodies. Or like that David Copperfield on television who made the Statue of Liberty disappear.

Cruising into the vacant parking area, Edgar drove to the place marked by the same silver Saturn that he now knew had been rented by Philip Magill. Edgar made a mental note to check the glove box of the vehicle for the name of the rental agency, so he could arrange its return. Let Magill worry about paying for it later.

The circus tent was collapsed on the ground, the charter bus long gone, and he was surprised to see the old horse-drawn wagon parked in the same spot, though empty of passengers.

When he got out of his car, he smelled the woody aroma of wet sawdust combined with a vague scent of fresh corn. Edges of the rain-soaked tent flapped in the wind, releasing sprays of steam against the sunlight.

Halfheartedly, Edgar bent over to study the ground, hoping for a charred circle in the earth to prove his eyes hadn't deceived him. But even the small pile of ashes had been blown away by the wind.

It was 7 am. He heard a rough, scraping noise and, when he turned around, he saw Old Claude hobbling toward him, leaning on his twisted sweetgum cane.

"Claude! What're you doing out here at this hour?"

"Ransom, he over there raking, Sheriff. We're out to catch the first light, 'fore we goes to church." The old man opened his palm. Sunlight glinted off the silver coins in Old Claude's hand. "Treasures! Come see what else we find."

Edgar followed him to the wagon. A plastic margarine tub with bolts, nuts, and nails. A plastic toy submarine. One rhinestone earring. A child's pink sweater.

"Well," he said. "Guess it's not against the law. Finders, keepers."

"What you doin' out here this mornin', Sheriff?"

"I guess Ransom told you what happened here Friday night. It was bad."

"Sure did. So did the grandbabies. Like to scared 'em to death, don't you know."

"If I could identify him, then maybe we could find him. Well, it's troubling me, like unfinished business keeping me awake all night. Don't know who he was."

"What'd you say his name s'pposed to be?"

With a smirk, Edgar said, "Adrian Lightfoot. At least that was the name he was going by."

Old Claude shook his head mournfully. "No Suh! That not be his name. Uh-uh-uh. I seed him my own self, in de fun'ral home when Miz Jerushia die. He was the Prophet Aaron, from when that church in Ridley burnt down. Seems he up and disappeared, jes' like before."

His worst fears confirmed by the old man's words, Edgar shook his head in a gesture of willful disbelief. "But now he's gone. At least I hope he is."

Old Claude hawked a wad of snuff and spat it out. Wiping his mouth on the sleeve of his tattered denim jacket, he said, "Don't you worry none, Sheriff. He be back."

From behind, "Hey there, Sheriff."

Edgar turned to greet the grandson Ransom, a tall handsome coffee-colored boy of sixteen whose penetrating green eyes reminded the sheriff of Old Claude. He saw wisdom there, a firm conviction of what life was all about. For a fleeting second, Edgar envied Ransom.

"Look like we g'wan have us a fine day," Old Claude said, shading his eyes to gaze up at the blue sky streaked with thin pink clouds reminding Edgar of cotton candy.

"Well, guess I'll be seeing you. Claude. Ransom." Edgar returned to his official vehicle, got behind the wheel, started the car and slowly drove away.

As he pushed at the outer boundary of the speed limit to get home, Edgar Wills thought of his old boss and good friend, Ray Hawke. In an unusual moment of weakness, at his retirement party when Ray had one too many beers under his belt, Hawke had told Edgar about the apparition he'd seen in the church fire about ten years ago.

Edgar had scoffed at him, thinking Ray was pulling his leg. Now he wished Ray was in town, so he could talk to him about it. But Edith was dying of cancer, and Ray had taken her out west to see the Grand Canyon while there was still time.

The only man who might understand Edgar Wills' present troubles as chief law enforcement officer of Keyser was Ray Hawke.

How can you apprehend a phantom, was what Edgar wondered.

And how do you live with yourself if you can't?

Epilogue

On a warm, balmy night in late June, April savored the fragrance of lilacs at the perimeter of the parking lot of an Applebee's restaurant somewhere in Ohio.

The restaurant was packed with travelers who had also stopped for a late dinner. While her mother waited in line to pay the bill, April volunteered to take Petey out to play on the swings and monkey-bars on the playground adjacent to the parking lot.

Pushing him on the baby-swing, with Petey yelling to go higher, April was amazed by how easily she'd grown to love the little boy, her half-brother. She liked caring for him, playing with him. Besides, it was good practice.

"More!" Petey squealed, laughing joyously as the chains of the wooden swing creaked above his head.

"Just a minute, Petey," April said, giving him one last push before turning away.

She limped to the bank of lilac bushes, bent over and vomited the remains of the pistachio ice cream sundae she'd had for dessert, topped by the two chewed halves of the maraschino cherry.

She didn't feel quite so sick anymore. Throwing up seemed to stop the fluttering in her stomach. She placed her hands on her abdomen and grinned: still flat as a board.

By the time her mother even noticed, it would be too late.

Nothing could be reborn until it had died.

At 8:30 pm, darkness descended. Petey called to her to lift him out of the swing. When he scooped up Strawbaby from the grass, she took his tiny hand and began to lead him toward the car.

"Wook!" Petey broke free and ran toward the dark green leaves of the bushes.

Like tiny jewels, fireflies signaled their mating dance, soft, bright, intermittent flashes against the leaves.

Petey ran from one to the next in delight, trying to catch them in his chubby hands. "Tars!" he cried.

She remembered words her mother had taught her so long ago. *Starlight, star bright, first star I've seen tonight…*

"Tars!"

"No, not stars. Those are fireflies, Petey. Aren't they pretty?"

"Fah-fies! Wink!"

"If we had a jar, we could take a firefly home and put it beside your bed. Then you could watch it wink at you in the night. Wouldn't that be neat?"

She could hear her mother calling her name. But for a few seconds longer April lost herself in Petey's innocent excitement.

Like the beacon from a lighthouse to ships on a dark sea, the fireflies continued to flash their cool light.

She could almost believe she heard them singing to her.

Haley!

Ha-ley!